SUNSHINE STATE

Also by D. P. Lyle

The Jake Longly Series
Deep Six
A-List

The Dub Walker Series
Stress Fracture
Hot Lights, Cold Steel
Run to Ground

The Samantha Cody Series
Original Sin
Devil's Playground
Double Blind

The Royal Pains Media Tie-In Series
Royal Pains: First, Do No Harm
Royal Pains: Sick Rich

Nonfiction
Murder and Mayhem
Forensics For Dummies
Forensics and Fiction
Howdunit: Forensics; A Guide For Writers
More Forensics and Fiction
ABA Fundamentals: Forensic Science

Anthologies
Thrillers: 100 Must-Reads (contributor); Jules Verne, Mysterious Island Thriller 3: Love Is Murder (contributor); Even Steven; For the Sake of the Game (contributor); Bottom Line

SUNSHINE STATE

STATE

A JAKE LONGLY THRILLER

D. P. LYLE

OCEANVIEW ⦿ PUBLISHING

SARASOTA, FLORIDA

ISBN 978-1-60809-336-6

Cover Design by Christian Fuenfhausen

Published in the United States of America by Oceanview Publishing

Sarasota, Florida

www.oceanviewpub.com

10 9 8 7 6 5 4 3 2 1

PRINTED IN THE UNITED STATES OF AMERICA

ACKNOWLEDGEMENTS

To my wonderful agent and friend Kimberley Cameron of Kimberley Cameron & Associates. KC, you're the best.

To Bob and Pat Gussin and all the wonderfully dedicated people at Oceanview Publishing. Thanks for your friendship and always spot-on insights, making my writing the best it can be.

To my writers group for helping make this story work. Thanks, Barbara, Terri, Craig, Donna, Sandy, and Laurie.

Thanks to Mary Sue Baker for her generous contribution to the Anaheim Public Library Foundation and for allowing me to use her name in this story.

Thanks to JoAn Pettite for her generous contribution to the Anaheim Public Library Foundation and for creating the name Erma Clemens and her dog Poochie for this story.

To Nan for everything.

SUNSHINE STATE

CHAPTER ONE

HERE'S THE DEAL. Ray thinks I'm a wimp. Has for years. The best I can remember it began around the time I left Major League Baseball. For several years, I pitched for the Texas Rangers. Could really bring the heat. A hundred miles an hour. Zip, pop. Loved that sound. Loved that the catcher would often shake his hand out after snagging one of my fastballs. That was me. Jake Longly, baseball stud. Everybody said so. Even the ESPN folks.

Not so Ray. He never actually used the word wimp. Pussy. That's the one he preferred. Four weeks ago being his most recent assessment.

Nicole Jamison, my current girlfriend, love interest, whatever she was, I wasn't sure yet, had laughed. Rude, but she does love getting her shots in. Besides, she just might've agreed with him. Mostly. Not in bed, mind you. I'm freaking Godzilla in the sack. Really, I am. I think she would agree. In fact, just last night, if I remember correctly, there was tequila involved, and she invoked God a couple of times. Or it could've been my echo. Lord knows I called on Him a couple of times.

Okay, I added the *zilla* part. So, sue me. No, wait, don't. The best attorney in town, Walter Horton, is married to my ex-wife, Tammy the insane. He'd already done a colonoscopy on my wallet. Probably wouldn't hesitate to encore that performance.

So, let's just say Nicole and I have fun.

Regardless, she and Ray conspired to enroll us in martial arts classes. Actually, some craziness based on Krav Maga and several other disciplines mixed into a soup of pain, mayhem, and considerable bodily harm. Taught by an ex-Mossad guy that Ray knew from back in the day. Ben Levitsky. Six-two, lean and muscular, the body fat of a distance runner, and no nonsense. No wonder he and Ray got along.

Ray Longly. My father. Owner of Longly Investigations. An outfit that, depending on your definition, employs Nicole. Speaking of employing, Ray has used every trick in his considerable bag of mischief to drag me into his business. But I prefer Captain Rocky's, my just dive-y enough bar/restaurant on the sand in Gulf Shores. I'd much rather hang out there with Pancake, who really does work for Ray. He also thinks I should sign on with Ray. Not going to happen. At least, not officially.

Seems like, despite this resolve, I repeatedly get dragged into Ray's world. And end up throwing baseballs at hit men, or whacking alligators with baseball bats, stuff like that.

Captain Rocky's is much safer.

Back to Krav Maga. It's a system of combat that is aggressive and can be lethal in the right hands—and feet—or whatever might be handy. Ben Levitsky ended his career with Mossad nearly ten years ago. I suspected he had done things that weren't nice, or legal, or even kosher. Now, he owned a studio in Orange Beach where he dispensed his knowledge to folks of all ages and skill levels. Nicole and I had already taken a gazillion lessons. Actually, three a week for four weeks, but my hands felt like a gazillion. They ached and making a fist was a process not an event. No way this was a healthy pursuit. I mean, I could hardly wrap my fist around a beer.

Nicole felt otherwise. She loved it. Her hands were fine. Fact is, all of her was fine. But that's another story.

We had completed our morning session of bag punching and kicking and spinning and thrusting and had downed a couple of breakfast burritos my cooks had whipped up for us, when I sat down at an umbrella-shaded table on the deck at Captain Rocky's with Carla Martinez, my manager. The one who really runs the joint. She had a stack of stuff for me to go over, checks and papers to sign, invoices and orders to review, inventory lists that blurred my vision. Paperwork is not my thing.

It was August and the daily temp, which was projected to reach well into the nineties, had begun to climb. I had already downed two glasses of sweet tea and was working on a third.

Nicole opted for a walk on the beach. In a red string bikini. Not enough material to wad a shotgun. An exhibitionist's dream. Which was another of her outstanding qualities. All that exposed flesh garnered a lot of attention. As she disappeared up the beach, every male head turned in her direction. Most of the women, too. She even brought a touch football game to a halt. Now, as she walked back our way, I saw she had attracted a couple of followers. Two old dudes with metal detectors. I don't think their focus was on finding coins any longer. Pervs.

Speaking of focus.

"Are you listening to me?" Carla asked.

"Sure."

"What did I just say?"

"That we needed to order more ribs and chicken."

She smiled. "And here I thought you were daydreaming again. Glad to know you can multitask."

"I can. I'm a multitasking freak."

"You're a freak, all right." She smiled.

Like Nicole, Carla enjoyed giving me a ration. Come to think if it, so did Ray and Pancake.

She twisted in her chair and looked up the beach. The direction of my gaze. Where Nicole was leaving a trail of footprints near the waterline. "I should've known."

I smiled. "Never get tired of that view."

"You're obsessed."

"Sort of."

"Definitely. But she is beautiful. If I swung that way, I'd do her."

I shook my head. She laughed and turned back toward me.

"No worry there though. I do like my dudes."

"That you do."

"Well," Carla said, "you can put all your awesome multitasking talent away, because that's all I have." She stood and gathered up the papers, stuffing them into a folder. "What's on your agenda today?"

"This. I think I'm done."

"It's ten o'clock in the morning."

"Long day." I smiled.

She gave me a look I'd seen all too often. The one that said I was incorrigible.

"Don't strain anything," she said. "I've got work to do."

Like I said, she really runs the place.

She started to walk away but stopped. "Oh, I forgot. Pancake called a little while ago. Wanted to know if you guys were here. Said he'd drop by."

"Any idea what's on his mind?"

"No one knows what's on his mind. What little he has."

That was true. Not that Pancake was dumb. Far from it. One of the smartest people I've ever known. But, for lack of a better word, he's quirky. And that's being kind.

Carla continued, "I asked but he said he wanted to see your face when he told you."

That didn't sound good.

"Guess you'll know soon." She laughed and headed toward the bar.

Nicole climbed the stairs to the deck and walked my way. And what a walk. Runway perfect. The murmuring of the late breakfast crowd dropped to near silence and gazes followed every stride and sway.

She slipped on the flimsy coverlet she had left hanging over one of the chairs and sat. "Did you get your homework done?"

"I did."

"Good boy."

Boy? I expected her to pull out some treats and pat my head. A reward for a job well done. She didn't.

That's when Pancake arrived. All six feet five and 280 lumbering pounds of him. His red hair looked windblown. His left cheek sported what looked like road rash.

"What happened to you?" I asked.

"Three Wild Turkeys and a bicycle."

No further explanation offered. I tried to picture him on a bicycle. Sure, he and I had terrorized the neighborhood on our bikes as kids, but he outgrew the tensile strength of a Schwinn before we reached high school. The only thing that could safely transport him now was his massive dually pickup. Apparently, a bicycle couldn't.

"Did you smear on any antibiotic ointment?" Nicole asked.

"Rubbed some dirt on it." He smiled. "That'll do."

Worked when we were kids, so why not?

"Ray's headed this way," he said.

"Really?" I asked. "Why?"

Ray avoided Captain Rocky's like it was a toxic waste site. Something must be up.

"He has a job for you guys," Pancake said.

"I don't work for Ray."

"I do," Nicole said. "What is it?"

Pancake laughed. "You're gonna love it."

"What?" I asked, not really wanting to know, even as a niggle of curiosity rose. Or was it dread? Whenever Pancake said something like "you're going to love it" or "wait till you hear this" or "here, hold my beer and watch this," what followed was never predictable, and often led to chaos and mayhem.

"I think I'll let Ray handle it. Wouldn't want to spoil it for him."

"That bad?" Nicole asked.

Pancake nodded. "Oh yeah. We've done a bunch of crazy shit, but this'll beat all."

"Cool," Nicole said.

No, probably not close to cool.

CHAPTER TWO

FIFTEEN MINUTES LATER, Ray arrived. He took a seat. Didn't say a word. Carla plopped down a cold can of Mountain Dew in front of him. Ray and Mountain Dew had a close relationship. Almost pathological. I think he drank a dozen a day.

"Anything else?" Carla asked.

"This'll do," Ray finally spoke. "Thanks."

"Give me a wave if you change your mind." She headed back inside.

"What's up?" I asked.

"Got something I want you two to check out."

"I don't work for you," I said.

He shrugged. "Nicole does. And you'll pretty much follow her wherever she goes."

I had no response for that. Mainly because it was true.

"So, what do you have for us, boss?" Nicole asked.

Boss?

"Damnedest thing I've ever heard of," Ray said.

Pancake laughed. "All that and a passel of howler monkeys."

"The suspense is killing me," I said.

"Me, too," added Nicole.

I guess I neglected to add enough sarcasm to my question. For her. Not for Ray. He gave me a look before continuing.

"I got a call from an attorney over in Jacksonville," Ray said. "He wants us to sit down with his client and see if we can help."

"With what?" I asked, immediately regretting it. I had no idea why I was engaging in this. Better to stay in the foxhole and hope Ray blows over.

"Prove he only killed five people instead of seven."

"What?" Nicole said.

Ray took a big slug of Dew. "You know the name Billy Wayne Baker?"

Nicole looked at him, then me.

"Sounds familiar," I said.

"A convicted serial killer," Ray said.

I nodded, his history starting to take root in my head. "I do remember him. Vaguely. Murdered some folks over in Florida."

"That's him. Seven victims. Doing multiple life sentences."

"Not the death penalty?" I asked

"Part of the bargain. He confessed to all the killings. Saved the state a bunch of money. Got seven life sentences. No parole, of course."

"He's the client?" Nicole asked.

"Sure is."

"How does a lifer have the money to pay you?" I asked.

"He doesn't. But according to his attorney—guy named Winston McCracken—there's a benefactor who's paying the freight."

Nothing about that sounded right. "Serial killers now have benefactors?"

Another slug of Dew. "Apparently Billy Wayne does."

"Who is it?" Nicole asked. "The money man?"

"Don't know. That's part of the deal. He stays completely anonymous."

I couldn't quite wrap my head around that. A serial killer, who confessed, now wants to backtrack, and he found someone to pony up the cash to reopen the investigation. Who the hell would do that? And why?

"That makes no sense," I said. "He wants us to prove he didn't kill two of the people he confessed to killing? What? Five life sentences is better than seven?"

Ray balled one fist and then opened it, spreading his fingers, examining them. "All I know is what McCracken said. That's why I want you to check it out."

The situations Ray had dragged me into in the past were quirkily weird. Or was it weirdly quirky? Same difference, I suspect. Ray had roped me into things like staking out the adulterous Barbara Plummer. Who, of course, did get murdered right under my nose. Okay, maybe not my best day. Or trying to figure out how Hollywood A-List actor Kirk Ford woke up with the coed niece of a New Orleans mobster dead in his bed. Those were indeed quirky and odd, but I had to admit this was something else entirely.

"I am intrigued," I said.

"I see a screenplay in there somewhere," Nicole added.

I shook my head. "Of course, you do."

She slugged my arm. My already sore arm from all that Krav Maga crap. Not to mention that my hands were too tender to hit anything. Apparently, not so for Nicole.

"Besides keeping Jake in line, what's the plan?" she asked.

"Me? In line?"

"No small task." She ruffled my hair.

"I can't help you with that," Ray said. "Lord knows I've tried. But on the case, the first order of business would be a sit-down with McCracken. See what's what. He said he could get you in to see Billy Wayne."

"Who is where?" I asked.

"Union Correctional Institute. Over near Raiford."

"We're on it," Nicole said.

Of course, we are.

"When?" I asked.

"Tomorrow afternoon. His office in Jacksonville."

"Short notice," I said.

"What? You got something else to do?"

I was sure I did but I couldn't think of a single thing.

CHAPTER THREE

WINSTON MCCRACKEN'S OFFICE was in Jacksonville's downtown business district not far from the famous Jacksonville Landing, a central entertainment, dining, and tourist hangout along the St. John River. Took nearly five hours to get there from Gulf Shores, Alabama. Should've taken longer, but Nicole was driving. I suspected the 450 horses beneath the hood of her white SL550 Mercedes were panting and lathered up by the time we let them rest in the parking deck. They emitted ticking noises and heat ripples into the already hot air above the hood.

The building was fairly generic. Concrete, plain facade, with one of those twirling glass-door entryways. I hate those things. I could never match my stride to the spin rate. Nicole had no problem and charged right through, while I had to do a hop, skip, and jump to avoid a whack in the butt. And even with that I caught a slight nip.

McCracken's suite consumed half the fourth floor. The waiting room was empty and the receptionist, a humorless young woman who seemed to be having a bad day, led Nicole and me to McCracken's office. Corner, with a view of other buildings. Lots of buildings. No water view. Maybe he wasn't high enough up the legal food chain to warrant one.

McCracken welcomed us and offered coffee or a soft drink, which we declined. He glanced at me, but his gaze lingered on Nicole. We shook hands and then sat in moderately comfortable chairs facing his desk. Massive law books filled the wall behind him, except for a single shelf where a dozen baseballs and a picture of a woman and three teenagers, girls, sat. Handsome family. McCracken had a full-house backfield of daughters. I felt a twinge for him. He was outnumbered and surrounded in his own house.

He seemed to wear it well, however. He looked to be mid-fifties, round face, intense brown eyes, half glasses resting low on his nose. He wore a white shirt, yellow tie, gold cuff links. His gray suit jacket hung on a hat rack near the wall to his left. The papers on his desk were neatly stacked and squared.

"Thanks for coming over," he said.

I nodded but said nothing.

Nicole said, "We at Longly Investigations are glad you called." She smiled. "And more than a little intrigued."

McCracken raised an eyebrow, and one shoulder. "It's definitely an unusual situation."

"Tell us what the story is," I said.

"Before we do that, I want to say what an honor it is to meet you."

"Me?" I asked.

"I'm a huge baseball fan." He gave his chair a half spin toward the shelves behind him and waved a hand at the line of baseballs that kept his family company. He swung back toward me. "I followed your career. You were great."

I loved this guy. He obviously was a sports aficionado. Nicole simply shook her head.

"Thanks, but that was many years ago."

"Still, you could really heave a fastball." He smiled. "And from what I read about that whole Victor Borkov thing, you still can." He laughed.

I shrugged. "We were in a pickle and baseballs were the only weapons I had."

Which was true. Borkov had captured us and taken us far out in the Gulf. Middle of the night. His plan was to tie us to an iron ring and toss us overboard. Into very black and very deep water. Not a pleasant thought. Who thinks up things like that in the first place? I managed to whack his two henchmen with baseballs. My speed was down to only eighty miles an hour but it was enough to stun them so that Nicole and I could fly off the back of the 100-foot yacht and plunge thirty feet into the cold water. Where Ray and his special forces buddies saved us and took out Borkov and crew. Hell of a night.

"Speaking of baseballs," McCracken said. "If you could indulge me." He pulled open a drawer and removed a bright, white, obviously new baseball. "Maybe an autograph?" He extended the ball and a marker pen toward me.

I signed the ball and handed it back.

He examined it, smiling broadly. He stood, placed it next to the others, and returned to his seat. "Thanks. A wonderful addition to my collection." He rubbed his hands together. "To business. I'm sure you know of Billy Wayne Baker."

"A little," I said.

"He's a confessed serial killer. Seven victims. Officially. I was part of his defense team. We never made it to trial—which is a good thing, I think. Had we, he'd probably be sitting on death row."

"No lawyerly tricks would've worked?" I asked.

McCracken smiled. "Point well taken. Sure, we had a few moves but, in the end, they likely wouldn't have been enough. The prosecution held all the cards. They had DNA in every case."

"So he really did all seven murders?" Nicole asked.

"You mean like the DNA doesn't lie?" McCracken raised an eyebrow and gave her a half smile.

She smiled back. "Something like that."

"He did confess to all the killings. Right?" I said.

"He did."

"And now he wants to recant?"

"On two of them, yes."

"Why only two?" Nicole asked. "He'd still be in jail for life."

McCracken nodded. "Actually, several lives." He scratched his chin. "Billy Wayne's an unusual character. A serial killer? Sure. Brutally so, in fact. But he has a deep sense of fair play."

"Really?" I asked. "Didn't he break and enter at night and then rape and murder his victims?"

"You've done your homework."

I shrugged.

We had dug into Billy Wayne's history. Actually, Pancake had. He had printed out forty pages on Billy Wayne's killing spree, which I had read aloud while Nicole flew across the Florida panhandle to Jacksonville.

McCracken slipped off his glasses and rested them on the desk. "Actually, he talked his way into some of the victims' homes. As you'll see when you meet him, there's more there than what you might think. He's smart, charming, very well read. Could've been anything he wanted. In fact, he was a straight-A student in prelaw at Florida State when he began killing. That was just over four years ago. He went on for around two years until his arrest and incarceration a couple of years ago."

"The fair play comes in where?" I asked.

"I know it sounds odd, but Billy Wayne does believe he's responsible for his own actions. Willing to pay that price. That's why he confessed and waived a trial."

"And to take the death penalty off the table," I said.

"That was my doing. What Billy Wayne really wanted was to tell the truth."

"And the truth is?" Nicole asked.

"He always said he didn't do two of the killings."

"Which ones?"

"He won't say."

"What does that mean?" she asked.

"Just what I said. Not only that, he says he knows who did them."

Nicole's brow furrowed. "But he's not telling?"

McCracken tapped an index finger on his desk a couple of times and shook his head. "No. He wanted to have his day in court. At the sentencing. Wanted to tell the judge he only killed five people."

"Did he?" I asked.

"Never got the chance. I stopped him cold."

"Why?"

"If Billy Wayne reneged on any of the killings, the prosecution would have pulled the plug on the deal. That wasn't up for negotiation." McCracken pinched the bridge of his nose and sighed. He looked up at me. "In the end, the prosecution didn't really care who killed whom but they wouldn't take the deal unless he confessed to all seven." He shrugged. "God forbid there were any open cases left behind. Anyway, we—me and the prosecution—met with the judge. Told him what Billy Wayne wanted. Of course, the prosecution made it clear that if he did recant on any of the killings the deal was off. I said Billy Wayne would confess to all but wanted it on the record that he didn't do two of the murders. The judge almost killed the deal right then and there. Said if Billy Wayne confessed to something he didn't do, maybe a trial was in order so he could prove it."

"But, he didn't," Nicole said.

McCracken shook his head. "Took some tap dancing, but I convinced the judge that Billy Wayne was comfortable—I actually used that word—with a full confession. Then, it took some arm twisting, but Billy Wayne finally agreed."

"Sounds like an honest citizen," I said.

McCracken smiled. "I can appreciate your skepticism. Were I in your position, I'd probably come to the same conclusion. But I know Billy Wayne. As well as anyone does." He picked up a black Mont Blanc pen from his desk, examined it, and laid it aside. "He's a sick young man, a brutal killer, but he does have a sense of responsibility, and, as I said, fair play."

"So why now?" Nicole asked. "His conviction, or confession, was years ago. Why stir things up at this late date?"

"While I was twisting Billy Wayne's arm on the deal, I told him he'd get his chance to tell his story sometime down the road. He countered that no one would believe him if he confessed to all of them, to which I said no one believed him anyway." He shrugged. "Not then and probably not ever, confession or no. That any recantation would fall on deaf ears. Unless some new evidence came up."

"Did it?" Nicole asked.

"No. But Billy Wayne is convinced it's out there. All it takes is for someone to find it."

"And that's where we come in?" I asked.

McCracken nodded. "So it seems."

"So, Billy Wayne bided his time and now has a benefactor," I said. "An anonymous one, I understand."

"I can tell you that this person has a keen interest in crime and forensic science and all things law enforcement. He's supported crime labs and police associations for years. Has one of the largest collections of first-edition crime novels in the country."

"A crime groupie?" Nicole asked.

McCracken smiled. "You might say that."

"How many people know Billy Wayne denied two of the killings?" I asked.

"Of course, the prosecutor and the judge do. But I don't think they really believed Billy Wayne. Or more likely even cared. I think they thought he was simply trying to mess with the system. Plus, the aftermath of the rumors and rumblings a couple of years ago. I suspect anyone who heard those has long forgotten that part of the Billy Wayne Baker story. So, in reality, only me and his benefactor."

"All this time he's been silent on the subject?" I asked.

McCracken nodded.

"Why? Seems like a newspaper or TV reporter, even some true crime writer, would listen to his story and run with it."

"All I know is that he said if he made too many waves, he wouldn't be safe."

"From other prisoners?" Nicole asked.

"Or the guards," McCracken said. "He said if he pointed the finger where it needed pointing, things could go sideways—his word."

"But now he's willing to take that chance?" I asked.

McCracken opened his hands, palms up. "That seems to be the case. He was clear that he didn't simply want to come clean, but rather he wanted proof that he was being truthful."

That actually made sense. On some level. Billy Wayne screaming his innocence, even on two of the murders, maybe especially on only two, wouldn't do much. Except possibly make him a prison target. But, if he had real evidence, proof, that might be different. What he hoped to accomplish, how that would change his life in any way, I still didn't grasp, but maybe it was the fair play thing. Whatever that was.

"How did this anonymous guy and Billy Wayne hook up?" Nicole asked.

"He sent Billy Wayne a letter. They began a correspondence. Billy Wayne apparently came to trust him and told him his story.

The guy believed him and decided to help. He then contacted me. To say I was surprised doesn't quite cover it. So, I called Ray and here we are."

"What's the next step?" I asked.

"I've got you a sit-down with Billy Wayne."

"When?"

"Tomorrow. Nine a.m." He looked at Nicole. "I'd suggest it only be Jake. Women visitors always create a stir inside Union Correctional." He smiled. "Particularly one that looks like you. It would no doubt create a riot."

"What's wrong with a little riot?" she said.

Good grief.

CHAPTER FOUR

THE UNION CORRECTIONAL Institute, an important part of the larger Florida prison system, housed the baddest of the bad. Definitely maximum security, it even had its own death row. It had been home to such pleasant citizens as Daniel Conahan, the Hog Trail Murderer; Danny Rolling, the Gainesville Ripper; and two of the Xbox Murderers, Troy Victorino and Jerone Hunter. It now also housed one Billy Wayne Baker—in gen pop, his confessions having freed him from death row.

Billy hadn't gotten a cute moniker like slasher or ripper or strangler, though strangulation had been his basic method for murder. I suspected the newspapers had mostly ignored old Billy Wayne because his killings took place in the less populated areas and smaller towns of northwest Florida. Not to mention that Florida had a laundry list of serial killers to choose from and there were only so many newspaper column inches available. They might buy ink by the barrel, but space could kick off a barroom brawl among reporters.

Maybe if he'd chopped up his victims or posed them in a bizarre ritualistic fashion, he would have garnered more attention. But simple rape and strangulation weren't worthy.

Not in the Sunshine State, anyway.

Union Correctional squatted along a two-lane road halfway between Jacksonville and Gainesville near the tiny town of Raiford. It was sterile and institutional and more than a little scary. Nicole felt the same way. I knew this because as we approached the facility, she said, "This place looks scary."

"That's why you're not going in."

On the drive down, she had said she was "damn sure" going in with me. I said no. She said I couldn't stop her. I said I could—and would. She said I was an ass. I agreed but that she still wasn't going inside.

"Why?" she asked.

"Because I don't want to have to watch out for you, and me, at the same time."

"There are guards there, I presume."

Presume?

"Yes, but they have their hands full. If the inmates get restless, they might just toss us out. Before we ever get to Billy Wayne." I could see her mulling that over and went on. "Besides, I don't want Billy Wayne distracted. The visit probably won't be very long and there are a few things I need to get from him."

She gave me a glance. "I hate it when you're right."

"I know."

"At least it's a rare event." She smiled.

She can be so funny.

When she pulled up to the entry gate, I got out and walked around to the driver's side. She lowered the window. "You going to hang around here or what?"

"I'll drive into town and find a Starbucks."

"Not sure Raiford is big enough for a Starbucks."

"Never seen a place without one."

She left.

I stood before the entry door and stared at it. Wasn't looking forward to being inside. What if they had a riot, or mistook me for one of the inmates, or lost the keys? Silly, but standing there, a sliver of claustrophobia reared its head. I looked up at the clear blue sky, figuring I'd miss it the most. That and Nicole.

I remembered the first time I was in jail. Eight years old. Me and Pancake. We had done something stupid. Spray-painted our names on Mr. Fletcher's garage. He wasn't happy. Neither was Ray. We couldn't deny it was us, our names emblazoned in red on the white clapboard. Like I said, something stupid.

Ray decided we were inveterate criminals. Destined to be outlaws. Not the first time he had said that but this time he added that we needed to learn our future. He knew a guy at the county jail. Ray always knew a guy, it seemed. Sargent something or other.

My mother was alive then. She defended us, saying we were just kids. Ray didn't listen. Said we either learned now or later the hard way. He finally won the argument by saying she should consider it a field trip with a lesson attached.

The sergeant was scary. Dark eyes, a thick mustache, and not a smile to be seen. He showed us the entire jail, with all its concrete walls and clanging doors, before locking us in a tiny cell. He and Ray then went for lunch. A long lunch. Seemed like days.

Ray's point was well taken.

I took a deep breath and entered Union Correctional. Fortunately, the guard had my name on his clip board. He didn't smile, probably universal for jailers, but he made a call. Five minutes later a uniformed officer named Rafael Lopez appeared. He led me into the entry building. After showing my ID, emptying my pockets, giving up my phone, and undergoing a search, he explained the rules, emphasizing that they were rigid and not negotiable. He didn't smile either. Not once. I then sat on a bench and waited for another guard to escort me inside to the visitors' area.

Last night, after Nicole and I checked into the Hyatt, we had a nice dinner, a stroll through Jacksonville Landing, and then a few drinks at the hotel bar. Back in our room, Nicole used me for her pleasure—really, she did—I only participated to be polite—and then she immediately rolled over and went to sleep. No cuddling, no pillow talk. She could be such a guy sometimes. I was too amped up for sleep so I reread Pancake's research on Billy Wayne Baker.

Billy Wayne was twenty-six. He had begun his killing spree four years earlier, a week before his twenty-second birthday. His first victim had been in Apalachicola. A young woman who lived alone. Killed in her apartment on a Sunday night. He left behind DNA and fingerprints. Lucky for Billy Wayne, and unlucky for the cops and the world in general, he wasn't in any of the databases, neither AFIS nor CODEX, so he remained anonymous.

Three months later, farther north, Wanda Brunner crossed paths with Billy Wayne. Late at night in her Santa Rosa Beach trailer. Her husband, a long-haul trucker, had been three states away at the time of her murder. After a thorough dusting, no prints were found in the trailer. DNA was and an analysis proved the Apalachicola and Santa Rosa Beach murders were connected. Florida now had a new anonymous terror on the loose.

Then Billy Wayne went quiet for a little over a year. Officials began to think maybe he had moved on. Or died. But he reappeared in Pine Key where three more victims breathed their last breath. All in a three-month period. Loretta Swift, owner, along with her husband, Peter, of a bakery/sandwich shop; bank teller Noleen Kovac; and Sara Clark, the wife of a local cop.

Then, a mere twenty-four hours after the death of Sara Clark, Billy Wayne emerged near Defuniak Springs for victim number six. Misty Abbott, who had worked in a nail salon. Then, four months later, he reached the end of the road. In Lynn Haven, just east of Panama City. His seventh and final victim was Della Gibson, like Billy an FSU college student, home for a long weekend to visit her widowed father, a local prosecutor. The end came because Billy Wayne was stupid and foolhardy. He was popped the day after his final murder, less than a mile from the crime scene, for shoplifting a pair of running shoes. When his prints were uploaded into AFIS, and they matched those taken from Marilee Whitt's Apalachicola home, Billy Wayne's career came to a screeching halt.

His entire reign of terror had lasted less than two years but it had sent a chill throughout northern Florida. All the killings happened in the victims' homes, where they should be sheltered from such evil. But with someone like Billy Wayne on the prowl, was anyone safe? That's the fear that led to many sleepless nights in that corner of Florida. Particularly for women who lived alone. Gun and security system sales had skyrocketed.

With his arrest, the nightmare ended and Floridians could finally breathe again. Until the next Billy Wayne appeared, anyway. And with this being Florida, that was inevitable. Only the when, where, and how many were in doubt.

The metal bench I sat on wasn't designed for comfort, and my butt felt like it had gone to sleep. Finally, a young black guard named Marcus McKinney appeared. Tall and fit with a warm smile. The first one I'd seen.

"You Mr. Longly?" he asked.

I stood. "Yeah." We shook hands.

"Let's go." I followed him through a pair of locked doors, opened from the inside by stone-faced guards.

"They go over the rules with you?" Marcus asked.

Lopez had. Stay with my escort, don't talk to anyone unless spoken to, and don't even think about trying to be cute. He hadn't really used that word but he had said that bending any of the rules, like attempting to pass something to Billy Wayne, or offering any form of nonverbal communication, or stirring up even a minor disturbance, and I'd get to see the business end of Union Correctional. Pleasant thought.

"Sure did," I said.

"Your first time here?" he asked.

"Yes."

He let out a soft laugh. "Looks like it. You're all bug-eyed."

"It's my natural look."

"Yeah, right."

To say that Union Correctional was disconcerting didn't cover it. The palpable undercurrent of violence was amplified by the clanking of doors, the shouts of the inmates, and the absolutely humorless demeanor of the guards, who in many ways looked more dangerous than the few inmates I saw. But I managed to stick with McKinney and was soon seated at a glass window, phone on the partition wall to my right.

I waited, and fidgeted, and waited. Finally, Billy Wayne appeared. He was smaller than I had pictured in my mind. Couldn't be more than five-eight, maybe 140. Thin and wiry but with a round face that still held its baby fat. He looked about fourteen. Pleasant and harmless. Hard to imagine this was the guy that had terrorized this neck of the woods.

Billy Wayne sat. He wore a white prison jumpsuit, the short sleeves rolled to his shoulders. No tattoos visible. He eyed me as if taking my measure and then picked up the handset on his side. I grabbed mine.

"Jake Longly," he said.

"That's me."

"I'm a big baseball fan. Know all about you."

Not what I expected.

He continued. "I have to admit I was impressed that you'd be the one I'd talk to."

"That was years ago. I'm sort of a P.I. now."

"That's what they tell me. Thanks for coming."

I shrugged. "I'd be lying if I didn't say I'm intrigued you asked to see us. This whole story is more than a little odd."

"True that." He smiled.

"And I've got to say, it crossed my mind that you might be doing this as a way to relive your crimes."

He huffed a smirk. "Look at you. The amateur shrink."

I couldn't suppress a smile. "Never been mistaken for that. But, still, the idea did pop up."

"I get that."

He hesitated as if considering what to say. Maybe he was contemplating ending the interview. Dropping the handset and walking away.

He didn't and continued. "I relive each and every one on a daily basis." He waved an arm. "Not much else to do in here. Lot's of time to think on things."

"Good or bad memories?"

Again, he hesitated. "A little of both."

I nodded. I suspected that was true. He probably had mixed feelings on everything he had done. At least I hoped he did. Remorse can go a long way toward saving your soul. And if anyone's soul needed redeeming, it was Billy Wayne's.

"Let's get to it," he said. "The guards have a habit of cutting visits short." He shrugged. "One of the many games they play."

"Okay. Tell me why I'm here."

"Didn't McCracken fill you in?"

"To some extent. But I want to hear it from you."

"Good enough. I guess you've looked into my career—so to speak."

"I have."

"What I want is for you to prove what I know to be true."

"That you only did five of the murders?"

"That's right."

"Can I ask you something?"

"That's why you're here," Billy Wayne said.

"How did a prelaw student, a good one from what I read, get mixed up in this? I mean, you were on a career path of a different sort. What happened?"

"I've asked myself that more than a few times," he said. "It was almost accidental that I uncovered that little slice of my personality."

The murderous slice. The thick glass separating us was suddenly comforting.

"How'd that come about?" I asked

"I was twenty-two. Almost. Still in college. Went down to see some friends on St. George's Island for the weekend. On the way back, I stopped in a bar in Apalachicola. Met this chick. We went back to her place. Things got hot and heavy, as they say, but then she backed down."

"Said no?"

"Yeah. I wasn't into her teasing. It was sort of like being mocked. Put down. And I'd had a few drinks. More than a few, actually. And some weed. That isn't an excuse, merely a fact. In the end, I more or less held her down. Threatened her. Did what needed to be done. Afterwards she got all crazy. Saying she was going to call the police. That kind of thing."

"So, you killed her?"

"Sure did. I could see law school going up in smoke if she talked. Afterwards, I was scared. Terrified would be more accurate. I blasted out of there and hit the road."

"A natural reaction to that sort of panic. When you realized you'd done something that couldn't be undone?"

He scratched the side of his nose. "It was sloppy. I never thought about DNA or fingerprints or anything like that. At least not at that moment. Later, after I was forty, fifty miles up the road, and my brain was functioning again, I realized that I should've considered those things and cleaned up. By then it was too late. No way I was going back. So, I just cut and ran." He shook his head. "Funny thing is that, right then, driving up the highway, I knew I'd get caught. Didn't know when, where, or how, but I knew it'd happen."

"But you also left evidence at each of the other scenes."

"Not for lack of trying. After I thought about it, I wore gloves and condoms." He gave a soft laugh. "'Course I never figured condoms would leak when you took them off." He shrugged. "Live and learn."

"So you altered your MO?"

"Not that it helped all that much." He rubbed one shoulder. "She, that first one, put up a fight. Scratched me up pretty good. So, next time I brought along a knife. A big scary one. Made for better cooperation."

"I imagine so," I said.

Billy Wayne's calm manner was disturbing. He talked as if relating a story that had little to do with him. Like giving someone the thumbnail of a movie he'd seen. I know this isn't unusual for sociopaths, but sitting here looking it in the eye was, for lack of a better word, unsettling.

"So, with the first girl, in Apalachicola—Marilee Whitt—you got angry and killed her. What about the others?"

He looked up at the ceiling for a couple of seconds, then back to me. "After I fled Apalachicola and was driving back up to Tallahassee, something odd happened."

He stared at me as if expecting a response. I didn't have one so he continued.

"The killing, strangling the life out of her, set something off inside. I don't know what exactly, but I liked it." He looked down, gave a slow shake of his head, and then looked back at me. "It doesn't make much sense, but it was like some dark obsession escaped from a Pandora's Box inside my head." He raised an eyebrow and gave a half shrug. "I know that sounds ridiculous. Even does to me. But that's the best way I can describe what it felt like. Anyway, that was the beginning."

"The others were to relive that thrill?"

He nodded. "Sounds overly simple, doesn't it? Almost a cliché. But that's the truth of it." He let out a long, low sigh. "Don't know where that came from, where it'd been secreted inside my head, but once that darkness escaped, it sort of took over. I fought it. Knew it was wrong. But a day didn't go by I didn't think on it." Another sigh. "Three months later I was back at it."

"Were these better planned? Did you case each place? Maybe stalk each victim?"

"Not really." He hesitated as if considering what else to say. "I mean, I came to town, I looked around, found an opportunity, and took it."

"No real preplanning?"

He shook his head. "Wasn't hard though. Opportunities are everywhere. People don't lock their doors. Leave windows open. And most of these little towns turn in early. Easy to do what I needed to do and get back home long before anything was discovered."

"After the second killing—Wanda Brunner—in Santa Rosa Beach—nothing happened for over a year. That's when you began in Pine Key. Why the quiet period?"

Billy Wayne rubbed his nose with the heel of one hand. "I was wrestling with it. That thing inside. I knew what I was doing was wrong, and, like I said before, knew one day I'd get caught. Always works out that way. So, every time the feeling, the need, I guess, reared up, I managed to arm-wrestle it away. But eventually, I gave up fighting it." He shrugged. "That's the best way I can explain it."

"And the end?" I asked. "The shoplifting?"

"Stupid, huh?"

"Some have speculated that you wanted to get caught. That you did that to end it all."

I had read that in Pancake's documents. Some psych type offered that opinion. A few others agreed.

"Shrinks say all kinds of stuff. Mostly psychobabble. Keeps them in business, I guess." He nodded back over his shoulder. "Trust me, no one wants to be in here."

"I suppose that's a fact," I said.

"The truth is that it was simply a bad choice. Several bad choices. First off, I stayed around the area. Not sure why. At some motel off the highway. Should've gone back home. Things are always calmer there. Not like when I'm on the road hunting. Who knows, maybe I would've found someone else regardless of where I was. Done another killing. Anyway, I hung around. Even bought a map, trying to decide where to go next." He shrugged. "It was worming around in my head, that's for sure. But, instead, I walked in that store. I wanted those shoes and took them."

"I'm curious. Why go through all this now? I mean, seven life sentences versus five doesn't seem like much of a victory."

"To me it is."

"I see."

"Do you? Or am I talking to the wrong person?"

"I suspect we'll see. Tell me what you believe and what exactly you expect from Longly Investigations."

"I confessed to all seven killings. Had to for the bargain. But the truth is two of them weren't mine. I expect you to figure out which ones and to prove it wasn't me."

"And that's what we'll try to do. But, can I ask which ones you deny doing?"

"Well now, didn't I just say that was what you're supposed to figure out?"

"It would help if we knew where to look."

Billy Wayne shrugged but said nothing.

"McCracken said you wouldn't tell him either. Said you knew who did it but had steadfastly refused to give up that information."

"Not going to now either."

"Why?"

Billy Wayne scratched at the stubble on his chin. "If I did, they'd say your investigation was biased. That rush to judgement crap. When this is all done, I want folks to know the truth. I want them to believe it. In my experience, knowing and believing don't always go together."

"I agree with you there."

"Look, I did some bad shit. I'm fucked up. Sick in the head. I know that. But I didn't do two of those killings."

"And you want the person who did them to face justice? Like you did?"

"Actually, I don't give a rat what happens to them. I simply want the record straight. So to be fair, I think you should dig it up on your own. Free of any bias. Real or imagined."

"So we'll have to earn our money?"

"Seems fair to me."

Just as McCracken had said, Billy Wayne believed in fair play. Not sure his victims would agree.

"It would save a lot of shoe leather and time if I had at least a hint."

"I got lots of time."

"I know you didn't tell your attorney, McCracken. What about your mysterious fan club? The guy footing the bill for all this?"

"Nope. Didn't tell him either."

"Who is he?"

Billy Wayne shrugged, said nothing.

"We can find out. I mean, all your mail is censored, records are kept."

"Won't do any good. He can't tell what he don't know."

I leaned forward, elbows on the countertop before me, my face only inches from the glass that separated us. "Look, Billy Wayne, we'd like to help. We like fair play and truth and justice, too. But a little help would be nice."

Billy Wayne smiled. "I hear you guys are pretty good. Sniff around. It'll become apparent, I think."

"Why are you so reluctant to help here? The potential bias aside."

"Let's just say, if I make waves, start pointing my finger at people, things could get uncomfortable in here." He glanced over his shoulder again, and then back to me. "Not like I got any place to hide."

"Like someone might do you harm?"

"Possibly." He shrugged. "Likely."

"How so?"

"If I was pointing fingers at a member of your family, or at you, wouldn't you try to make things more than a little unpleasant for me?"

"I wouldn't even know how."

"Well, some folks do. I'll leave it at that."

I stared at him. "If I'm hearing you correctly, that also means that no one can know we're working on your behalf."

"That's part of the deal. Even a hint that I started this, or was in any way involved, could blow back on me." He gave me a half smile. "Once you dig up the facts, find the evidence, and do so independently, so to speak, I won't have to say a word. Everyone will know. And they'll believe. I won't have to point fingers or make trouble for myself. I'll only have to nod and say, 'Yeah, that's how it was.'"

I nodded but said nothing.

Billy Wayne leaned back, folded his arms over his chest. "So, you going to help or not?"

"Let me talk to Ray. He's the boss man. We'll let you know."

"You'll do it," he said.

"Maybe."

"You will. I see curiosity all over your face."

CHAPTER FIVE

ONCE I LEFT Billy Wayne and made my way back through the final locked door, the gate guard returned all my stuff. I stepped outside, into the sunlight. I honestly felt as if I'd been freed from a dark cave. One inhabited by monsters. The shouting and clanking and danger-thickened air evaporated and I could breathe again.

I called Nicole.

"Be there in fifteen minutes," she said.

"Where are you?"

"You were right. No Starbucks in Raiford. I guess a population of a couple of hundred doesn't fit their business plan. Yet they have them on every street corner in New York and LA. Go figure. I'm in Lake City. Just up the road. No Starbucks here either, but I found a cute little mom and pop coffee shop. On my way."

While I waited, I called Ray and brought him up to speed on everything Billy Wayne had to say.

"He wouldn't tell you the names?"

"Nope."

"That'll make our job more difficult."

"So, you're going to take the case?" I asked.

"Too interesting to pass up."

"That's what Billy Wayne said. That he saw curiosity all over my face."

"That's why you're a terrible poker player." Ray laughed. "But, got to admit, I'm curious, too. Not to mention that, from what McCracken said, the pay is good."

"We're leaving in a few minutes." I glanced at my watch. "We should be there before five."

"Pancake and I'll start sniffing around. I'll call McCracken and get the paperwork going."

"Sounds good." I ended the call.

Nicole showed up. I hopped in.

"Where to?" she asked.

"Ray's."

And we were off. Gravel pinged the undercarriage and a thin dust trail lifted in our wake as she turned north toward state highway 121 and, after a few dips and turns, I-10.

"How'd it go?" Nicole asked.

"Interesting."

"That doesn't tell me much."

"He's an odd cat. Certainly doesn't look the part. More like a shy, quiet college kid. Maybe only high school."

"Who just happens to rape and murder?"

"Well, since you put it that way."

She whipped around an eighteen-wheeler, the turbulence rocking the Mercedes, before she settled back into the right lane. The speedometer read 95.

"I still think I should've gone in with you."

"If you had, you'd wish you hadn't. Lots of very angry and unhappy folks inside. And that's just the guards."

She gave me a look. The one that said I was a wimp. That she could've handled it. Probably true, but still. I started to suggest she keep her eyes on the road but thought better of it.

"So, do we have a job?"

"We do. Ray said it was too interesting to pass up."

She smiled. "I agree."

Again, it should have taken six hours to reach Gulf Shores. For Nicole, four hours and forty-five minutes. She actually got pulled over for speeding. Eighty-five in a sixty-five zone. While the officer extricated himself from his patrol car and sauntered up to her side of the Mercedes, I gave her a bunch of grief, to which she replied, "Watch and learn." Really?

She undid a button and thrust out her chest, smiled that smile, and got a warning. Are you kidding me? I'd probably be hauled back to Union Correctional, but she not only got off, the patrolman actually, I swear to God, apologized for stopping her.

Not sure what I was supposed to learn from all that, since I lacked the required physical attributes, but I had to admit, it was impressive. Infuriating, but impressive.

She smiled and thanked the officer, promised to hold it down, and we were off. Two miles down I-10 we were back up to 85 and cruising.

We reached Gulf Shores around four thirty, where we found Ray and Pancake in Ray's office—the round teak table on his deck. Both had computers open. A rock, painted like a sea otter, sat on a stack of papers near the center of the table. The umbrella offered shade and a soft on-shore breeze made the deck tolerable. Still hot, but not a true sauna.

Pancake held a beer in one hand, a stack of papers in the other. The road rash on his cheek was healing nicely. A nearly empty can of Mountain Dew sat near Ray's laptop. He was intently typing something so said nothing, but rather waved us to sit. We took the two empty chairs.

In the corner behind Ray, a white marker board stood on a light-weight aluminum easel. I recognized Pancake's block script in bright red.

Billy Wayne's Timeline:

#1—August 2014—Marilee Whitt—Apalachicola

#2—November 2014—Wanda Brunner—Santa Rosa Beach

#3—December 2015—Loretta Swift—Pine Key

#4—February 2016—Noleen Kovac—Pine Key

#5—March 2016—Sara Clark—Pine Key

#6—March 2016—Misty Abbott—Defuniak Springs

#7—July 2016—Della Gibson—Lynn Haven

Before, the victims had been an abstract. A group of unknown people that offered no real hint to the level of Billy Wayne's damage to his corner of the world. Even reading about them in the pages Pancake had printed felt distant. Not real. Like a term paper or something. But seeing the names listed, in stark red letters, the dates of their demises, like an obituary, brought a degree of focus. And sadness. Each had been living a normal life, and then Billy Wayne showed up. Just like that, their individual movies ended. With a terror I knew from the materials I had already read. Sitting here, looking up at that board, I felt as if I was in the presence of true evil.

Nicole felt the same. I knew from the way her hands squeezed my arm, the way her eyes widened as she studied Pancake's chart.

And yet, when I recalled sitting there across from Billy Wayne, seeing his round childlike face, easy demeanor, almost innocent eyes, his small, delicate hands casually holding the phone, he seemed incompatible with such depravity. Yet, I knew it was true. That those hands had murdered—how many? Seven? Five? Did it really matter in the scheme of things?

The thought crossed my mind that Billy Wayne might be playing us. Maybe he really killed each of the people on the list. Maybe he was simply bored in prison and this was a game he wanted to play. Maybe he was looking for extra privileges. Or visits from newspaper and TV people. Maybe he needed to rekindle the notoriety that had once haloed him. Maybe he wanted to make fools of us all.

What did he really have to lose? And as he had said, he had time.

Ray dragged me from those thoughts.

"How was the trip?" Ray asked.

"Harrowing," I said

He raised an eyebrow.

"Nicole's driving."

"Wimp," she said.

"She did get pulled over though. On I-10."

"Really?" Pancake asked.

"I was only doing eighty-five," she said with a head shake.

"Didn't get a ticket," I said.

"I can't imagine why they let her off." Pancake laughed and looked at her. "Darling, I want you to be my chauffeur."

She smiled. "As long as I don't have to drive that behemoth you call a truck."

"Uh, never mind."

"How did things go with Billy Wayne?" Ray asked.

I told him more of our conversation. "He's a bright guy. And he's adamant about not telling us the name of the victims he says weren't his work."

Ray nodded.

"Where do you want to start?" I asked.

"Pancake and I've been looking into the victims, but we have more to discover. And I want to wait until we get the contract and the retainer before we move forward."

"How long will that take?" I asked.

"I suspect we'll be good to start our planning tomorrow."

"One thing," I said. "Billy Wayne said he wouldn't reveal the names because it could make things tough for him in prison."

"How so?" Ray asked.

"He wouldn't say."

"What I have so far," Pancake said, "is that the father of Della Gibson in Lynn Haven is a local prosecutor. Sara Clark in Pine Key was the wife of a cop. And Misty Abbott in Defuniak Springs had a brother who's a guard over at Took Correctional in Daytona Beach."

"Any of them could make things uncomfortable for Billy Wayne," Ray said. "With a simple phone call."

"They'd do that?" Nicole asked.

Ray shrugged. "Sure. Law enforcement types take care of their own. One, or more, of these guys could have a line to the guards at Union. And prison guards only need the slimmest excuse to lean on the inmates."

From what I saw at Union Correctional, that seemed plausible. The few guards I saw looked like they weren't overly thrilled with their lot in life. And with a captive audience, I suspected they wouldn't hesitate to flex their authority from time to time. Newspapers and TV often promoted such tales, sometimes almost gleefully to make a point, but seeing the environment firsthand added credibility to those stories. Being confined to a cage was bad enough, but if that confinement included beatings and stabbings and worse, that could truly be a living hell. Not that I felt all that sorry for Billy Wayne, but even he shouldn't be tortured. Much.

"Makes sense," I said. I stretched. "Anybody else hungry?"

"I am," Nicole said.

I looked at Pancake. He was always hungry. But to my surprise he shook his head, saying, "Me and Ray had pizza an hour ago."

"Actually, you had a pizza and a half," Ray said.

Pancake smiled. "Man's gotta eat."

I stood. "We'll head over to Captain Rocky's. Be happy to bring something back."

"We're good," Ray said. "Let's meet here tomorrow around noon and plan our approach."

"Will do."

Nicole scraped her chair back and stood. "Come on. Feed me."

"Yes, ma'am. Whatever you say."

"Whatever?" She smiled. "In that case, after we eat, I have a few more instructions in mind."

Am I the luckiest SOB on the planet?

CHAPTER SIX

NICOLE AND I shared a Cobb salad and a pair of shrimp tacos before Pancake's goofy-ass, grinning face lit up my iPhone screen. I licked my fingers, wiped them with a napkin, and grabbed it from the table.

"Changed my mind," he said. "I'm hungry."

Of course he was. I couldn't remember a single minute of any day he wasn't.

"What would you like?" I asked.

"A ribeye with Bordelaise sauce, potatoes au gratin, Caesar salad, and Bananas Foster."

"You have the wrong number."

"And you need to upgrade your menu."

"Never heard you complain before," I said.

"That's 'cause the price is right."

"Not to mention the food. All your favorites."

"Hard to argue with that," he said.

"What'll it be?"

"Surprise me." Then he said something to Ray I didn't catch. "Ray'll have the same."

"Will do."

I waved Carla over. "Pancake's hungry."

"I'll alert the media."

"Ray, too. Maybe a pair of oyster po'boys."

"That means extra oysters on both and a pile of jalapeños on Pancake's." She nodded. "I'll have them up in a few."

While Nicole and I waited, we talked about the case.

"What do you make of this?" Nicole asked.

"I'm not sure. Basically, we're being asked to prove a guilty man is only partly guilty."

"I'd say he's beyond guilty. Partly or otherwise. He's a serial killer, after all."

"Billy Wayne's an unusual character for sure. In spite of his history, he actually comes off as a pleasant guy."

"Not the word I'd choose," she said.

"Maybe not the best choice. But he's smart. And, believe it or not, engaging, even charming on some level. I can see how he talked his way into those women's lives."

"My image of him doesn't include charming."

"If you saw him, you might feel differently," I said. "Baby faced. Innocent-looking. He even has small hands."

"And that's important how?"

"I don't know," I said. "It's just that, as he held the phone, his hands looked more like they should be playing a piano than strangling someone."

"But he did. Several times."

"The point is he's not a brute. Definitely not a snarling animal. That's what makes folks like him so dangerous. Serial killers aren't the creepy, crawly miscreants folks picture. At least not visually. Like Ted Bundy. Smart, pleasant, charming."

"Scary thought."

I nodded. The oyster po'boys arrived. Along with a large bag of extra crispy French fries and onion rings. Because an overloaded oyster po'boy was never enough for Pancake was Carla's take.

On the way out, I grabbed a bottle of Patron tequila from the bar.

"Put this on my tab," I told Carla.

She laughed." Everything's on your tab." She nodded at the bottle. "You two have a nice evening."

Nicole took the tequila from me. "Once I get some of this in him, he'll be defenseless."

Carla laughed. "Go get him, girl."

Nicole did. Eventually.

We dropped the food by Ray's, and then drove to Nicole's place out on The Point, a pricey enclave off Peppermill Road in Perdido Beach. The multimillion-buck mansion didn't belong to her, but rather to her uncle, Charles Balfour. The home sat thirty feet above the Gulf, a gently sloping collection of sand dunes and sea oats separating it from the sugary beach. We stayed there a lot. More so than my place, which was nice and also on the beach, but several million dollars less impressive.

We shed our clothes and sank into the deck jacuzzi, where we consumed half the Patron. Didn't take long before I was indeed defenseless and at Nicole's mercy. She took advantage. Twice. First there in the warm water, then on the cool sheets of her bed.

Now she lay in the crook of my arm, her cheek against my chest. Neither of us spoke for a while, letting our hammering hearts return to normal. I could feel her warm breath against my skin.

Finally, Nicole spoke. "I've been thinking about Billy Wayne."

"You were thinking of Billy Wayne during that?"

"I can multitask."

I was sure I had some incredibly witty comeback, but if so, it evaded me. I simply said, "What about Billy Wayne?"

"It makes no sense that he won't reveal the names of the two victims he denies are his. Or who he thinks killed them."

"His thinking is that if we uncover the truth, he'll simply have to agree with our findings. Our independent investigation. And not make waves or put himself in any danger."

"Which means that the killer is someone who could do Billy Wayne harm."

"Like a prosecutor or a cop or a prison guard?" I asked.

"Exactly."

"The question then becomes, which of those had a motive to kill?"

"And frame Billy Wayne," she said.

"Which would actually be clever."

"How so?" she asked.

"If I wanted to off someone, and a serial killer was at work in the area, the best cover would be to make it look like the victim was simply another one along the trail."

"I'll keep that in mind." She pinched my ribs. "In case you ever get mad at me."

"I'd need a serial killer first."

"That could be difficult. This is Alabama, not Florida where they have plenty to go around."

"Maybe we could borrow one," I said.

"Like a cup of sugar?"

I laughed. "More like an exchange program. We can ship them a couple of liquored-up good old boys complete with pickup trucks, and they could send us a serial killer."

"You've thought about this," she said.

"You brought it up."

"No, you did."

"Regardless, the next question," I said, "besides the motive, is who could effectively frame Billy Wayne? His DNA was found at each crime scene."

"True." Her hand slid across my chest. A finger made small circles.

I went on. "If we assume Billy Wayne's telling the truth, who could commit a pair of murders, and then plant evidence? Who would have access to Billy's Wayne's DNA?"

"You mean other than Billy Wayne himself?" she asked.

"You saying he really did do all the murders and is simply messing with us? Playing some sort of mind game?"

"Don't you think that's possible?"

"Sure do," I said. "But that's not how I read him."

"Then that leaves lovers, or friends, or his cleaning lady. Someone with access to his toothbrush."

"I'd bet on the cleaning lady. Not sure what her motive would be though."

She laughed. "Maybe she got tired of picking up his dirty underwear."

"Speaking of DNA."

"You're gross."

"You started it. Again. But, getting back to reality, I'd suggest someone like a cop, or a prosecutor, or even a prison guard—though that would be less likely, I imagine."

"Or someone at the crime lab," she said. "Wouldn't they handle all the evidence? Couldn't they mix it up?"

"Good thought."

"Of course it is," she said.

"I'd bet on the cop. The crime lab doesn't seem reasonable. For that line of reasoning to be true, a lab tech, say a DNA analyst, would have to kill two people in Billy Wayne's hunting grounds and then manipulate the evidence. To me, that would be far-fetched."

"Unless it's a conspiracy of sorts," Nicole said. "The killer had help inside the lab. Someone who would plant evidence for him."

"Or her."

She hesitated as if considering that. "I don't think so. This is a guy deal."

"We get blamed for everything."

"Not without reason. It's all that testosterone. Guys are serial killers."

"Aileen Warnos was a chick," I said. "And in Florida."

"She was pissed. At men in general. Her victims were simply opportunity."

"I didn't realize you were such an expert on serial killers."

"I can read." She pinched my ribs again. Harder this time. I was sure it'd raise a bruise. Maybe collapse a lung. I took a deep breath. Everything seemed to be in working order.

"A local cop makes the most sense," I said. "More so than a lab tech, or a prosecutor, or a guard. He'd already be in Billy Wayne's domain and would have easy access to the crime scenes and the evidence."

"The only place with more than one killing was Pine Key. Where the cop's wife was killed."

"That's what I'm thinking. If Billy Wayne's being truthful, the first Pine Key victim could be his; the other two could've been done by someone else. Like the cop. He'd have the DNA from the first victim and could plant it on the other two."

"Clever."

"Sure is."

"I mean you coming up with that's clever," she said.

"That's me. Clever and then some."

"You wish."

"I was slick enough to get in your pants."

I felt her head give a shake against my chest. "You got that backwards, I think. If memory serves, I got in yours."

"Let's say it was mutual."

"Let's. So, if the cop is the bad guy, why would he do it?"

"That's what we've been hired to find out."

Nicole propped up on one elbow and looked at me. "Which means we could be walking into a dicey situation."

"More like a hornet's nest," I said. "If we go in there and start asking questions about cases that were long ago solved, and that pointed the finger in another direction, say at a local cop, things could get wonky in a hurry."

"Unless we have a cover," she said.

"Like what?"

"I have an idea. At least I think I do."

"What is it?" I asked.

"I'm not ready to tell you yet."

"So, it's one of those days? Where you keep secrets?"

She smiled. "That's every day."

"That seems a little unfair."

"Life's unfair, Jake. Deal with it."

"And manipulative."

She laughed. "It's what we girls do."

"My point."

"Jake, do you really believe that all those years you wooed all those women that you were in charge? That they weren't the ones doing the manipulating?"

"Wooed?"

"Is that what you got from that?"

Uh-oh. I must have missed something. I gave a tentative nod. "Yeah."

"That's why you're so easy."

"I thought you liked that," I said.

"I do. Saves me buying you dinner."

"So, you're really not going to tell me your big idea?"

"Let me think about it. Maybe sleep on it."

"You ready to go to sleep?"

She rolled on top of me. "Probably not."

CHAPTER SEVEN

THE NEXT MORNING, I awoke refreshed. Last night had been one of those deep REM sleeps. No dreams and I'm not sure I even moved since I stirred in the same posture I had been in when everything faded. Tequila, a hot tub, and a few rounds of Nicole always guarantees a coma. At least I hadn't drooled on the pillow.

I stretched and rolled over. No Nicole. Out of bed, I slipped on my jeans and headed to the kitchen. Still no Nicole. Then, I saw her. On the deck. Curled in a lounge chair, wrapped in a white terry-cloth robe, cup of coffee in her hand. I stepped outside.

"I was about to come in and give you a shake," she said.

"I'm too tired for sex."

"No, you're not. But we have a class this morning."

I don't feel well, Mommy. Can I stay home from school today? That's what I thought, but I said, "Cool."

I flexed both hands. Two days away from Krav Maga classes had done wonders. I could actually make a fist without pain. Almost.

The class lasted an hour and a half. We finished around ten thirty. Next stop, my place, which was much closer than driving back out to the Point. We showered, dressed, and then headed to Captain Rocky's.

"Looks like you survived the tequila," Carla said, as we came in.

"Only drank half of it," I said.

She shook her head. "Only half?"

I smiled. "We'll work on the rest tonight."

"I'm starving," Nicole said. "We have to hook up with Ray and Pancake. What's quick and easy?"

"Breakfast burritos," Carla said. "That work?"

"Totally."

We grabbed a table on the deck.

"Should be interesting to see what Ray and Pancake've come up with," I said.

She nodded. No reply.

"What?" I asked.

"The idea I mentioned last night?"

"What about it?"

"I think it just might work."

"Tell me."

"I need to talk with Uncle Charles first." She glanced at her watch. "He should be in his office now."

"What does Uncle Charles have to do with Billy Wayne Baker?"

She stood. "You'll see." She walked to the far end of the deck, cell phone to her ear.

What was she up to? What I knew was that Uncle Charles, that's mega, A-List, Oscar-winning, Emmy-winning, DGA President, director/producer Charles Balfour to you, was under a lot of stress right now. I mean, his star, Kirk Ford, even though he was innocent, remained under the shadow of Kristi Guidry's murder. Kirk's co-stars, twins Tara and Tegan James, were looking at life-without for doing the actual killing. And Uncle Charles' crown jewel, the *Space Quest* franchise, was up in the air. More like a couple of billion dollars had been tossed into a hurricane. It was anyone's guess if the franchise could be saved, and more importantly, how much of the money would find its way back home.

He had left a major production in Paris and jetted to New Orleans to see the twins and help prep, and pay for, their defense. No easy task since they had confessed. Then, on to LA to hopefully salvage the latest *Space Quest* episode, the one being filmed at the time of Kristi's murder, and to do damage control for Kirk Ford, the face of the franchise. The only face now that the wildly popular twins were out of the picture. No pun intended.

I didn't envy him. Particularly since Nicole now had a "plan." Whatever it was. I couldn't imagine Uncle Charles relishing something else on his plate.

Took all of ten minutes for the crew to whip up our burritos and for Nicole to finish her call.

Carla set out plates in front of us as Nicole sat.

"I'll make a couple of others for you to take to Pancake and Ray when you leave," Carla said. "Actually, I'll make three. The big guy never stops at one."

"Good thinking," I said.

After we each took a couple of bites, I asked, "What's your idea?"

"I'll tell you at Ray's."

"I don't get a preview?"

She took another bite. Around a mouthful she said, "Eat."

I did.

We woofed down breakfast, grabbed the other burritos, and headed to Ray's. On the way I asked again what her idea was and she just smiled. I hate it when she does that. Not smile, that's good, but keep secrets. I tried to pout. Didn't work. She laughed, muttering something like, "Poor baby."

We, of course, found Ray and Pancake on the deck, each with a laptop open, Ray a Dew in one hand. I handed Pancake the bag.

"Carla made some burritos for you guys."

Pancake retrieved one and slid the bag toward Ray.

"I'm good," Ray said.

"Great," Pancake said. "More for me."

"What's happening?" I asked

"Lots," Pancake said. "We followed up on what Billy Wayne said. About someone being able to make his life a little less fun."

I started to say that Nicole had an idea, but she gave me a look. The one that said I'd be better served to stay silent. I hated when she did that, too. Knew what I was going to say almost as soon as I did. I simply said, "And?"

"You already know one of the victims was a cop's wife and another the daughter of a prosecutor," Ray said.

I nodded.

"And the girl killed over in Defuniak Springs, Misty Abbott, had a brother who works in the prison system," Pancake added.

"That's right," I said. "But of the three, I think he would be the least likely to frame Billy Wayne." Ray gave me a slow nod, so I went on. "Not sure how he would have access to the evidence. Be able to plant it."

Ray smiled. "That's exactly what Pancake and I thought."

"Last night, Nicole and I discussed that a lab tech at the state lab could be involved. Either as the killer, which I seriously doubt, or maybe manipulating the evidence for someone else."

"It's a good thought," Pancake said, looking at Ray. "Of course, that requires a conspiracy. Multiple players. At least two, probably more."

"Still possible," Ray said. He took a slug of Dew. "Since fingerprints were found at the first scene, in Apalachicola, I think that one is ruled out altogether. Not only because it was the first one, so no one would know that a killer was at work, but also because prints are difficult, almost impossible, to plant. DNA's a different story."

Pancake nodded. "Anyone with access to a sample could easily plant it on the bedsheets. Which is where it was found in every case except the first one. That was the only one with vaginal DNA."

I had told them earlier what Billy Wayne had said about changing his MO—wearing gloves and using condoms.

"That's why I think the most likely candidate is the cop," I said. "He would be local to the crimes and have access to the evidence."

"And spouses are always the first suspect," Pancake said.

"To me, that's the only thing that makes sense," I said. "Frank Clark, the cop, and the husband. The first killing in Pine Key, Loretta Swift, was Billy Wayne. That would give Clark access to the DNA. The other two are on him."

Now Ray eyed me. "Came up with that all on your own?"

"He did," Nicole said. "He's clever. Told me so last night." She nudged my elbow. "Something about being clever enough to get in my pants."

"A fact I can't get my head around," Pancake said.

Nicole laughed. I didn't.

Pancake continued. "I mean look at you, and him. Don't make much sense."

My friend. My girlfriend. My life.

Pancake leaned back in his chair. "So, you're thinking, maybe start with the murder of the cop's wife down in Pine Key and see what shakes out."

"And the other victim," I said. "Number two in Pine Key. Noleen Kovac."

"Why that one?" Ray asked.

I shrugged. "Billy Wayne was one and done everywhere else. I suspect he could have returned to Pine Key, but somehow that feels wrong."

"He say anything like that?" Pancake asked. "Like he never backtracked?"

I shook my head. "No."

Ray finished his Dew and crushed the can. "I agree. My take on this is exactly that. Billy Wayne was a mover. He showed up, did his thing, and left. No rearview mirror. No bounce back. And it doesn't make sense that two staged killings took place in separate locations. Everything comes together in Pine Key."

"Exactly," I said.

"So, Clark's our initial focus," Ray said. "We'll need to find a connection between Noleen Kovac and Sara Clark."

"Don't see it so far," Pancake said. "'Course we ain't been down there sniffing around yet."

"Which could be delicate," Ray said.

"True," Pancake added. "If we assume it's Clark, we'll be rubbing up against him."

Ray tossed the crumpled Dew can into the wastebasket behind him. "And ruffling his feathers could get out of hand."

Pancake shuffled through the pages in the folder before him and handed one to me. "Frank Clark. Been on the force there well over a decade."

"Good cop? Bad cop?" I asked.

"No real issues from what I can tell," Pancake said. "At least there's nothing out there in the world."

"Could be something internally," Ray said. "Something the department kept under wraps."

I examined the page that included a fuzzy photo of Clark. Square face, strong jaw, buzz cut, hooded eyes. He looked like a cop. A tough cop. Hell, he looked guilty.

"But why?" Nicole asked. "What would be his motive?"

Ray shrugged. "That's what we've been hired to find out."

"The motive for the wife could be easy," Pancake said. "Maybe he and the missus had issues. Maybe he had a little something on the side. Maybe there were money problems. Any or all of those could work. The bottom line could simply be, he saw an opportunity and jumped on it."

"That makes sense to me," Nicole said.

Pancake smiled. "Of course it does, darling. You're smart. And great minds run in the same circle."

She laughed. "Now, if we could only get Jake up to speed."

"You two are funny. Maybe a sitcom is in your future."

Another one of those wonderful laughs from Nicole. "You're pretty. You don't have to be smart."

"I thought you said I was clever?"

"You are. And pretty."

Pretty? I can't win.

Bringing the discussion back to reality, I said, "Maybe he also had issues with Noleen Kovac. Maybe something as simple as an affair. That sort of thing. Took the opportunity to get rid of both his wife and his mistress."

"We'll have to take a hard look at that," Ray said.

I nodded. "This really could get tricky. If Clark's the bad guy, we would be sniffing around in his world. He'd definitely have home court advantage."

Pancake nodded. "Tricky doesn't quite cover it." He nodded to the photo. "Dude looks like he don't take much shit."

That was true. Not only did his face look tough and hard, but his chest and shoulders looked thick, muscular. And the badge on his uniform shirt placed the law squarely in his corner.

"How should we approach this?" Pancake asked.

Ray hesitated, glanced out toward the Gulf, and then said, "Not sure yet. Let's do some more digging and maybe we can figure out a strategy."

I looked at Nicole. Gave her a slight nod.

"I have an idea," Nicole said.

Ray and Pancake stared at her.

"I might have a way to avoid a confrontation. Even make Clark an ally of sorts."

Ray glanced at me.

"Don't look at me," I said. "She wouldn't tell me."

Nicole shook her head. "I had to talk with Uncle Charles this morning before it would even be possible."

"Okay," Ray said.

"When we talked yesterday, the cop, the prosecutor, the victim's father in Lynn Haven, and Misty Abbott's brother, the prison guard, were the ones of interest. Each of them still in play. But last night Jake and I talked about this. We decided the cop was the most likely candidate."

Ray nodded.

"And now, if I hear everyone correctly, we've sort of settled on that conclusion—the cop is the place to start."

Ray shrugged. "The only one that really makes sense."

"If we go in there asking questions," Nicole continued, "and if Clark has something to hide, he'll fight back. Maybe the entire department over there will."

"You can bank on it," Pancake said.

"What if we went in as if we were doing a documentary on serial killers?"

That got Ray's attention. He leaned forward, elbows on the table.

Nicole continued. "A documentary that focused on the victims. And their families. The collateral damage that such killings always bring. Then we could make Clark an ally. A chance for his story to be told. Make him a victim of sorts."

Pancake gave a slow nod. "From what I read, he was distraught over the murder of his wife. I saw a few videos of him talking to local media. He made a good victim. Cried and all that. And when

Billy Wayne was arrested, he was interviewed in his home. Said he was glad that a serial predator had been taken off the streets. That Billy Wayne shouldn't have been allowed to bargain his way out of a death sentence. That he deserved to die for what he had done."

"Did you believe him?" Nicole asked. "Or was he acting?"

"Hard to say. You and Jake take a look and see what you think."

"If we go in this way," Nicole said, "as if we accept all the killings are Billy Wayne's work, Clark might see it as a chance to be a hero. And solidify his dirty work as being in Billy Wayne's lap."

"I like this approach," Ray said. "How do you want to put it together?"

"Uncle Charles is on board. In fact, he liked the idea as a real production. So we go in as if we are doing preliminary research on the story. To see if it has legs. Do interviews, review the cases, that sort of thing. Talk to the people who live there. And, of course, the family members of the victims. Who knows? We might uncover a love triangle, or something, to connect the final two victims."

"And find evidence to implicate Frank Clark," Pancake said.

"Exactly," Nicole said.

Ray gave a slow nod. "I like it."

"Uncle Charles liked it so much he's going to go ahead and began assembling a production crew. At least loosely."

"Already?" Pancake asked.

"He never waits until the last minute to do anything. One of the reasons he's so successful. All he's going to do is see which producers, directors, writers, film crews, and things like that are available. Nothing concrete."

"Oh," Pancake said, "that's all?"

Nicole laughed.

"I think this could really work," I said. "And keep us low key."

"Hell," Ray said, "it could make us the guys in white hats."

It crossed my mind that that could easily be the case. Right up until we had to expose our real agenda. And sooner or later, if Billy Wayne was telling us the truth, we would. What would the town think then? I kept those thoughts to myself.

"Good." Nicole smiled. "I need everyone's shirt size."

"Why?" Ray asked.

"Uncle Charles' production company is Regency Global Productions. RGP, for short. He's going to overnight some golf shirts with the name and logo." She smiled. "Then we'll be official."

"You've given this a lot of thought," Ray said.

"When Jake wasn't snoring." She laughed.

Ray stared at Nicole for a few seconds. "You keep amazing me."

She gave a mock bow. Or was it a curtsy? I could never keep those straight.

"Trying to be helpful," Nicole said.

"Something you should teach Jake."

How did I become part of this?

"He's beyond hope," Nicole said. She punched my arm. "But he's cute."

Was cute a demotion from pretty?

Ray shook his head. "His major asset."

"Are you guys finished?" I said.

"Probably not," Pancake said. "But let Ray and me noodle on this idea and see if we can come up with a plan."

The meeting was over.

CHAPTER EIGHT

TWO DAYS LATER, Ray had the plan hammered out. Nicole and I were in her SL headed to Pine Key. "To get the lay of the land" and "sort out the players" as Ray put it. He and Pancake would follow, after a stop in Jacksonville to see attorney Winston McCracken and gather the information he had on Billy Wayne's plea deal, which contained details on each crime he had confessed to. They would then visit the nearby regional crime lab where the DNA evidence against Billy Wayne had been processed. Ray wanted to talk directly, and discreetly, with the lab's director. Get the details on the evidence—and do so off the radar. Apparently, the director was the friend of a friend of a friend of Ray's. Of course. Ray seemed to have very few degrees of separation between himself and anyone in law enforcement.

Pine Key nestled along the western Florida coast on a spit of elevated land that seemed to float on the Gulf's edge. It was sandwiched between the Gulf to the west and, to the east, an estuary that coalesced three small rivers before it swung around the town's north end, cut through the sandy shoreline, and emptied into deeper waters. It also separated the town from the mainland where Highway 98 sliced through farmland and ferried folks north to Panama City and south to Mexico Beach. The southern edge of town was defined by a network of swampy wetlands, sand dunes, and areas of low scrub brush. At least that's what the aerial photos I had seen looked like.

We turned off Highway 98 on to a weather-worn, two-lane black top, where a sign indicated Pine Key was a mere four miles away. I felt a dose of trepidation—yes, that's the word that popped up in my brain—I do know some big words—a few anyway. I mean, we were going to dig into the life of a police officer, maybe even the entire department. In a town where we would be strangers. Where we didn't know friendlies from foes. Where any waves could slap back at us.

I liked Nicole's idea for a documentary as our cover and believed it could work. Might even give us a degree of celebrity. Hollywood still had cache' in most of America, particularly in small towns. But, the truth was, I just didn't know. We could be viewed as inter-lopers, even scavengers, trying to make hay out of the town's tragedy. Not entirely untrue, but profit wasn't our motive. Not re-ally. Ray was being well paid, but this had morphed into something else. A quest for truth, justice, and the American way. At least we told ourselves that.

Another troubling point was that I wasn't entirely sold on Billy Wayne being an honest broker of facts. His story of being framed seemed far-fetched on the surface. I mean, his DNA was found at each scene. He said he didn't kill two of his victims. Two, who like the other five, he had confessed to strangling. If those people had indeed lived in Pine Key, which had suffered three killings, Billy Wayne still darkened this town. Once or three times was the only question. I had no illusions that Billy Wayne was anything but a stone-cold killer. Actually, he was worse than that. Despite his in-nocent and calm demeanor, he was as evil and predatory as any of his predecessors. Whether he murdered five or seven wouldn't change that an ounce.

But, if he was being truthful, there was another killer out there. Maybe still roaming the streets of Pine Key.

Maybe wearing a badge.

And carrying a gun.

As the winding road turned back west, a welcoming sign appeared:

WELCOME TO PINE KEY
A Pleasant Place to Live And Play
Population 3234
Elevation 24 feet

Beyond it, a narrow bridge bumped over the waters of the estuary and dropped us into town.

"Want to go check in?" Nicole asked.

Pancake had gotten three rooms at a small hotel called The Tidewater. I had no idea where it was, but in a town this size, how hard could it be to find?

"Let's take a look around first," I said.

Six blocks deep and a dozen long, Pine Key occupied the bulk of a flat plate of land and seemed to be laid out in cocoon-like layers. At least on three sides. Like one of those Russian nesting dolls. I remembered my mom had one. Ray had brought it back from one of his adventures.

The downtown area along the Gulf was enveloped by several blocks of peaceful tree-lined and well-kept residential streets, all encased by a shell of evergreens and other trees, which added to the town's sense of isolation.

Nicole zigzagged among the residences before reaching Main Street, Pine Key's commercial center. Shops, restaurants, bars, and several small hotels and B&Bs bordered each side. My research told me that The Famous Pine Key Boardwalk, as it was called, lay behind the buildings that lined the Gulf side of Main Street. It was ten blocks long and marked the western edge of the plateau the town sat upon. Several signs indicated passages between the businesses led to the popular tourist attraction. I also knew that The Boardwalk looked out over the Pine Key Marina, famous for fishing and boating. I had done my homework.

Everything about Pine Key felt relaxed, slow-moving, comfortable, and safe. I wondered how much Billy Wayne's visit had eroded those feelings among the residents. I suspected deeply and permanently.

"Nice place," Nicole said.

"Sure is. Looks like tourism is the major business."

"Lots of shops and restaurants."

"And tourists from everywhere."

She glanced at me. "How do you know where they're from?"

"The pale ones are from up north."

She laughed. "Or Canada."

"True, eh."

We finally arrived at our hotel, The Tidewater. White-trimmed, gray-clapboard, two-story, it sat near the north end of Main Street and faced the Gulf. The air held a salty must, and a gentle breeze came off the water. The sky was blue and pockmarked with wads of fluffy clouds.

As we checked in, I asked the young lady behind the reception desk, "What's the favorite local gathering place around here?"

"That would be Woody's. It's just down The Boardwalk. You can't miss it."

She wore jeans and a plain white shirt, untucked, sleeves rolled to her elbows, and gold loop earrings. Her name tag indicated she was Monica. She looked late twenties. Brown hair, brown eyes, pleasant smile.

"Thanks, Monica," I said.

"You guys here to fish?" she asked.

"No. We're actually here to research a documentary."

She nodded toward the logo on my shirt. "That the name of your company?"

Uncle Charles had overnighted a box of Regency Global Production shirts. Various colors in each of our sizes. I wore a navy blue one, the logo a large pale blue R within a circle constructed of the full name in script. Nicole's was lime green with a dark green logo. Went well with her white jeans. Of course, everything looked good on Nicole. Even nothing. But, that's for later.

"Yes, it is," I said.

"You guys done anything I might've heard of?"

"*Space Quest*," Nicole said.

"Really?" Monica's eyes lit up. "You guys did *Space Quest*?"

"The company did," Nicole responded.

"That's so cool. I mean, like, I love that series."

I smiled. "Glad to hear it."

"What's this thing you're working on?" Monica asked.

"A story on Billy Wayne Baker."

"Oh." Her shoulders straightened. She actually took a half step back. "What about him?"

Nicole laid a hand on the counter, leaned forward slightly, and smiled. "We're not here to glorify Billy Wayne. Or do some gory sensational crap."

"What does that mean?" Monica asked.

"We're exploring a piece on the victims and their families. We call it *Aftermath*. We think the collateral damage people like him leave behind is a story that needs to be told."

Monica sighed, seemed to relax a notch. "It sure tore up this town. Real bad." She glanced out toward the street. "Even now, after all these years, folks still feel off balance." She shook her head. "Awful stuff just don't happen here."

"Unfortunately," I said, "evil can show up anywhere."

"I suppose. But I'm here to tell you, no one around these parts ever thought they'd see something like that." She smiled. "We're pretty boring. We like it that way."

"Which is exactly why we want to do the documentary," Nicole said. "Focus on how someone like Billy Wayne Baker can alter the lives of the victims' families and friends, even an entire town."

"We might want to interview you," I said.

"Really? Why?"

"How long have you worked here? At The Tidewater?"

"My whole life." She laughed. "My mom owns it. I was raised here."

"That's why we'd like to talk with you. And your mom. I imagine as the owners of the best hotel in town, you two know everyone."

"We are the best." She laughed. "And Mom, for sure, knows everyone."

"Then we want to talk with her."

"She's up in Panama City today. Visiting her sister. My aunt. She'll back in the morning."

"Who else should we talk with?" I asked. "Who knows the most about the town?"

"That's an easy one. Betty Lou Thompson. She owns Woody's. She knows everyone and everything."

"Cool," I said. "Thanks for that."

"No problem." She pushed her hair back with both hands. "Let's get you guys in your room. I have a nice one for you. Corner. Overlooking the Gulf."

"Perfect."

CHAPTER NINE

RAY STOOD BESIDE Pancake's dually pickup, waiting for the big guy to fish his keys from his pocket and chirp open the locks. They were in the parking deck behind Winston McCracken's office. He pulled the door open and climbed into the passenger's seat.

They had visited McCracken, signed the agreement between Longly Investigations and Billy Wayne's anonymous benefactor, and retrieved the records of Billy Wayne's defense and sentencing hearing. While Pancake drove, Ray shuffled through the pages. The Florida Department of Law Enforcement, FDLE for short, crime lab was only a few blocks away. Took ten minutes to reach the two-story, green-roofed facility and slide into an empty space.

Ray closed the folder. "I'll dig into all this later, but on first blush, I didn't see much we don't already know."

Pancake grunted. "Figured as much."

Inside, they approached the reception desk where a young woman looked up. Short brown hair, round black-rimmed glasses, pleasant smile.

"Ray Longly. We have an appointment with Director Gaines."

"Yes, he's expecting you." She raised a finger. "Just a sec." She picked up the phone, punched the comm line, and spoke briefly. She smiled. "Someone's on the way to escort you to Director Gaines' office."

"Thanks."

Thirty seconds later, a young man in jeans and a gray tee shirt beneath a white, knee-length lab coat led them through a door and down a hallway. He held the door as Ray and Pancake entered the Director's office.

Robert Gaines stood from behind his desk. "Ray Longly?"

Ray had never met him. He had reached out to someone he knew in the FBI to arrange the meeting.

Ray nodded. "This is Tommy Jeffers. Folks call him Pancake."

"Pancake? Never heard that one before."

"Me, either," Pancake said.

They shook hands. Gaines offered them the two chairs that faced his desk.

"What happened to your face?" Gaines asked Pancake.

"Pavement one. Me zero."

"Ouch." Gaines sat. He raised an eyebrow. "It's not every day I get a call from the FBI Regional Director."

"An old friend," Ray said.

Gaines nodded, hesitated as if considering that. "I understand you're interested in the evidence from the Billy Wayne Baker case."

"That's right."

"Mind if I ask why?"

"This isn't for public consumption. In fact, we hope no one will know why we're here. Or even that we've been here."

"I see."

"Is that a problem for you?"

"Not at all." Gaines leaned back in his chair. "The Regional Director assured me you were discreet. And could be trusted implicitly. So, no, nothing will leave this room."

Ray nodded. "Good."

"I trust that discretion goes both ways?"

"It does."

"But I have to admit, I'm curious as to why a P.I. outfit is interested in Billy Wayne Baker."

Ray held nothing back and explained what they were doing. How Billy Wayne denied two of the killings. Wouldn't say which ones. What they had been hired to do.

Gaines nodded. "I had heard that. Back before his sentencing. As far as I know he gave up on that ploy and confessed to all seven." He looked at Ray. "Unless something's changed I don't know about."

"Not really. According to his attorney, Winston McCracken, Billy Wayne confessed to avoid a trial and to take the death penalty off the table. At McCracken's insistence. But Billy Wayne apparently never wavered on his assertion that two weren't his doing."

"And your job is to see if that's true and to discover which two weren't his work?"

"That's right."

"And maybe find out who did do them?" He cocked his head to one side. "If it wasn't Billy Wayne all along." He leaned forward. "I'm sure you've considered that he might just be pulling your chain?"

"We have."

Gaines gave a half smile. "Sure don't envy you your work." He shook his head. "I take it Billy Wayne's your client?"

"Sort of. He has an anonymous benefactor who's paying the freight."

"Anonymous?" His head swiveled between Ray and Pancake. "Who?"

"We don't know," Ray said. "That's part of the arrangement."

"I see," Gaines said. "Strange doesn't quite cover it."

"Sure don't," Pancake said. "But, if Billy Wayne's telling the truth, and not just blowing smoke up our asses, there's a murderer still out there. Getting a free ride."

"Which ones does he claim he didn't do?"

"He won't say," Ray said.

Gaines hesitated as if considering that, and then said, "That makes no sense."

"It does to Billy Wayne," Ray said. "Seems he doesn't want to bias our investigation."

"Boy, you sure got your work cut out for you."

"So it seems."

"What can I do to help?"

"Take us through the evidence. What you found and didn't find."

"Okay. First off, he left behind a forensic trail a mile wide. DNA, fingerprints. But those aren't very helpful with nothing to compare them to. Too bad he wasn't in any of the databases or we might've nabbed him sooner. Saved a few lives."

"The DNA in each case was semen. Right?" Ray asked.

"Correct. Except in the first one—the Marilee Whitt case—we also found his DNA in her fingernail scrapings." Gaines opened a folder on his desk. "I grabbed our test results on each of the seven cases. We did all the work here. The DNA was unquestionable. Once we had a sample from Billy Wayne, the odds for the least good sample was on the order of fifty billion to one. Pretty solid."

"Where were the samples found?" Pancake asked.

"One from vaginal swabs. And, like I said, nail scrapings. The first case. Marilee Whitt. Down in Apalachicola. But DNA was located on the bedsheets in all seven."

"Fingerprints in only the Apalachicola case, right?" Ray asked.

Gaines nodded. "Correct."

Ray related what Billy Wayne had said to Jake about changing his MO.

"Like he learned something?" Gaines said. "Wouldn't be the first time these guys altered their methods. Which, of course, explains why there was no vaginal DNA or fingerprints in any of the other cases."

"So we have vaginal and nail scraping DNA and prints at the first scene and bedsheet DNA at the others?" Ray asked.

"Yes. But I'd have to say, despite his changed methods, Billy Wayne didn't seem overly concerned about leaving tracks. Sort of like he wanted to get caught."

"Or was just plain stupid," Pancake said.

"Not from what I heard," Gaines said. "The investigators told me he's a pretty smart guy. They seemed to have no doubt there. So maybe he was cocky, maybe just sloppy. Regardless, he dropped a lot of breadcrumbs."

"Any of the evidence seem odd to you?" Ray asked. "Anything that gave you pause?"

Gaines gave him a quizzical look. "Not sure I follow you."

"Maybe not exactly as you'd expect. Any that looked planted?"

Gaines studied the pages before him. "Not really. I guess it would be odd that no vaginal DNA was found in any of the other victims. But, since Billy Wayne decided to wear condoms with the later victims, not surprising. But, as I said, in all seven it was on the bedding. Probably spilled some while removing the condom." He shrugged. "Seen it before."

"That's how we figured it," Ray said. "I take it no condoms were found at any of the scenes?"

"None were ever recovered. He must've taken them and disposed of them elsewhere. Again, common."

"Let me ask you something," Ray said. "And I don't mean to impugn your lab."

"We're used to it," Gaines said with a smile. "Defense attorneys have been impugning us for years."

"I hear you. Is it possible someone here, one of your techs, could've colluded with a killer? Maybe tampered with the evidence?"

Gaines folded his hands before him. "Anything's possible. But that would be unlikely. All the testing is reviewed by two techs. And in this case, being it was so high-profile, by me personally."

"Possible that the DNA could have been cross contaminated?" Pancake asked.

"Sure. It's possible." He sighed. "But I have a good crew here. I trust each of them." He closed the folder before him. "We have excellent protocols and we follow them strictly." He leaned back. "Also, the evidence came in weeks, months, even years apart. Billy Wayne's active period lasted just under two years."

"Would the techs have access to the old evidence? Maybe grab something from an old case and incorporate it into a new one?"

Gaines shook his head. "Not easy to do. If someone wanted to do that, access any old evidence, it would require a requisition, sometimes even a court order, either of which would have to be reviewed and approved by me. Nothing like that happened."

"I see."

"And there would be a record," Gaines continued. "The evidence would have to be signed out and then signed back in. That never happened either."

"After the original testing, was the evidence ever re-analyzed?" Ray asked. "Maybe in anticipation of presenting it in court?"

"No. We would have, of course, had a trial been set, but Billy Wayne confessed before those wheels could be put in motion." Gaines looked at Ray, Pancake, back to Ray. "You guys thinking that someone did the other killing and then used someone here to help frame Billy Wayne?"

"Truth is," Ray said, "I don't think that's the case. But we have to at least consider it."

Gaines nodded. "I'd suspect that if any shenanigans were in play, it would have happened before the samples reached us."

"I do, too," Ray said.

Gaines sighed. "The questions then become, who and why?"

"Assuming Billy Wayne ain't lying," Pancake said.

Gaines moved the folder to one side. "That wouldn't surprise me." He looked at Ray. "Any idea where you'll start looking?"

"Pine Key. With three victims there it would afford a better opportunity to plant the DNA. Better than if it were in separate locations."

Gaines gave a slow nod. "You thinking someone in law enforcement?"

"The last victim there was a cop's wife."

"That's right," Gaines said. "Frank Clark."

"Do you know him?" Ray asked.

"Peripherally. Crossed paths with him at a few conferences over the years. But the three Pine Key cases were the only times I ever worked with him professionally. He seemed on top of everything. Particularly for someone from a town where murders aren't all that common. My overall impression? I'd be surprised if he was involved in anything like that." He shrugged. "But I've been surprised before."

"He would have access," Ray said. "The evidence did go through his hands."

Gaines sighed. "Boy, you guys are going to be walking on egg shells."

"And trying not to make an omelet," Pancake said.

Ray stood, ready to thank Gaines, and leave, but another thought brought him back into his chair.

"One more thing," Ray said. "After the first victim, the others were restrained. Anything useful from the ropes used?"

Gaines shook his head. "Simple ski-type. Blue. Cheap and easy to come by. The gauge, color, and manufacturer matched in each."

"No way to trace them?"

"The FBI looked into that. Way too common."

CHAPTER TEN

OUR ROOM, A mini-suite, was perfect. In the living area a stone fireplace, a deep comfy sofa, a pair of plush chairs, and two large windows, one facing the marina and the Gulf, the other aimed up The Famous Pine Key Boardwalk. The bedroom had a king-sized, four-poster bed with a thick down comforter and a second fireplace.

I sat on the bed, patted the comforter. "Want to test-drive this thing?"

"No. I'm hungry." She shifted her shoulder bag to the other side. "Feed me."

We strolled down the crowded Boardwalk, weaving our way through people of all ages. Older couples walking hand in hand, teenagers laughing and eating ice cream and taffy, or hanging near the railing looking purposefully cool, and a handful of kids running wild.

It looked just like the pictures I had seen. The Boardwalk hung on the plateau's edge, businesses lining its inland side. Half a dozen wooden staircases led down to a parklike area and beyond that the marina, filled with boats, both sail and power. No wonder The Boardwalk was the town's main attraction.

Woody's was toward the far end, anchored between a clothing store and a candy shop. It reminded me of Captain Rocky's, my place in Gulf Shores. A large deck bordered The Boardwalk and opened into the restaurant proper, the entire place designed for food, drink, and fun. Even at two in the afternoon, it was busy, and noisy. A group of a dozen women gathered at a long, centrally located table—obviously celebrating a birthday if the balloons and gift bags were any indication. From the empty margarita pitchers that littered the table, I suspected their workday was done.

Their decibel level dropped as we walked by. I smiled, but their collective attention was directed at Nicole. She had that effect on every living creature, it seemed.

We found an umbrella-shaded table on the expansive deck, near the rail that separated it from The Boardwalk. You could literally reach out and touch the people who strolled by. Nestled against the umbrella's support pole, a metal tray held mustard, ketchup, Tabasco, and a couple of other hot sauces. The wooden armchairs were wide, cushioned, and comfortable.

Our waitress, young and trim, wore white short-shorts that covered very little and an orange halter top that covered less. Her light-brown hair was pulled into a short ponytail and secured with a turquoise clasp. Her name tag read: Sherry.

She dropped a pair of menus on the table. "Welcome to Woody's. You having lunch, or just drinks?"

"Food," Nicole said. "I'm starving."

Sherry laughed. "You're at the right place. Anything to drink?"

Nicole nodded toward the party. "The margaritas look like a hit."

"That's our speciality. We have the standard eight ounce, a sixteen-once schooner, or if you want to catch up with them, a thirty-two-ounce pitcher."

"Regular size for me," I said.

"Traditional, strawberry, banana, peach, watermelon, or blackberry?"

"I'm old-fashioned," I said. "Traditional, no salt."

"I'll go with the watermelon," Nicole said. "Sixteen ounces."

Oh, yeah. A couple of those and she'd be ready for that four-poster. A nice thought, but, really, what was I thinking? She could drink me under the table. That bottle of tequila we had had the other night at her place? She put a much bigger dent in it than I did. And handled it way better.

Sherry scribbled on her pad, said she'd be back in a sec. I watched her go.

"Did you enjoy that?" Nicole asked.

"Enjoy what?"

"Undressing her with your eyes."

I smiled. "Sure did."

"I'm so jealous." She gave me a mock pout.

"No, you're not."

"I could be."

"Can't think of a single reason why you should be."

"Since you put it that way." She smiled. "I like this place."

"Better than Captain Rocky's?"

"Wouldn't say that. But, from what I've seen so far, I like this town. Small, quaint. Seems friendly."

The margaritas arrived. Sherry suggested the shrimp tacos, as they were "to totally die for." We went with her recommendation. And they were great. When she delivered our second round, I asked if the owner was there.

"Betty Lou?" Sherry said. "She's always here."

"We'd like to meet her," Nicole said.

And we did. Five minutes later a middle-aged, blocky woman with graying hair, large round blue eyes, and a pleasant smile walked up. "Sherry said you guys wanted to introduce yourselves."

"I'm Jake. This is Nicole."

"Betty Lou. Nice to meet you." She nodded to our empty plates. "Everything okay?"

"Perfect," Nicole said.

"It better be." She laughed. A real laugh. One that shook her entire body and collapsed her eyes into slits. "Or I'd have to kick some butt."

"Not necessary." Nicole propped a forearm on the table. "Monica over at the Tidewater said you were the one we needed to chat with."

"Chattin's one of my favorite pastimes." Another laugh. Easy, natural, as if laughing was another of her favorite activities. "What you want to jaw about?"

"We're with Regency Global Productions."

Betty Lou scraped back a chair and sat. "From Hollywood? You two look like you're from Hollywood."

"We are," Nicole said. "We're doing some preliminary research for a documentary series."

"About what?"

"This segment would be about Billy Wayne Baker."

"Oh." Betty Lou's smile evaporated. Furrows appeared in her brow.

"Not what you think," I said. "We're doing a series on the effects folks like him have on victims' families and communities."

Nicole picked it up from there. "The series is definitely not focused on the killers. It's about the collateral damage they do. We're calling it *Aftermath*. We'll look into several serial killers, including Billy Wayne Baker. And since three of his victims were here, we want to feature this community."

Betty Lou looked from Nicole to me and then back to Nicole. She gave a half nod. "I like it. Everything I've ever seen about that boy has made him into some kind of celebrity."

Nicole nodded. "That seems to be universal in shows about these guys. It's the Hannibal Lector effect. Like these predators are somehow special."

"Billy Wayne Baker was special, all right. A special kind of evil." She gazed out toward the marina. "He sure as hell put this town through the ringer." Her gaze moved back to us. "Even though it's been a couple of years, folks still ain't back to normal. Not sure they ever will be."

"We want to tell their stories," Nicole said. "The people of Pine Key."

"Well, what did Monica think I could do for you?"

I smiled. "She said you knew everyone in town and could direct us to the right folks."

Betty Lou's laugh returned. "That's true. I do know just about everyone. I mean, people got to eat. And drink." She waved an arm. "They all find their way in here sooner or later."

"Based on the margaritas and the shrimp tacos, I can see why," I said.

"My folks in the kitchen, and bar, do a good job." A burst of laughter from the birthday party grabbed her attention. "It's Mary Green's birthday. She owns a gift card shop down the way. I hope I don't have to eighty-six them. Or drive them home."

A young man, a busboy, gathered our plates from the table.

"Thanks, Paul," Betty Lou said.

He dipped his head, smiled, and walked away.

Betty Lou squared her shoulders. "I do like the concept of what you're doing so I guess the question is what exactly can I do to help out?"

"We want to talk with some members of the victims' families," Nicole said. "The ones you think can handle reliving things."

"Not rightly sure anyone around here wants to revisit Billy Wayne."

Nicole leaned forward. "You know what I mean. We're not here to cause any unwarranted pain. But, if anyone wants to share their story, we'd like to listen."

Betty Lou nodded, smiled. "I like your attitude. Tell you what, let me noodle on it and I'll write down a few names for you."

"That would be great," I said.

"I think we'd like to start with you," Nicole said.

"Me?"

Nicole smiled. "You'd be great on camera. And I suspect you know Billy Wayne's story better than most."

Betty Lou shook her head. "Me? On camera? I just might break the damn thing." Another body-shaking laugh.

CHAPTER ELEVEN

HIS NAME WAS Jason Levy. Billy Wayne's benefactor. Wasn't hard to uncover his identity. Took ten minutes. A call to the Union Correctional warden, dropping the right names, and Ray discovered he had exchanged dozens of letters with Billy Wayne and visited him a total of eight times. He accomplished all this sitting in Pancake's truck outside the FDLE lab.

Pancake then took the ball. Another ten minutes working his iPhone and he discovered that Levy was thirty-eight and had earned his pile of cash in real estate and Wall Street investments. Net worth north of eleven million. He also lived nearby. Ray gave him a call, explaining he wanted to talk about Billy Wayne, and the fact that he knew Levy was paying the freight for Ray's investigation. Levy hesitated, as if he might deny he was the one, but then, probably sensing that would be a futile tact, agreed to meet.

Pancake plugged his address in the GPS and they headed that way.

River Road bisected a spit of land between Lake Marco and the St. Johns River south of downtown Jacksonville. Multimillion-dollar neighborhood, including Levy's multilevel, stark-white stucco and glass structure that looked over the river. Palm trees hugged a circular drive that curled around an eight-foot, three-tiered fountain, breeze-blown water rising another five feet in the air. Levy stood in the doorway as they climbed from the truck.

After an exchange of greetings and handshakes and a brief chat about Pancake's name and facial scrapes, Levy led them inside. Soaring ceilings, magnificent views through a wall of thirty-foot windows. Beyond, an infinity pool. They sat at a table on the deck beneath a green-and-white-striped umbrella.

"I have to say, your call was a surprise," Levy said. He wore khaki cargo shorts and a pale blue golf shirt, expensive black leather sandals.

"Why?" Ray asked. "Didn't you think we could uncover the benefactor?"

Levy shrugged.

"You hired us because we know how to do this. Right?"

"Yes. I did."

"So, we're doing our job."

Levy smiled. "I'm curious. How'd you find out about me?"

Ray shrugged. "It's what we do. More specifically, friends of friends." He left it at that.

"I see." Levy glanced at Pancake and then back to Ray. "Who else knows?"

"You're looking at it," Pancake said.

"I hope it stays that way. I wanted to be anonymous for a reason." He looked out toward the water. "I'm afraid most people wouldn't understand."

"We have no reason to reveal or alter your relationship with Billy Wayne in any way," Ray said. "Besides, you're the guy footing the bill." Ray smiled.

Levy nodded. "Good. Good." He spread his hands on the table before him. "What do you want to know?"

"How and why did you hook up with him?"

"I'm sort of a true crime buff. I collect first-edition novels in the genre. Just over eight hundred and counting."

He hesitated as if waiting for an attaboy or something of that nature, but Ray said nothing.

"Billy Wayne was, of course, a big story. I heard from a friend of mine, a local prosecutor, that Billy Wayne had suggested he didn't kill all of those folks. He thought it was all so much BS, Billy Wayne messing with the system, that sort of thing, but I was curious. So I wrote him. We became pen pals, I guess you'd say. The more I communicated with him, the more my curiosity grew. Have you met him?"

Ray shook his head. "My son Jake had a chat with him. But me? No."

"Jake Longly. The baseball player." It wasn't a question.

"That's right. He works for me now."

"I know." He smiled. "I did my homework."

Ray waved a hand at the house. "I suspect you always do."

Levy gave a soft laugh. "That I do. I talked with Billy Wayne. Yesterday. He was impressed with Jake."

"Good to hear."

"As I was with Billy Wayne," Levy said. "Despite his proclivities for murder and mayhem, he's actually an amazing guy. Smart. Quiet. Soft-spoken. Definitely not the mental image I had before I met him."

"That's what Jake said." Ray leaned forward, resting his elbows on the table's edge. "What do you expect to get out of this? Digging into Billy Wayne's life? Hiring us?"

"The truth." He forked his fingers through his unkempt light brown hair. "I mean, isn't this a fantastic story? What if Billy Wayne didn't kill all of those people? What if he's being truthful?"

"Is he?"

He opened his hands, palms up. "Honestly, I don't know. But it's worth a look."

"What's your gut tell you?" Pancake asked. "You probably know him better than most."

"I believe him. Enough to spend some money to find out."

"And then what?" Ray asked. "What if he's being truthful? What's the next step for you?"

"I know a couple of crime writers who'd jump at the chance to tell the story." He smiled. "One even wants me to cowrite it with him." He raised an eyebrow. "Can't say I'd mind seeing my own name on one of the books in my collection."

Ray liked that. An honest and straightforward answer. No wavering or tap dancing. Of course, Levy wanted something out of the deal. Something more than satisfying his curiosity. Curiosity was fine, but results paid the tab for his mansion and his lifestyle. Ray was curious, too. And if Levy was willing to pay for satisfying their collective inquisitiveness, then it was a win-win.

"And if he's lying?" Ray asked. "Jerking everyone off?"

"It's still a story, isn't it?" Levy sighed. "But, honestly, I don't think he is."

CHAPTER TWELVE

TWO SIXTEEN-OUNCE MARGARITAS worked. Nicole was lit up. In a good way. The four-poster never had a chance. Neither did I. Also, in a good way. As we lay there, recovering, Ray called. They were fifteen minutes out, would check in, and be good to go in about thirty. I told Nicole. She rolled over, doing that cat-like stretch of hers, saying it was time for another margarita anyway. Where the hell does she put it?

It was just after six p.m. when we met Ray and Pancake in the lobby and headed out. The descending sun lit up The Boardwalk while burnishing the gently rocking sailboat masts in the marina. Oddly hypnotic, they looked like a series of synced metronomes. It was warm with a light breeze off the Gulf adding a welcome hint of evening chill.

Ray and I fell in behind Nicole and Pancake. She had hooked his arm with hers. I smiled. I liked the fact that over the past few months they had developed a special bond. Not exactly brother-sister, but close. I think they had a mutual respect for each other's smarts. To a casual observer, neither gave that impression on first blush. Pancake was a big-ole lumbering dude, and Nicole, well, just look at her. Stereotypes being what they are. I had known since we were kids that Pancake was smarter than the average bear, and Nicole continually amazed me. I mean, this whole documentary cover she conjured up was pure genius. And if Monica back at The Tidewater and Betty Lou were any indication, it was working.

If I had harbored any ideas that The Boardwalk wasn't the center of Pine Key's social actives, tonight would have quashed them. It was packed with people strolling over the warped wooden planks and filing in and out of shops, bars, and restaurants, everyone at an easy pace.

I imagined Billy Wayne here, mingling unnoticed with the "normal" folks. Like a shark in murky water, seeking prey. No one the wiser. Billy Wayne's innocent face would definitely have blended in. I saw many such faces flow by. Was one of these the next Billy Wayne? Like sharks, serial killers seemed to possess a knack for locating victim-rich hunting grounds. If Billy Wayne found Pine Key, someone else could.

I pushed those thoughts aside. The evening was too nice for that brand of darkness.

We ended up back at Woody's. Nicole had apparently told Pancake how good the food was, so he insisted. Besides, Nicole wanted another giant margarita. An idea I wholeheartedly supported.

Nicole did indeed order another sixteen ouncer, this one peach. I was sure she had a wooden leg. Or a cast-iron stomach. Maybe both. Either way, she could handle her alcohol. Pancake opted for the same size, only blackberry. I had the regular margarita, Ray bourbon.

Our waitress this time was Laurie Mae. Said so right on her name tag. Tiny would be the word. Barely five feet and a hundred pounds soaking wet. She wore cutoff jeans, frayed at the edges, and a plaid shirt, the hem tied to expose her middriff. Feisty would be the other word. She had a certain electricity about her.

"You the folks from Hollywood?" she asked.

"We are," Nicole said.

"Mom said to take good care of you."

"Mom?" I asked.

"Betty Lou. She's my mom."

Now I saw the resemblance. Same large, active blue eyes, and infectious smile. Laurie Mae simply a much smaller, slimmer version.

She looked at Pancake. "You look like you fell down some steps." She fingered the side of her own face.

"Sort of," Pancake said. "Alcohol and bicycles don't mix."

Laurie Mae laughed. "You're cute."

"That I am."

Laurie Mae gave him a lingering smile. "Mom'll be over in a minute." She glanced toward the bar, where Betty Lou sat talking with a guy. "Actually, several minutes. She's having an issue with one of our beer suppliers. He wants to raise the rates." She leaned down, lowered her voice conspiratorially. "Ain't going to happen. He just needs to learn you don't try to snooker Mom." That got a laugh from everyone. "Anyway, she's got that list you wanted."

"Good," Nicole said.

She pulled a pad and pen from her hip pocket. "What can I get you folks?"

Nicole had another shrimp taco, but I passed, still full from our late lunch. Ray followed Nicole's lead. So did Pancake, except he ordered four. Along with a bowl of clam chowder, a Caesar salad, extra dressing and croutons, and a side of onion rings.

While we waited, Ray went over their visit to the crime lab. He concluded with, "So, DNA was found in every case. Vaginally in only the first victim, and on the bedsheets in all seven. Prints also only at the initial scene."

"That fits with what Billy Wayne told me," I said. "After the first one, he wore gloves and used condoms."

"Director Gaines also said the first victim put up a fight," Ray said. "They found blood and skin beneath her nails. DNA there also matched Billy Wayne."

"Billy Wayne said the first victim, Marilee Whitt, was almost an accident. He picked her up and when she backed out of having sex with him, his temper got the best of him."

"So, he took what he wanted," Pancake said. "But good for Marilee for putting up a fight." He gave a half shrug. "Not that it did her much good."

"Her fighting sure freaked Billy Wayne out," I said. "He simply ran away. Leaving her there."

"He also left a forensic trail," Ray said.

"Again, thanks to her fighting him," Nicole said.

"He told me the trip back to Tallahassee was a blur. He was panicked. Knew he'd made a huge mistake. Knew he should have stayed long enough to clean things up. He said it didn't occur to him until he was a ways up the road. He considered going back but knew that wouldn't have been wise. Better to just run with it. But he also said he knew right then that somehow, someday, he'd get caught."

"He was right," Ray said.

I sighed. "Unfortunately, that murder also woke up some demon inside him."

"That's an understatement," Nicole said.

"The evidence Gaines went over with us correlates exactly with what Billy Wayne told you," Ray said. "The first was a frenzied accident, of sorts, the others were planned."

Our food arrived. Good thing I hadn't ordered anything because this discussion was definitely an appetite killer. Not so for Pancake. But then, I've never seen anything come between him and food. Between mouthfuls, he laid out his thoughts.

"From everything I've read and heard, no one around here remembers seeing Billy Wayne. Before or after. At least no one came forward if they did. Means he's very sneaky, or simply blended in well."

"If you met him, you'd see why no one remembers him," I said. "Even if they saw him. He appears pretty innocuous. Wouldn't stand out in a crowd."

Pancake dabbed clam chowder from his chin. "Likely means he didn't hang around here between the killings. If he had, you'd think someone would remember. Even vanilla folks register if they keep showing up. Probably went back up to Tallahassee to cool down."

"I didn't think to ask him," I said, "but that makes sense."

"But, did he return to Pine Key?" Nicole asked. "If he's lying, he came back and committed two more murders, and if that's the case, why would he return here when he didn't anywhere else?"

"Could be easy hunting," Pancake said. "Seems like the kind of place where folks turn in early."

"I guess some towns are too laid back," Nicole said.

"So it would seem." Pancake popped an entire onion ring in his mouth. "But if he's being straight up with us, he didn't come back. Someone else picked up the ball."

Ray nodded. "The question is who? And how are the other two murders connected? Right now, I don't see it."

"Me, neither," Pancake said. Another onion ring. "I can see Clark being good for the killing of his wife. But the other murder? Noleen Kovac?" He shrugged. "If he did that one, too, there's a connection. We just have to find it."

By the time we finished our meal, including the pecan pie and ice cream Pancake added to the tab, Betty Lou showed up. I introduced her to Ray and Pancake.

"You guys don't look Hollywood." Betty Lou laughed. "No offense."

"None taken," Ray said. "We're private investigators."

A look of concern laid across Betty Lou's face. "P.I.s?"

"Ray is Jake's father," Nicole said. "He has a P.I. firm. Over in Gulf Shores. But that's not why he's here. He and Pancake are technical consultants. To help us understand all the police stuff. Investigation, evidence, that sort of thing."

"If that don't beat all," Betty Lou said. "You guys think of everything."

"We try." Nicole smiled. "We need to understand the crimes if we're going to show how they affected everyone."

"Makes sense." Betty Lou pulled a piece of paper from her pocket and unfolded it. "Here's the list you wanted." She handed it to Nicole.

"You got time to talk?" Ray asked.

"Sure." She looked around. "A might bit noisy in here. Let's take a walk, and I'll go over it with you."

"Sounds good," Ray said. "As soon as we clear the bill."

"On the house," Betty Lou said.

"No," Ray said. "We'll pay. You got a business to run."

"Want me to introduce you to a beer distributor? One that thought he could negotiate with me?" She laughed that great laugh of hers.

Ray raised his hands. "You win. Thanks."

We stood. I tugged a couple of twenties from my pocket and laid them on the table for Laurie Mae. Betty Lou noticed and gave me a wink.

"You guys like cigars?" Betty Lou asked.

"Sure," Pancake said.

"Me, too." She waved Laurie Mae over. "Grab some of those R and Js and pour me a bourbon. Knob Creek." She looked at us. "Anyone else want a bourbon for the walk?"

Sure, why not.

"Hell, just bring me the bottle and some glasses."

The sun had dipped into the Gulf, the western sky now dark blue, and the crowd had thinned. We followed Betty Lou along The Boardwalk to a staircase that descended to an expanse of thick green grass near the southern edge of the marina. An array of redwood picnic tables flanked an ornate, white, octagonal gazebo. We settled around the gazebo's central, white wrought-iron table on the matching bench seats. Concentric rope lights beneath the canopy cast shadowless light over us.

Betty Lou doled out the bourbon and we fired up our Romeo y Juliette cigars. Even Nicole had one. I swear I had no Freudian thoughts. I swear, I swear.

Nicole passed around the list Betty Lou had given her. While each of us looked it over in turn, Betty Lou talked.

"I think you'll want to talk with Peter Swift, Loretta's husband, of course. But also, Charlaine Anders. She's Loretta's younger sister. Helps run Swift's Bakery. With Peter. He needed the help and she stepped up. She and Loretta were only a year apart so they were more like twins. Very close. Losing her sister was a big blow. She ain't recovered yet. Peter neither for that matter."

No one responded. Not much to say.

"Then I'd chat with Tommy Lee Kovac. He's Noleen's brother. He runs a fishing charter." She pointed toward the marina. "His boat's out there on Pier Three. Near the end. Got himself all sideways with the cops. Blamed them for not finding Billy Wayne earlier. Before he killed his sister."

"Which cops?" I asked.

"Hell, Tommy Lee blamed all of them. But mostly Frank Clark and Terry Munson, his partner."

"Clark's wife was the third victim," I said.

"Exactly. And that cooled Tommy Lee off in short order." She knocked an ash from her cigar. "Mostly, anyway."

"Mostly?" I asked.

She clamped her cigar with her teeth. It bobbed as she spoke. "Tommy Lee ain't the kind to back down. Or admit he was wrong. Ain't in his nature. But, for the most part, Frank losing his wife settled him considerably. Overall, I'd say they're copacetic now."

"What's Clark's story?" Ray asked.

"He's been here, on the force, for quite a while. A dozen years at least. He and Munson handle most of the major stuff. Major for us. We don't get murderers around here. Fact is, I think there's only been one in the last ten or more years. If you take Billy Wayne Baker out of the equation. It's more like burglaries, break-ins, occasionally an assault. Nothing very big."

"I take it Clark and Munson are the top dogs around here?" Ray said.

Betty Lou smiled. "You could say that. Don't think Chief Morgan could run the department without them. I mean, most of the other officers are good old boys. Do an okay job. But those two are pros. Don't miss much as far as I can tell."

"Sounds like you admire them," Nicole said.

She nodded. "I do. I think most folks do. Leastwise those that don't get sideways of them. They take lawbreaking seriously. You don't want them sniffing around your dirty laundry." She flicked another ash and laughed. "Relentless, I'd say. We like that around here. Makes those who plan to do something stupid reconsider their choices."

"How did Clark take his wife's murder?" I asked.

"Not well. Not well at all." A puff, two, from her cigar, a sip of bourbon. "They were close. All the way back to high school. One of those situations that everyone knowed they'd end up together."

"So no trouble in paradise there?" I asked.

She looked at me. "Why'd you think that?"

I shrugged. "No reason. Just trying to get a feel for everyone involved."

The question was a mistake. Nicole thought so, too. She kicked my leg under the table. But my answer seemed to satisfy Betty Lou.

"Frank and Sara are, were, pillars of the community. She worked on about every board you can think of. Parks, planning, school, even the tourism board."

"Did they have any kids?" Nicole asked.

Betty Lou shook her head. "No. I think they tried, but it never worked out." Another sip of bourbon.

"You think he'd talk with us?" Ray asked.

"I'm sure he would."

"What about Munson?" Pancake asked. "What's the deal with him?"

"Terry Munson is God's gift to women." She laughed. "Don't believe it, just ask him." Another laugh. "Actually, he's okay but he does have a rep for chasing the ladies." She nodded back up toward her restaurant. "Seen him work his magic right up there many times."

"I take it he's not married," Nicole said.

"Nope." She watched the smoke rise from her cigar for a few seconds, and then said, "I think he was engaged, or at least had a regular, for a while. I forget which. Anyway, she moved away and since then I don't think he's had another long-term relationship." She gave a quick nod. "I could be wrong on that."

The list now lay in the middle of the table. Nicole slid it toward her and examined it. "Charles Morgan? He the police chief?"

"Yep. Good guy. Been the chief forever and a day." She looked out toward the Gulf. "Over thirty years now."

"Who's Gwen Olsen?"

"She's the mayor. Over twelve years now. I suspect she and Charlie can offer some insights on all this craziness."

"Anyone else we should talk with?" I asked.

She glanced out toward the marina, as if thinking. A slow shake of her head. "Those should give you a good start. If I think of anyone else, I'll let you know."

"This is a huge help," I said.

"Glad to do it," Betty Lou said. "Like I said before, I like your idea for the documentary. Showing the other, less sensational, side of the story."

"That's the plan," Nicole said.

CHAPTER THIRTEEN

THE NEXT MORNING, just after eight a.m., I called to arrange an appointment with Mayor Gwen Olsen. Her secretary had just gotten in and said the mayor had twenty minutes at nine thirty. She also knew who we were.

"You're the ones from Hollywood?" she asked. "Making that film?"

"We are," I said.

"Cool."

The small-town grapevine up and running.

Last night, after our meeting with Betty Lou broke up, and while we walked back to the hotel, Ray suggested that Nicole and I take the lead on any interviews. His thinking was that we offered a "more benign face." Less likely to cause any of the wrinkles that naturally follow the designation P.I. Even the moniker technical consultant might prove confusing and off-putting. As Pancake saw it—keep the temperature low in Pine Key. Ray and Pancake would remain in the background and handle any research or outreach to other jurisdictions.

A chunk of their research pinged my laptop as I hung up from the mayor's office. It indicated that Gwen Olsen had served as Pine Key's mayor for over twelve years, surviving a highly contentious first election, then easier reelections, the most recent four uncontested. Must be doing a good job. She and her husband, Ralph, owned a hardware store on Main and lived on Elm Street, just three blocks down from City Hall, which housed her office. I liked that. She could walk to work. Of course, anywhere in Pine Key was walking distance. Made me envious. With the sticky traffic in Gulf Shores, most days I wished I could walk to Captain Rocky's. Sure would make life easier. But then, the mayor had to actually show up; with my manager, Carla Martinez, I rarely had to make an appearance. Except that Pancake, when he wasn't at Ray's, considered Captain Rocky's his office. He was there most days and he enjoyed, actually expected, my company. Carla did, too. An unchaperoned Pancake usually resulted in mischief.

This morning, I opted for tan slacks and a navy blue RGP shirt; Nicole black slacks and a pink RGP shirt. We looked the part, now we had to play the role. Hollywood producers on the job. We were, in fact, stealthy spies digging for information.

Longly, Jake Longly.

When we stepped outside, the sky was clear and the temperature mild. I knew it was headed up, the high predicted to be near ninety by midafternoon.

City Hall was a white clapboard building, black trim, crushed shell walkway, and a gallery porch that extended its considerable width. Two pairs of white, slat-backed rockers flanked the front door, taking advantage of the shade. Two sixty-something ladies relaxed in the rockers to the left, one working a crossword, the other knitting. A small black dog lay between the two. They looked up and smiled as Nicole and I approached.

The knitter said, "Nice morning, ain't it?" She wore baggy tan pants and a dark blue sweatshirt, *Visit Panama City* in white script across the front, sleeves pushed to her elbows.

"Sure is," I said.

"Where you guys from?" the puzzler asked. Also clad in tan pants and a dark blue sweatshirt, this one stating *Cats Rule*. I wondered what the dog thought of that.

"How do you know we're not from here?" I asked.

The knitter took that one. "'Cause we know everyone in town and we ain't seen you before."

I smiled. "Gulf Shores."

"Well, welcome. I'm Mary Sue," the knitter said. "This here's Erma."

"Nice to meet you," Nicole said. She squatted and looked at the dog. "Who's this?"

"That's Poochie. She's a bit spoiled." The dog looked up at hearing her name, tail offering a couple of lazy wags.

"And whose fault is that?" Erma asked.

"Yours," Mary Sue replied. She flashed a mischievous smile.

Erma fanned herself with the crossword book. "She's mostly a liar." She laughed.

"You do your fair share of spoiling," Mary Sue said.

Erma shrugged.

Poochie had shuffled over to Nicole, who scratched her head. "She's sweet."

"You guys the ones doing that movie thing?" Erma asked.

"That's right," I said.

"We heard some about it. Heard it concerns Billy Wayne Baker."

"Not exactly," Nicole said. She stood. "It'll be mostly about his effect on this town."

"How much film you got?" Erma asked. "It's a long and sad and sordid story."

"We know."

"You here to see the mayor?" Mary Sue asked.

"Yes," I said.

Erma pointed to one of the porch cover support poles. "Tell her it's about time to repaint things around here."

I saw a few curls of old paint lifting way from the wood. "Will do."

"She won't listen to us. Maybe she'll do something if movie folks complain." She laughed.

We said our goodbyes to Mary Sue and Erma and entered. Quiet, the reception desk unoccupied. A sign indicated the "Mayor's Office" was down the hallway to the right. We headed that way and found the door open. Gwen Olsen sat behind her desk. I recognized her from the picture on the city's webpage.

Based on the birth date on her bio, I knew she was thirty-seven. Meant she'd first been elected mayor at twenty-five. No small feat, I imagined. She looked younger. I suspected that when she first ran for office she would have appeared to be fourteen. Must have run a hell of a campaign. Energetic blue eyes looked up from beneath her short, curly blond hair.

"Can I help you?" she asked.

"Jake Longly and Nicole Jamison."

"Oh, yes." She stood, glanced at her watch. "Is it nine thirty already?"

"I think we're a few minutes early," Nicole said. "We can come back."

"No, no, please come in."

She circled her desk and we shook hands. Her grip was firm. She wore gray slacks and a white blouse, a simple gold chain necklace visible at the open collar. She directed us to the sitting area to the left of her desk. A sofa, two wingback chairs, a coffee table. We sat on the sofa.

"Can I get you some coffee or juice, anything?"

"We're good," I said.

She sat in one chair. "I take it you met Mary Sue Baker and Erma Clemens out front."

"The two young ladies?" I asked.

She laughed. "They'd love to hear that. They're sisters. Both widowed. Live together a block from here. They're our de facto welcoming committee. Here every day."

"They did look comfortable." I smiled.

"We used to have a bench out there—for folks to sit out in the fresh air—but we brought in the rockers just for those two. Other folks, too, of course, but Mary Sue and Erma definitely have staked their claim."

"Seems to work," Nicole said.

"They asked us to tell you the porch needs repainting," I said.

Olsen smiled. "They've been harping on that for a couple of months. As soon as I find the money, we'll get on it."

Small-town budgets.

"So, you're the Hollywood folks?" Olsen asked.

I smiled. "Yes."

"And you're doing a documentary?"

"News travels fast," Nicole said.

"Most things around here move slowly, but news? It's like electricity." She smiled. "Particularly if Betty Lou has news."

"Ah," I said. "She's the source."

She gave a soft laugh. "She does love a good story."

I nodded.

"She called me last night. Gave me a heads-up that you were coming by." She smiled. "She sure liked you guys."

"We liked her, too," Nicole said. "Funny lady."

"That's one of her many good qualities." Olsen leaned back, settling into the chair. "By the time I got to breakfast over at McGee's Cafe this morning, she had everyone buzzing."

"I hope in a good way," I said.

"I'd be lying if I didn't say some folks have concerns about resurrecting Billy Wayne Baker. That's someone we'd as soon forget." She sighed. "But for the most part, I'd say people are curious."

"Not unexpected," I said.

"So, tell me what this's all about."

Nicole explained the documentary and our proposed slant on it.

Olsen seemed to give that some thought, then asked, "Why here? Billy Wayne ranged far and wide around this part of Florida."

"Three of his victims were here," Nicole said. "Seemed like the logical place to start."

She nodded but remained silent.

"This documentary series will be called *Aftermath*," Nicole said. "We'll ultimately have eight to twelve episodes. That hasn't been decided yet. Each will focus on a different community. A different killer. One principle of storytelling is to tell a small story as a means of telling a big one. Such murders in big metropolitan areas—like LA or New York—rarely make a blip. Comparatively speaking. Back-page stuff. But, their effects on small towns are catastrophic. Visceral. More personal."

"Since in small communities, everyone knows everyone else?" Olsen said

"Exactly." Nicole nodded. "The victims aren't simply random names."

"That was the case here." She brushed a curl off her forehead, shifted slightly in her seat. "I like it. It might be the final healing we need."

"That's what we hope."

She took a slow breath. "What do you need from me?"

Nicole uncrossed and recrossed her long legs. "We're doing preliminary interviews right now. Later we'll put together a shooting schedule and get a crew in to do the actual filming. Since you were mayor at that time, that would put you at ground zero. We want your take on that time. What it was like around here."

Another breath, as if gathering her thoughts. "The first murder was a shock. Like a punch to the gut. Had everyone on edge. The second and third knocked this town way off balance. Staggered the entire community. Everyone was literally terrified. With the events taking place at night, in people's homes, where they were supposed to be safe, the tension became unbearable. You could taste the fear. Everyone was distracted, confused. Gun sales went up. Home security systems, too." She waved a hand. "The traffic through my door increased dramatically."

"A universal reaction," I said.

She nodded. "Charlie Morgan, our police chief, did a magnificent job. Calming everyone as best he could given the circumstances. He added patrols. We dug into the city coffers for the overtime pay he needed."

"I know the final victim was the wife of one of his officers," I said.

"Sara Clark. One of the nicest and sweetest people you'd ever meet. And being Frank's wife, it made Charlie's job even harder. Folks seemed to think that if the home of our best cop wasn't safe, whose was?"

"I understand Frank Clark and his partner lead the investigation," Nicole said.

"That's right. Frank and Terry Munson."

"From what we've heard, they're good at their job."

"We're lucky to have them. Both are sharp and dedicated to this town."

"We also heard that Frank Clark was broken up over his wife's death."

"He was. Understandably. He and Sara were one of those couples. The ones everybody points to as ideal. But Frank manned up. Bit the bullet and did his job." She smiled. "That's the kind of guy he is. Tough as nails."

"We'd like to talk with him," Nicole said. "And his partner."

"That shouldn't be a problem."

I nodded. "And the chief, too, of course."

Olsen smiled. "Charlie loves to talk so that's an easy one. I'll give him a call and let him know."

"We'd appreciate it."

"I do have a question," Olsen said. "I understand you have a couple of P.I.s with you."

I smiled. To put her at ease, but more to cover the unease I felt growing inside. For the lie I was about to tell. This was a good town, a nice place to live. This was a good mayor, a good woman. I only hoped that in the end, when the truth came out, as it would have to if Billy Wayne was telling the truth, she'd understand. Even forgive us. But, right now, the game had to continue.

"Ray's my father," I said. "He's a P.I. over in Gulf Shores. He and his partner are here as technical consultants. Help us understand the investigative side of this."

Nicole jumped in. "That's common with these types of documentaries. We always employ consultants. So we don't mess up the technical stuff. Otherwise, believability goes out the window. Viewers won't trust any of the story if they think we don't know what we're talking about."

I could feel the same unease in Nicole's voice. Apparently, Olsen didn't.

"Makes sense. I'll give Charlie a call."

She stood and walked to her desk. She punched a button on the desk phone, waited a few seconds, then, "Charlie? Gwen. Yeah, just fine. I had a chat with Jake Longly and Nicole Jamison, the two from Hollywood." Pause. "Yeah, they seem like nice folks." She smiled at us. "They want to have a sit-down with you." Pause. "Will do. Thanks." She hung up. "He said come by now. He's got time."

We stood. "Thanks," I said. "That was nice of you to do."

She smiled. "I have an ulterior motive."

"Oh?"

"Remind him we have a meeting later this morning. He sometimes forgets." Her smile broadened. "Accidentally on purpose."

CHAPTER FOURTEEN

REACHING THE POLICE station took a half a minute. It was right next door. Also white clapboard with black trim, it was essentially a mirror image of city hall. Slightly larger but the design and color carried on the city's chosen theme. Clean, functional. The major difference was it had no front porch, only a small stoop, and no rockers. No Mary Sue or Erma. No Poochie either. A gray cat sat on the lawn near the walkway, bathing. It ignored us.

I immediately liked Chief Charles Morgan, or Charlie as he asked us to call him. Almost before he said a word. He reminded me of everybody's favorite uncle. I knew he was sixty-three. He had a round face and a thick body, carrying a good thirty pounds of extra weight. His gray hair and matching mustache were thick; his blue eyes and smile bore a hint of mischievousness. Probably had some hell-raising in his background. Before he pinned on a badge.

He offered us coffee, but we declined and took the chairs that faced his desk.

"Gwen said you guys wanted to talk."

"We do," I said. "Thanks for seeing us."

He gave a slight wave of his hand as if to say it was no problem. "Betty Lou told me at breakfast this morning you're doing some film, or something, on Billy Wayne Baker."

"Betty Lou gets around."

He gave a soft laugh. "That she does. But it seems you two made quite an impression and she ain't easily impressed. I'd say she's a big fan."

"As we are of her," Nicole said. "I love her straightforward sense of humor."

He smiled. "That's her in a nutshell. So, tell me about this project."

"It's a documentary series," Nicole said. She laid out the gist of the project.

He tugged one edge of his mustache and nodded. "So, this ain't another one of those that makes Billy Wayne Baker look like a criminal genius? Or a celebrity of some sorts?"

"The opposite," Nicole said. "This isn't a story about Billy Wayne, it's about the damage people like him leave behind."

"I've got to say that normally I wouldn't give anybody who wanted to talk about Billy Wayne the time of day. Wouldn't even let them through the door." His gaze moved back and forth studying us. "Unless they wanted to tell me he got himself killed up there in Raiford." He hesitated. "But, you two seem different from the newspaper types who try to shoehorn their way in here."

"We are," Nicole said. She smiled. "We want to hear, then tell, the stories of the people in this town who he affected. The stories newspapers tend to ignore."

That uneasy feeling rose in my chest again. I could see in Chief Morgan's eyes that he believed, maybe even trusted us. But would he if the path we were exploring led to one of his best officers? Would he feel used? Duped? Probably. We could only hope that, if indeed a killer was still in this community and if we were able to prove that, the end would justify our devious means. My discomfort was tempered to some degree by the counter feeling that this would be a real documentary. It would tell the stores of real people.

It could serve as a tool for healing. Or was that simply the lie I was telling myself?

Morgan shifted in his chair. It creaked under his weight. "I suspect you'll find most people around here willing to talk about it. A few won't." He shrugged. "I guess that's expected."

"Maybe even those will come around once they know the slant of the documentary," Nicole said. "After they get comfortable with what we're doing."

"Could be." He tapped an index finger on his desk top. "I suspect you want my recollections on that whole deal."

"We do," Nicole said. "We're in the research stage. Preliminary stuff. We'll then set up a video interview. If that's okay."

He smiled. "The missus always said I was so funny I should have my own TV show." One eyebrow gave a quick bounce. "But I think she was being sarcastic."

I laughed and glanced at Nicole. "I understand completely."

She gave a mock surprise look.

Morgan laughed. "So you two are more than just coworkers?"

"We are," Nicole said. "Jake needs taming. That's my job."

"I suspect my wife'd say the same thing." The finger tapped again. "So, let's get to business. Before someone out there in our fair city does something stupid and my whole day goes south."

"Tell us about that time," Nicole said. "How you became embroiled in Billy Wayne's world."

"Embroiled. I like that word. That's what it was, too. Or maybe entrapped. Like we were tangled up in a fishing net and sinking fast." He leaned back and laced his fingers over his belly. "The first murder—Loretta Swift—was a big jolt. We'd only had one killing around here in memory. Must've been over ten years earlier." He glanced down at his desk top, gathering his thoughts, maybe envisioning something from the past. He sighed, his head giving a slight bob. "Loretta was a great lady. She and her husband, Peter, owned a bakery just over on Main. Swift's Bakery. Stop by. They make the best muffins and pastries in town." He patted his stomach. "I can vouch for that."

"We'll do it," I said.

"She was killed in her home. Right?" Nicole asked.

"That's true. Peter was at an Elk's meeting. Up in Panama City. Got home about eleven. Found Loretta dead. When I got there, it was obvious she'd been dead for a couple of hours at least."

"From what we've read, at that time, you had no idea Billy Wayne Baker was involved," Nicole said.

"The guys up in Jacksonville had already linked up the two earlier killings. That young girl in Apalachicola and the woman over in Santa Rosa Beach. Those were a good year before Loretta got killed. So, we never gave a thought that her murder might be part of that. Things like that happen elsewhere. Not here." He shook his head. "Man, were we ever naive. Anyway, when the DNA matched those two cases, it put Billy Wayne right here in our own backyard. Things got crazy around here in a hot minute."

"I suspect it did change the town's mood," I said.

"It's funny," Morgan said. "It was sort of a dichotomy. Is that the right word? Anyway, it's true that the fear level around here jumped off the charts when Loretta was killed. But linking it up to those earlier murders actually lowered the hysteria a tad."

"How so?" I asked.

"Each of the other killings had been in different cities. I think that made folks feel the killer was more or less itinerant. Not someone local. Meant that if he'd struck here then he'd likely've moved on. Gone. Never to be seen again. Better than having a killer living here among us seemed to be the mood."

"Until the next time," I said.

"You can say that again. It was like someone had poured gasoline on smoldering embers."

"From what we've read," I said, "no one around here remembers seeing Billy Wayne. Before or after the murders."

"That's correct. And we asked everyone in the whole damn town. Nothing. Like he was a ghost."

"In many ways he was." I looked at him. "I met him. Talked with him up at Union Correctional."

"Bet that was pleasant," Morgan said.

"Unexpected. Billy Wayne seemed calm, passive. Even harmless."

"A case of the book not matching its cover?" Morgan asked.

"Exactly. But it might explain why no one remembers seeing him. He really does look benign."

Morgan seemed to consider that for a few seconds. "Maybe so. I always figured he came to town, did his dirty work, and headed back to his lair up in Tallahassee. Where I hear he lived during his spree."

"That's what he told me," I said. "I wasn't sure he was being entirely truthful." Morgan raised an eyebrow. "He came into strange towns, strange to him anyway, and got out without being detected. In short order. Seemed to find his victims quickly. That didn't feel right to me so I questioned him on it. His assaults seemed to be well planned. Like he'd have to spend at least a few days getting the lay of the land, so to speak. Finding a vulnerable target. He flatly denied that was the case. If he's being truthful, it seems to me he was very lucky to stumble on just the right victim. Seven times."

Morgan nodded. "Some predators are good hunters."

And there it was. Billy Wayne was definitely a skilled hunter. He knew, or felt, or whatever, the vulnerability of others. I suspected this was true of killers like Bundy and Gacy and many other multiple murderers. Each had that sixth sense that sniffed out the vulnerable, the trusting, or from their point of view, the weak. And if Billy Wayne was being truthful, he was smart enough not to hang around. Or return to a place where he had killed. Kept moving. Stayed off the radar. Unless he really did all three killings here. Maybe found Pine Key to be the ideal hunting ground. I wasn't sure yet what I believed.

"Since you had three victims here," I said, "he must have found something he was comfortable with in Pine Key."

Morgan sighed. "That's what I've wrestled with since then. Are we too comfortable around here? Not vigilant enough? Should we be more wary of strangers?" His shoulders dropped a couple of inches. "Truth is, I'd hate for the town to become cynical. I'd hate to be the one that pushed folks in that direction. But, in the end, isn't that my job? Ain't I the one that's supposed to keep the town safe? To forewarn them of danger?" He took a deep breath and let it out slowly. "It weighs on me, I'll tell you that."

It did. I could see it in his face, his body language. I suspected that three years ago he looked ten years younger. I did not envy Charlie Morgan his job.

"I'm sure it didn't help that the last victim here was the wife of one of your officers," Nicole said.

"No, it didn't. Sara Clark. Frank's wife."

"How did that change the public's mood?"

"A couple of ways. It definitely ramped up the hysteria. As you mentioned, people began to wonder if the killer had taken a special liking to Pine Key. Sort of like that shark in *Jaws*. Found a feeding ground where he was comfortable. On the other hand, it settled down Tommy Lee Kovac. His sister Noleen was the second victim. He got it in his head that we weren't doing our job. Made a ruckus. Dragged a few others into his circle. Made things a shade more difficult. But when Sara was killed, that seemed to diffuse his anger a little."

"What about Frank Clark?" I asked. "How'd he take it?"

"Damn near killed him. He and Sara were close. Very close. He sat right there where you are and cried his soul out. Broke my heart. He's been with us a long time. Our best guy. And almost like a son to me."

"Did it affect his job performance any?" I asked.

"Sure did. He and his partner, Terry Munson, were leading the investigation into the other two murders. When Sara became number three, it knocked Frank all sideways. Distracted, emotional, not sleeping, all the stuff you'd expect." He opened and closed one fist as if limbering it up. "But, I'll tell you, he still did his job. Terry helped him a lot. We all did."

"Do you think he'll talk with us?"

"Don't see a reason why not. He ain't here right now, but he and Munson shouldn't be too far away. Or too busy. Quiet day so far. I'll give him a call."

"We'd appreciate that."

"One thing," Morgan said. "I hear you got a couple of consultants with you? P.I.s? That true?"

"Yes," I said. "My father and his partner. We hired them to help sort out the investigator stuff. Make sure we understand everything that happened here."

"That'll help us better portray the effect these murders had on the town and the victims' families and friends," Nicole added.

Morgan gave a slow nod. "Makes sense. Frank and Terry can walk you through all that. They know these cases better than anyone."

"We'll do our best to not get in the way," Nicole said.

Morgan smiled. "The truth? I like what you're doing. It just might be the thing this town needs. I know the mayor feels the same way. If everyone who lost someone can get their story out there, vent it as it were, then maybe it'll help put Billy Wayne Baker in the rearview mirror once and for all." He gave another brief nod. "We could use that."

"Oh, speaking of the mayor," Nicole said, "she asked us to remind you of your meeting this morning."

He glanced at his watch. "It's our annual budget wrestling match." He smiled. "I want more and she always wants to give me less." He gave a quick nod. "Guess I'd better grab another cup of coffee before I mosey on over there. Gwen's a tough cookie."

CHAPTER FIFTEEN

RAY HAD JUST finished a phone conversation with an attorney back in Gulf Shores. A case that had nothing to do with Billy Wayne Baker. Ray had worked with the guy before, a young up and comer in the local legal world. He wanted Ray to look into some business shenanigans in a real estate firm where one of the partners was suing for unlawful termination, defamation, loss of income, the usual stuff. Seems his partners, who would be the clients, felt the dismissed colleague had bent the rules a little too far and had placed the company in legal jeopardy. The attorney used words like fraud, predatory practices, kickbacks, bribery of inspectors—things that to Ray were the typical under-the-table shuffles that go on in the mega-buck real estate world. The kind of case that could be a quick in and out, thank you very much, or turn into a multi-tentacled monster that sucked up time and effort like a Hoover. Ray wasn't overly enthusiastic but agreed to look into it and decide whether he could help or not.

That's when Jake called. After giving him the thumbnail of what he and Nicole uncovered from their talks with Mayor Gwen Olsen and Chief Charlie Morgan, not much, Jake said Morgan was arranging a chat with Frank Clark and his partner, Terry Munson. Both were on their way to the station.

"The chief okay with me and Pancake snooping around?" Ray asked.

"Seems to be on board. Just remember, you guys are technical consultants."

"I know the game," Ray said.

"And wear your RGP shirts."

"That I might not have remembered. Thanks." He disconnected the call.

Fifteen minutes later, Ray and Pancake arrived to find Jake and Nicole in the reception area. Almost immediately, Clark and Munson came in. Ray recognized them from the department website photos as well as the materials Pancake had dug up on each. Introductions followed. Clark led the group down to Chief Morgan's office. He was ensconced behind his desk.

Morgan had a no-nonsense air and a firm handshake. He carried his extra weight well, but his chair creaked as he sat.

"What happened to you?" he asked Pancake.

"Asphalt," Pancake said.

"There's a story there."

Pancake shrugged. "It's better now. Should've seen it a few days ago."

Clark and Munson had moved to Morgan's left side and turned to face them. They adopted wide stances as if forming an impenetrable wall. The blue wall. The one that said we're in charge here.

Clark was a bull. Big chest and shoulders, dark eyes, square jaw, buzz cut. He looked tough. Looked like a cop. Munson was slighter of build, light brown hair that flopped over his forehead, and hazel eyes. Sort of a pretty boy. Went with his ladies'-man rep. Both were pleasant, if a little reluctant. Understandable. They were cops. Suspicious by nature. First instinct always to circle the wagons, say little, gather intel before revealing anything. Ray respected that. He was of the same mold.

Nicole managed to dent their armor. First off, her mere presence laid a patina of school-boy nervousness over their hard faces. Quick smiles, looks away, all the reactions guys of any age have when facing a beautiful woman. Boys/men never change. She sure had that effect on Jake. He and Pancake, too, for that matter. Nature of the beast it seemed.

Still, Clark and Munson didn't exactly melt. But, when she explained the project, the slant, how the documentary would tell the town's and the victims' stories, not Billy Wayne's, the tension in the room dropped several notches.

Munson eyed her. "What's your position in all this?"

Nicole smiled, reeling him in. "I'd be the project manager. Probably the host of the show."

Munson nodded, glanced at Morgan. "Can't say I hate the idea." He smiled.

Nicole gave a soft laugh. "Well, that's a start."

A few more minutes of casual conversation followed, both Clark and Munson relaxing, warming to the idea, or at least to Nicole. Ultimately, a plan was formed. Jake and Nicole to sit down with Clark while Munson took Ray and Pancake through the cases.

As the meeting was breaking up, a man stuck his head in the door.

"Peter," Morgan said. "Let me introduce you to some Hollywood folks."

Peter proved to be Peter Swift, the first victim's husband, the owner of Swift's Bakery, the name printed in white script on the side of the large, flat, pink box he juggled as he shook hands with everyone. He flipped open the box, exposing an array of muffins, pastries, and cookies. "Brought these over for the crew."

Morgan laughed. "Peter comes by almost every day trying to fatten us up."

"Community relations." Peter smiled. He extended the offerings. "Any takers?"

Everyone declined, except for Pancake, who lifted a bear claw and took a bite.

"Wow," he said. "These are good."

"We do our best."

"Mr. Swift," Nicole said. "We're sorry for the loss of your wife."

Peter nodded. "Thanks."

"We'd like to stop by and talk with you later."

He looked at her, then scanned the other faces in the room. "About what?"

"A project we're working on," Nicole said. "If it's okay, we'll drop by after we finish here. I can explain it then."

"That'd be fine," Peter said. "You know where the bakery is?"

"Just follow the smell," Morgan said with a laugh.

"That's true," Peter said. Then, to Morgan, "Is Angus here?"

Morgan nodded, smiled. "Ain't he always here?" He glanced at Ray. "Angus Whitehead's our town drunk. Every place has one, I suspect. He's harmless, and actually smart enough to wander over here to sleep it off whenever he gets a snoot full. Which is often. Hell, he spends more time here than I do. But that beats him trying to drive home. So we keep a cell open for him."

"Sounds like an interesting character."

"Oh, yeah. He is that."

"He's a pain," Clark said.

"And annoying," Munson added.

Morgan smiled. "Frank and Terry ain't big fans of Angus. Me? I sort of like the guy." He then nodded to Peter. "He's in the back. I'm sure he needs the sugar about now." As Peter turned to leave, Morgan added, "Tell him it's time to go home. We ain't the Holiday Inn."

Peter gave the group a nod before retreating down a hallway toward the rear of the building.

"I'm going to leave you guys to it," Morgan said. "While I have the pleasure of a sit-down with our mayor." He looked around. "Now, where'd I leave my coffee?"

"That one?" Nicole said, indicating a stainless mug on the corner of his desk.

Morgan wagged his head. "Jesus, I'd lose my head if it wasn't attached." He scooped it up and circled his desk.

"Tell her we want a raise," Clark said. "Ain't had one in so long I can't remember."

"I'll be sure to add that to my wishful thinking list." He gave a soft laugh. "Later."

CHAPTER SIXTEEN

RAY CLIMBED INTO the passenger's seat of Munson's gray Chevy sedan, Pancake in back.

"I think it's best if we visit the scenes in order," Munson said. "Maybe that'll help you get a feel for what we were up against."

"Sounds good," Ray said.

Munson pulled from the station lot, swinging onto Main Street. Traffic was light.

"You'll find out just how small this town is," Munson said. "Each of the scenes is within four or five blocks of the others. Made everyone feel like the murders took place right in their own backyard." He whipped a left. "Literally."

"Bet that kicked up the community fear level," Pancake said.

"It was more than that. Folks were terrified. Panicked might be a better word."

"Made your job easy, didn't it?" Ray said. Not really a question.

"You got that right." Munson shook his head. "I'd never seen anything like it. Every time a pine cone fell on someone's roof, or a raccoon rummaged in a trash can, or, hell, even if the rain pattered a little too hard against a window, we'd get a call." He brushed his hair back from his forehead. "And me, or Frank, or one of the other guys'd have to check it out." He glanced at Ray. "Sleep became a rare commodity."

Munson pulled to the curb in front of a well-maintained house only three blocks from the station.

"This is where Peter Swift lives. Where his wife, Loretta, was murdered."

The house, the entire street, was pleasant, and quiet. Safe. Thick green grass, flowering shrubs, fat shade trees. The kind of place nothing bad could ever happen. The kind of place Peter Swift would live. Having just met Peter, Ray's first impression was that he was a quiet and welcoming man. One of those who went about his business and likely never harmed, or even insulted, anyone. Passive, almost meek. He fit this neighborhood well.

"Peter had been up in Panama City at an Elk's meeting," Munson said. "He's a big muckety-muck in those circles."

"I hear he got home late and found his wife's body," Pancake said.

"That's right. We got the call about eleven, eleven thirty, something like that. Frank was on first call but when he learned it was Peter's wife, he called me. We both came running." He sighed. "Loretta was one of the nicest people you'd ever want to meet. Her murder shook this town like an earthquake."

"How'd Peter react?"

"Crushed. Beside himself. Kept pacing the floor, muttering, crying. We tried to get him to leave, or at least sit down, but every time he settled on the sofa, he'd pop back up. He was frantic."

"Understandable," Ray said.

"You see, he and Loretta were together since high school. Actually, before that, I think. Everybody knew even back then they'd end up together. Nothing else seemed possible."

"You knew them back then?" Pancake asked.

"Sure did. Frank did, too. We all went to school together. Peter and Loretta were a couple of years ahead of us, but around here everybody knows everybody else anyway."

"I understand she had a sister," Ray said.

"Charlaine Anders. A year younger, but they looked like twins. She, like Peter, was destroyed. She and Loretta were inseparable. Charlaine ended up in the ER that night. Hysterical. The doc over there sedated her. Kept her overnight to keep an eye on her." He shook his head. "It was a tough time."

"She now helps run the bakery, doesn't she?" Pancake asked.

"Sure does. She was working over at the hardware store but she quit and stepped in to keep the bakery working."

"And the scene here?" Ray asked. "Any sign of a break-in?"

"Nope. She apparently had left the back door unlocked. Front door, too, for that matter. According to Peter they rarely locked anything. Never had a reason to."

"She was found in the bedroom, right?" Ray asked.

"Yes. The sheets were a bit messed up, but there was no real sign of a struggle. Later we learned Billy Wayne used a knife to force compliance. So, it'd make sense there wasn't a struggle." He stared at the house for a few seconds. "Of course, Billy Wayne tied her to the bed. Both wrists and both ankles. So fighting him wasn't an option." He shook his head. "Loretta wasn't a fighter anyway. At least, she never seemed that way to me." He looked at Ray. "More like Peter. Nice folks."

Ray knew most people under those circumstances weren't fighters. They'd let an intruder restrain them before they'd resist physically. Always hoping it was simply a robbery and that no harm to them was the intent. Hope can be dangerous sometimes. But how was someone to know what was best? Fight a guy with a knife, or some other weapon, tooth and nail, maybe to the death, or hope and pray that being tied would be the worst of it? If they knew what was coming, they'd react differently. At least most people would, he believed. So, Billy Wayne likely used the knife and probably some sweet talk to convince them to let him tie them up. Probably saying he was there to rob them and wasn't going to harm them. He wasn't the first killer to use that tactic. Wouldn't be the last.

"What'd he use for restraints?" Pancake asked.

"Blue ski rope."

"Same with the others?" Ray asked.

Munson nodded. "The FBI guys said that was his standard MO. They were able to determine the manufacturer but never could trace the purchase site. Too common and too many sources out there." Another brush back of his hair. "They even sell the same stuff over at the hardware store."

"No evidence Billy Wayne shopped there?" Pancake asked.

"Nope. Besides, he'd already used the same type of rope up in Santa Rosa Beach." He shrugged. "And then the same thing after he left Pine Key. The other two killings."

"So, all but the first one," Ray said. "The one in Apalachicola?"

"That's what the FBI said. That young lady wasn't restrained at all. And she fought back."

Ray nodded. "That's what we understand."

"One thing you can say about Billy Wayne—he learned from his mistakes."

"Sort of," Pancake said. "He did leave his DNA everywhere."

"That he did," Munson said.

"And the only real evidence you found was a small semen stain on the bedsheets?" Ray asked.

"That's right. No fingerprints, or shoe prints. Nothing else."

"And it took a few days for that to be connected to Billy Wayne Baker?" Pancake asked.

"Yep. Until the lab up in Jacksonville did its testing. Then the hysteria around here really ramped up." He looked at Ray. "Anything else you want to see here?"

Ray shook his head.

Back in the car, Munson pulled from the curb and after zigging a couple of blocks, turned into the drive of another pleasant house on another pleasant street. This one smaller, tan brick, shaded by a pair of maple trees. They climbed out and moved to the front of the car.

"This is where Noleen Kovac lived. Looked like Billy Wayne cut through a screen door that entered off the back patio. She wasn't found until the next day. A good twelve hours after the murder. When she didn't show up for work over at the bank—she was a teller—and didn't answer her phone, her boss called and asked us to check on her. Frank took the call since he'd had the duty the night before. He found her in her bed, nude, tied with the same rope, and strangled. He called me and Chief Morgan. Again, no prints, only a semen stain on the bedsheets."

"I assume you considered this was Billy Wayne's work from the beginning?" Ray asked.

"More than that. We knew. I mean, we couldn't definitely say that until the DNA came back, but we knew." He pointed toward the house. "What we saw in there was a carbon copy of Loretta Swift. In essentially every detail."

"I hear her brother made some waves," Pancake said.

"Tommy Lee. Sure did. He gathered a few sympathizers and basically marched on city hall. Said we were incompetent. Called us Keystone cops. That sort of thing."

"How'd you guys take that?" Ray asked.

"Like you'd imagine. We were pissed off. Big-time. But we kept telling ourselves he was a grieving brother. Still, wasn't easy to sit back and let him trash us."

"The job's never easy."

"You got it."

"Tommy Lee have a history of that sort of thing?" Pancake asked.

Munson shook his head. "Not really. He went to school with us, too. Back in the day. Frank and I both knew him. We were friends back then but later drifted apart. He was on his boat all the time, and me and Frank were pretty busy, too." He brushed his hair off his forehead again. "You might say life got in the way."

"No bad blood?" Ray asked. "Between him and either you or Frank?"

"Not before Noleen's murder."

Ray nodded.

"After Sara Clark was killed, he softened a notch. Still thought we were incompetent, but since one of our own had lost a wife it settled him down."

Ray walked up the drive to the garage that sat at the end. The door, the entire structure, could use a new coat of paint, but it otherwise looked solid. Closed up. In the backyard, there was a well-maintained garden demarcated by railroad ties, a blue and silver swing set, and a small, round inflatable pool. A green garden hose hung over its edge.

Ray returned to where Munson and Pancake stood. "Who lives here now?"

"Tommy Lee inherited the property from his sister. I think he toyed with idea of renting it, but in the end, didn't want anything more to do with it. He sold it to a young couple. Of course, knowing that a murder had happened here brought the price down."

"Sounds like Tommy Lee and his sister were close."

"Sure were. Noleen was older by a couple of years. They lost their parents in a car accident. Down near Orlando. A few years ago."

"That's a tough one," Pancake said.

"Sure was. The only silver lining was the parents left them a chunk of money. And a house. They sold the house. Neither of them wanted that one either."

"How much money we talking?" Ray asked.

Munson looked at the house. "I've heard it was around three-hundred thousand. In that neighborhood. They split it." He kicked at a loose stone. It skittered across the drive. "I understand it was in an account at Noleen's bank. Given her financial background, she handled it. Made some good investments. Grew it some from what I understand."

"I assume Tommy Lee inherited it from his sister," Ray said.

Munson looked at him. "Don't see that that's relevant."

"Just trying to get a handle on Tommy Lee," Ray said. "Before we talk with him."

Munson nodded. "I don't think either he or Noleen ever took any of the money out. Neither needed it. She had her career and Tommy Lee runs a successful charter business."

"I see."

Munson eyed him. "You sound like a cop."

Ray shrugged. "P.I. thinking. Old habit."

"I hear you," Munson said. "Do that myself all too often." He sighed. "That much money could be a motive for murder. But not here. Tommy Lee and Noleen were close. Besides, Billy Wayne Baker killed Noleen. Not much doubt about that."

CHAPTER SEVENTEEN

"I'VE BEEN BURNED by reporters before," Detective Frank Clark said. "So I think my caution is understandable."

He sat across the centrally located, dull, metal table from Nicole and me. We were in "the box," as he called it. The interrogation room. No windows, one door, a video camera near the ceiling in one corner, aimed at us but not active, and three hard, uncomfortable chairs. The table was bolted to the floor and a thick chain attached to a pair of handcuffs hung off the edge to my right. The overheads were fluorescent and harsh. Not a comfortable situation if the focus was on you. Hell, I felt guilty. And I hadn't done anything. Well, other than spinning a yarn about our real agenda and lying to everyone, including the police.

I eyed the cuffs. I had worn a pair before. More than once. The first time being just after my seventeenth birthday. Me and Pancake. Bar fight. Two a.m. Intoxicated. Angry police. Ray even angrier. He actually let them take us to jail. Got Pancake's folks in on the whole deal.

This visit was nowhere near the few hours Pancake and I stewed in jail as kids. While Ray went to lunch. Underage drinking and fighting was, to Ray, more egregious than spray-painting a neighbor's garage. Hard to argue with his logic there. Still, the object lesson was more or less the same—if you do stupid shit, there are bad consequences. He did arrange for us to have our own cell. Two bunks, one toilet. Which was good since the other inmates looked like serious criminals. The night had been long and cold. Even though it was summer in Gulf Shores, something about concrete and iron dropped the temp. The flimsy sheet and blanket and painfully thin mattress offered little help. Not my favorite memory.

To his credit, Clark had apologized for using "the box" for our chat. Said it was the only place around the department with any real privacy. He added that he suspected our questions might enter areas he didn't want to reach the gossip mill. I understood.

Nicole had a notepad before her and had placed her iPhone on the table to record the interview.

"We aren't reporters," I said. "We're here to make a documentary."

The lie was getting easier.

"We want to tell your story," Nicole said. "This isn't a hit piece. I promise."

Clark stared at her. Also, to his credit, he hadn't visually undressed Nicole. Not once. In my experience that was rare. In fact, I couldn't ever remember it happening before. Us guys are just like that. Can't help it. I took Clark's lack of leering to mean his head was somewhere else. Maybe back to the day his wife was murdered. By Billy Wayne? By Clark himself? We didn't yet know which.

"Why me? Why Pine Key?" He folded his hands before him. "Lot's of others lost loved ones to Billy Wayne."

"Every story needs a focus," Nicole said. "A sharply defined one. If we simply told the tales of all the victims, the impact would be lost. Viewers would yawn and change the station." She smiled. "When we did our research, we got the feeling the murders hit this town harder than the others where Billy Wayne prowled. Partly because those towns he only visited once. Here, he seemed to . . ." she hesitated as if searching for the right word . . . "linger."

Clark nodded. "That he did. And you're correct. It hit this community hard." He gave a half shake of his head. "We still haven't recovered." He sighed. "Just so I understand this, it's your uncle who's doing this. Right?"

"Yes. Charles Balfour."

"A name everyone knows." He offered a half smile, then looked at me. "And Ray and Pancake? Your father and his partner? They're technical consultants?"

"That's right," I said.

"Technical consultants are fairly standard for documentaries," Nicole said. "Regardless of the topic. They prevent us from making silly mistakes. Help avoid messing up the facts. In this situation, Ray and Pancake understand your world, your professional world, much better than we do."

He scratched the back of one hand, then nodded. "Okay. Ask your questions."

"Tell us about your wife. What she was like? How did you two meet? That sort of thing."

He remained silent for a good half a minute as if gathering his thoughts. "She was special. Kind, gentle, smart, devoted to this town. Everyone loved her. Even the ones she locked horns with over some issue or the other." Another hesitation, a half smile, as if remembering something. "We met in the seventh grade. That's when her family moved here. She was the prettiest thing I'd ever seen. But I was shy back then. Took three weeks to even speak to her. Then, another two months before I asked her out. To the movies." He took in a breath. "I knew right then she was the one."

"She feel the same way?" Nicole asked, smiling.

That drew a full smile from Clark. "Maybe not right then. But after a few more dates we were what they called 'an item.'"

"When did you get married?"

"Two weeks after graduating high school." He jerked his head to his left. "Right down there by the marina."

"You never had children, I understand."

"We tried. For a while. But it became apparent that children weren't in our future."

"How'd she take that?" Nicole asked.

"She, both of us actually, were disappointed. But, ultimately, we gave up that dream. She did a ton of community service work, and I joined the force. We focused on those things."

"How did you end up on the police department here?"

"Charlie, Chief Morgan, hired me to do odd jobs around the office. Everything from sweeping the floors to going out for coffee and lunch to filing. Whatever was needed. After a year, he was looking to hire a couple of more officers, so he hired me and Terry Munson."

"You and Officer Munson close?" I asked.

"Very. We've been friends since grammar school. Neither of us had siblings so we were more or less brothers." He smiled. "Not always well behaved, but we at least avoided doing anything too bad." Another smile. "Or at least getting caught."

They sounded like Pancake and me. Brothers-in-arms so to speak. I told him so.

"How come he joined your father but you never did?" Clark asked. "Or so I hear."

I shrugged. "Not that Ray didn't try. Over and over. Not my thing though. I own a bar and restaurant over in Gulf Shores. I'd rather do that than rummage around in other folks' dirty laundry."

"Yet, here you are."

"True. But this is different. This seems a worthy cause." I glanced at Nicole. "Besides, Nicole and her uncle are hard to refuse."

Clark nodded. I felt that he was beginning to relax. His initial reluctance seemed to be waning.

"Tell us about that day," Nicole said. "The day your wife was murdered."

"At first, the day was typically boring. Not much happens around here. But, by nightfall, things got a little crazy. Terry and I had to break up a fight. Over on The Boardwalk. Four guys got into it. All were well lubricated. Words and then fists flew. We broke it up. Didn't arrest any of them but gave them, let's say, a stiff warning. Then we had a shoplifting crew move in. Three teenage girls. One would occupy a merchant while the other two snatched stuff. Clothing, jewelry, that sort of thing. Those we arrested. While booking them, we got a TA—traffic accident—call. Over on the bridge. Terry took off to handle that. I got stuck with three crying and begging young ladies. Said they'd give everything back if we'd just let them go. Promised to never do it again. Something I've heard about a thousand times. Pleaded with us not to call their parents. If I remember it right, they were from Mexico Beach. Here for the weekend." He rubbed his chin. "'Course I told them it didn't work that way. They were sixteen. They stole several hundred dollars' worth of merchandise. Told them we couldn't let that ride. So, their parents drove up and we let them go home with them—after the parents promised they'd be back to face the judge in a couple of weeks."

"Did they?"

"Sure did. The judge gave them each six weekends of community service. Here, locally. So for the next month and a half they spent every Saturday and Sunday in our care. They cleaned the park and the roadsides and spent Saturday nights in the jail. I think they learned a lesson there."

"When did you discover what had happened to your wife?" Nicole asked.

"After I informed the parents of what their daughters had done, I got the girls all locked down and headed out to help Terry with the

TA. It was a little more than a fender bender. But, fortunately, no one was hurt. A few bumps and bruises. It snarled traffic for a couple of hours though. We got back about the time the parents arrived. Must have been around ten or so." He took a deep breath, released it slowly. "When I got home, I found her. Tied up in bed. Strangled."

I tried to read him. He seemed in control, as if reciting from a police report. His hooded eyes weren't exactly hard, maybe more sharp and focused. As if they were absorbing everything. Probably the look others had seen when being interrogated here in "the box." I suspected few could stand up under Frank Clark's glare. But was that sadness I saw behind his eyes? In the creases at their corners? Maybe remorse? For what—was the question.

"Did you know it was related to Billy Wayne then?"

"Obviously, I couldn't be sure. Not until we got the DNA back—that took a couple of weeks—but yeah, based on the other two killings we had, and the others up the road, all his hallmarks were there. Nighttime B&E, restrained with those blue ropes, strangled." He nodded. "So, yes. I knew."

"Must have been awful," Nicole said.

He sighed. "Worst day of my life."

"What happened then?" I asked.

"The FBI had already been here. Looking at the other two cases. So I called them and they showed up the next morning. They took over the investigation." He tapped the tabletop with one index finger. "They let Terry and me help, but it was their show. No doubt about that."

"How'd you feel about that?" Nicole asked. "The Feds taking over."

"Earlier, before Sara—" Again his, voice cracked. "I resented them coming in and swaggering around. But in truth, after Sara was killed, I was grateful. I needed the distance."

"Did you take some time off?" I asked.

"Sort of. Charlie wanted me off duty for a couple of weeks, but I convinced him that that would only make things worse. I needed to stay busy. So I was in and out. There were times I simply went home and cried." He looked down at his hands, now folded again before him. "Terry was great. He picked up the slack without hesitation. Charlie, too. Everyone did." His gaze fell to the table and he held it there for several seconds. He looked up. "The worst part, after I scrubbed away all the fingerprint powder, was packing up her stuff. Dresses, makeup, jewelry. Everything. That's when it hit the hardest." He forked the fingers of both hands through his hair. "Guilt, anger, the whole nine yards."

"Guilt?" Nicole asked. "About what?"

"I should've been home. I should've protected her."

"You were working," I said.

"Yeah, I tried telling myself that a million times. Didn't help. So, I worked. Not very well. My mind was fuzzy. Couldn't think straight. Couldn't sleep. Probably drank a little too much."

Frank Clark was a good cop. I had no doubts about that. His face, body language, everything, gave away nothing. Not that I could see anyway. A personification of Ray's "be cool" philosophy. Don't give anything away, say little, gather intel. Never let the other guy know what you're thinking. Keep the advantage. Frank Clark possessed all of that.

Raised a few questions about his actions in the weeks after his wife's murder. The crying in front of Chief Morgan, the inability to perform his duties well, the drinking. Real, or was he simply playing his role? A shaken husband, or a killer making his case for innocence?

"But it seems you survived it," I said.

"Didn't really have a choice." He shrugged. "You know what they say, time heals all. But that's a lie. Time lets you handle it better.

Bury it some. But, a day doesn't go by that I don't miss her." He looked back down. "She was everything."

After a few more questions, we thanked Clark for his time and his candor. As we stepped out of "the box," I ran into a man coming down the hallway. He staggered and I grabbed his arm.

From behind me Clark said, "Angus, you still here?"

"Looks that way, don't it." He offered a lopsided grin. "Just heading to the head." He laughed. "Heading to the head. I must be a poet or something."

"You're something, all right," Clark said. Then to us, "This is Angus Whitehead. The one Chief Morgan was talking about earlier. He drinks. A lot. Don't you, Angus?"

Angus' eyebrows bounced. "Ever' chance I get."

"And he ends up here sleeping it off most nights," Clark continued. "And some days."

Angus directed a quick nod to Nicole and me, then to Clark, and said, "I'll be out of here before too long."

"You better be. The chief's wandering around somewhere. And you're still on his list from last week."

Angus shrugged. "Weren't my fault." He gave a brief wave and weaved done the hall.

"Angus was involved in a ruckus last week," Clark said. "Over on The Boardwalk. A misunderstanding with a couple of tourists. They apparently didn't appreciate his inability to walk straight."

"He seemed harmless," Nicole said.

"He is. Just annoying."

CHAPTER EIGHTEEN

RAY STOOD AT the curb in front of Frank Clark's home. A small red brick structure, white trim, dark green front door. Several oak trees shaded the well-kept lawn. It and the entire neighborhood, like the other two they had visited, felt peaceful, normal. No hint of the violence that had visited.

Terry Munson hiked one hip on the trunk of his car, jacket flapping open, revealing his service piece, holstered beneath his left arm.

"This here's the reason I was reluctant to talk with you guys."

"Why so?" Ray asked.

"Look, the chief said this—what you guys are doing—could be a good thing. A final healing of sorts. Let everyone tell their stories. Flush the demons is the way he put it."

"You don't see it that way?"

"Some, I guess. For the town. But this whole ordeal nearly killed Frank. Sure, he soldiered on. Stayed on the job, did what he could. But, his head wasn't in it. He'd tear up at a moment's notice. Drank too much. His pain was contagious. We all felt it."

"He seems to have recovered," Ray said.

"Mostly, I guess. But he's different."

"In what way?"

"Just not the same old Frank." Munson slid off the fender and took a couple of steps toward the house, out onto the grass. He stared at nothing for a good half a minute. "You'd have to know him to see it, but he's not the same guy." He turned back to Ray. "I don't want him to go through that again. Relive all that." He shook his head. "This time he might not make it back."

"Don't you think he lives with it every day anyway?" Pancake asked.

"Sure, he does. I can feel it. Like his pain is radioactive and sending out waves. But thinking about it and talking about it's two different things." He released a deep sigh. "I don't want him to suffer any more damage."

"You two are close, I take it," Ray said.

"We grew up together. Like brothers. Lived on the same street. Just a block from right here. Known each other since forever." He looked back at the house. "It's been a difficult few years."

"He and his wife were also close, I hear," Pancake said.

Munson shoved his hands in his jeans pockets. "Sure were. Ever since Sara moved here. We were in the seventh grade. They were inseparable." He shook his head. "We all were."

"You knew her well, then," Ray said.

He nodded. "Sara was one of the kindest and sweetest people you'd ever want to know. Even as kids, she was one of the guys. A tomboy of sorts. Frank and I dragged her into our mischief. She never batted an eye." He smiled. "Truth is, she took the rap for us more than once."

"Childhood friends'll do that," Pancake said.

"She sure did." He jerked his head toward the house. "Can't tell you how many times we cooked steaks or ribs or whatever on the grill out back. Drank beer. Laughed. Those were good times."

"Tell us about the scene here," Ray said.

"It'd been a busy night. More so than usual, for sure. A fight broke out on The Boardwalk, then we nabbed a trio of shoplifters. Three young girls. Sixteen, I think. From Mexico Beach. Up here for the day. Snatched a bunch of clothes, jewelry, that kind of thing. We, Frank and I, herded them over to the station. Then, a couple of cars tangled on the bridge, so I left to handle that. Frank came out later to help. The traffic was awful. Hard to get the tow trucks in there to drag the cars out of the way. About the time we got back to the station, the parents arrived so we packed the girls off. In big trouble. The parents weren't happy. Anyway, we finished all the paperwork and Frank headed home. Ten thirty or thereabouts. That's when he found Sara."

"What happened then?"

"He called and me and Charlie came over. Frank was collapsed on the living room floor. On his knees. Crying uncontrollably."

"Understandable."

"Sara was in bed. Tied to the frame. Obviously strangled."

"Did you immediately think it was Billy Wayne's work?"

"Absolutely. There'd already been two killings here that had been connected to him. This one had all his signatures. The ropes, the strangulation. So, yeah, we knew it was Billy Wayne." He removed one hand from his pocket and scratched an ear. "'Course that was later proven by the DNA, but we knew from minute one."

"Was Frank able to help you guys work the scene?"

"Not even close. He, of course, wanted to. But that's Frank. Charlie essentially ordered him to go outside. Sit on the stoop and let Charlie and me do the work. Didn't want him to see her that way. 'Course, he had, but he was still in shock. So we bagged everything up—the bedsheets, the ropes—and dusted for prints. An ambulance picked up Sara, took her over to the hospital morgue. I took Frank to my place. He stayed in the spare room that night. No way I would let him sleep in his house alone." He shook his head. "Next day the FBI came in and took over. Of course, the next night Billy Wayne struck again. Up in Defuniak Springs. So, the FBI crew headed that way pretty quickly."

"The knots?" Pancake asked. "Was the rope tied the same way in each of the cases here?"

Munson nodded. "Sure were. They were pretty standard. That's what the FBI guys said." He shrugged. "I don't know much about knots. Just what I learned in Cub Scouts." He smiled. "But I know the FBI lab looked at the ropes and the knots in every case. I heard that they determined everything was the same. Consistent." He looked at Pancake. "Good question."

Pancake nodded. "Just thought of it. But it'll make a good visual for the documentary."

"I suspect so," Munson said.

"Let me ask you," Ray said. "I understand no one ever saw Billy Wayne around here. Is that right?"

"That's correct. We talked to everyone in town. Literally, it seemed. Nothing. Like he was a ghost." He looked up toward the sky, then said, "Actually, a couple of folks said that they might've seen him. One sighting at Woody's, the other at a truck stop out on the highway. But neither ever worked out. The security camera at the truck stop did show a guy about Billy Wayne's size, but we found him." He smiled. "Fairly easily. He worked in the diner there. So, in actuality, no one ever saw Billy Wayne."

"Why do you think he came back?" Pancake asked. "All the other killings were sort of one and done. But here, Pine Key, he returned."

"He probably felt safe here. Found us to be an easy hunting ground."

"Any signs of forced entry?" Ray waved a hand to Clark's house.

"No. And in Sara's case, that would be unusual. I know she was security conscious."

"Did they have an alarm system?" Pancake asked.

Munson shook his head. "The irony is that Frank had scheduled an installation. But that was a couple of weeks away when Billy

Wayne arrived." He glanced at the house. "Too bad. It just might have saved Sara. So, no alarm system. Apparently, the back door was unlocked. We think he came in that way."

"But no evidence of that for sure?"

"The door wasn't damaged. No broken windows or anything like that. We found the door unlocked when we worked the scene. So, that looks like the most likely explanation."

Ray scanned the house one last time. Amazing how murder scenes can seem so normal after all the dust settles. He turned to Munson. "Thanks for showing us around and talking with us."

Munson gave a quick nod. "I just hope it doesn't come back to bite us. Frank, anyway."

"We're not here to pressure him. More to give him an opportunity to tell his story."

Munson sighed. "Let's head back to the station. See how he and your son got along."

CHAPTER NINETEEN

NICOLE AND I finished our chat with Frank Clark and escaped "the box." That's what it felt like. There seemed to be more air in Chief Morgan's office where we now sat, having coffee with him and Clark. Ray, Pancake, and Munson returned.

"How'd it go with the mayor?" Munson asked Morgan.

"The usual. Woman can be stubborn." He smiled. "But I got you guys a raise."

"Really?" Clark asked.

"Not much, but it's something."

"What about the new patrol car?" Munson asked.

"That's a no go. Said the city simply didn't have the money."

I think that's the main woe of many smaller towns. Not enough money to go around. Small tax base and mounting expenses. Not to mention the many mouths to feed: police, schools, parks, infrastructure maintenance, city hall, and all the beneath-the-radar costs of running a town. And here in Pine Key, the marina and The Boardwalk, which were surely city property. All that made a new car a luxury the town couldn't afford.

Nicole apparently felt otherwise.

"We might be able to help you there," she said. All eyes turned her way. "I can't promise anything but I'll talk with my uncle. His budgets always have padding." She smiled. "All Hollywood budgets do. Since we're here asking for your help and disrupting your work, a car seems a reasonable fee for that."

"You can do that?" Morgan asked.

She shrugged. "Maybe. Again, no promises, but let me see what I can do."

How does she do that? Keep coming up with amazingly simple ideas. Well, simple if you have a Hollywood budget in your pocket. Where the price of a car, a big deal to the city of Pine Key, was simply a line item for a production company or studio. Especially one the size and weight of Regency Global Productions. Oscars and Emmys will thicken your bottom line.

But, with that single promise, or possibility, she had just hooked the entire Pine Key police department. Probably the mayor and city council, too. It was written all over Chief Morgan's face. Not that he and Clark and Munson hadn't been helpful, and welcoming, but this would go a long way toward cementing that relationship.

I caught Ray's eye. He raised an eyebrow and gave a half smile.

"I can't even imagine you'd do that," Morgan said. "It's a very kind offer."

"If we can pull it off, it'll be our pleasure," Nicole said.

After a moment of almost stunned silence, Morgan nodded. "Anything we can do to help you right now?"

"Maybe show us around your department," Pancake said. "Sort of give us a feel for how you guys work."

Morgan glanced at Clark, who then said, "Glad to."

Munson nodded his agreement.

"I think we'll leave you guys to that," I said. "Nicole and I are going to head over and have a talk with Peter Swift."

"Sounds good," Ray said.

"Bring me something," Pancake said.

Of course.

Nicole laughed. "What would you like?"

"Something big. And sweet."

Now, Morgan laughed. "Peter has a bunch of stuff that'll fill that bill."

And we were off.

The aromas that greeted us when we entered Swift's Bakery were intense. Rich and buttery. Pancake might not be the only one getting something big and sweet. Behind the counter stood a woman who looked eerily like the photos I had seen of Loretta Swift, Billy Wayne's first victim here in Pine Key. Had to be Charlaine Anders, Loretta's sister.

She looked up and smiled. "Morning."

"Smells great in here," Nicole said.

"We just finished a fresh batch of croissants."

The door that connected to the kitchen swung open as Peter backed through, maneuvering a large metal tray filled with fat golden-brown croissants and other pastries.

"Hello," he said. He placed the tray on the counter and wiped his hands on the dark blue apron he wore. He nodded to the woman. "This is Charlaine. Loretta's sister."

Charlaine smiled over the counter. "It's a pleasure."

"I see the resemblance," I said.

"I'll take that as a compliment."

"As it was meant to be."

"We're so sorry for your loss," Nicole said.

She gave a brief nod. "Thanks." She picked up a hand towel and wiped the top of the pastry case. "Can I get you something?"

"Maybe later."

"I think they're here to talk with me," Peter said.

"Oh?" Charlaine said.

"Actually, both of you," I said. "If you're willing."

"I assume its about that film you're working on?"

"That's right."

Charlaine looked confused. "What film?"

Nicole explained what we were doing. The slant of the documentary. How we wanted to tell their story, the town's story, not Billy Wayne's.

The lie lived on.

Or was it a lie? The deeper we got into this the more I understood why Uncle Charles might see this as a serious project. We were looking for a killer, Uncle Charles for a moneymaker. I had to admit I was buying into it. Or was I trying to convince myself that a partial truth saved a lie from being so manipulative? Regardless, the further down this road we moved, the more this documentary seemed real. Tangible. And, in the end, a good thing for this community.

Peter nodded, wiped his hands on the towel again. "I'd heard about it but didn't really understand it all." He smiled. "I was skeptical, but, now that you've explained it, I like it. Everything else I've seen on him has made him into some sort of hero. Like he was just a misguided guy and not a killer."

"That's why we're doing this project," Nicole said. "It seems that every serial killer becomes a cult hero. Makes no sense but it's true. I think a lot of it's that the public doesn't really know what happened. Thinks it's like a movie or something. And they have no idea what the collateral damage is." She waved a hand toward the pair. "How it affects the survivors."

"It's the late morning lull," Charlaine said. "It'll be a little while before the lunch crowd shows up." She turned toward Peter, laid a hand on his arm. "I'll get Whitney to man the counter." She looked at us. "Whitney's our baker." She nodded toward the glass display case and the pastries inside. "She's responsible for most of this." She nodded toward Peter. "Of course, Peter taught her everything she knows."

"From the smell," Nicole said, "you taught her well."

"Why don't you take them in back?" Charlaine said to Peter. "I'll be along in a minute."

Peter took a deep breath and let it out slowly. "Okay."

Even though he had bought into the idea, I could sense his reluctance to revisit the past. Dig into feelings long smoothed over. Somewhat. Can't say I blamed him.

CHAPTER TWENTY

"THIS HERE'S WHERE Frank and I hang out," Munson said. "When we ain't out doing real police work."

Ray looked around the room. Small, two desks, facing each other from opposite sides of the room. One held neat stacks of papers, the other undisciplined piles.

Munson nodded toward the disordered one. "That's Frank's." He gave a short laugh. "Not the neatest creature on the planet."

"Works for me," Clark added.

"Felix and Oscar," Pancake said.

Munson nodded. "We are the odd couple for sure. Been that way forever. You should've seen his locker at school. And out at the field house when we played ball together. I swear to God small creatures lived in there."

"Neat freaks make me crazy," Clark said. He glanced at Munson. "But Terry knows not to mess with my stuff."

"Couldn't find anything in there anyway," Munson said. "Not to mention catching some deadly disease."

Clark smiled. "Terry hung one of those hazmat signs above my desk one day. I think he was trying to tell me something."

Munson raised a shoulder. "Simply warning others to steer clear."

Ray studied the two men. No doubt they were close. As advertised. Able to give and take the mutual needling. Ray found himself liking each of them. Sure, Munson might be a little too much of a pretty boy for his liking, but he seemed okay. Clark, on the other hand, was a guy's guy. No doubt. Closer to Ray's temperament.

Of course, Clark might be a killer so that mitigated things. Though he seemed relaxed, not trying to hide anything, his dark eyes were hard to read. Was it simply his cop's deadpan, or something deeper, more malignant?

Ray glanced at Pancake. "Pancake can be a little disordered, too."

Pancake shrugged. "There's a method to the madness."

"Exactly," Clark said. He nodded toward the door. "Come on. Let's do the tour."

Ray and Pancake followed Clark and Munson down a hallway. On the left were two more offices, and to the right a breakroom/kitchen affair. Coffeepot, stacks of paper cups, a microwave, open cabinets filled with bags of coffee, crackers, cookies, and rolls of paper towels. Everything the staff needed to make it through the day. Or night.

Just beyond that, a storage area. Munson pushed open the door and they stepped inside. Along one wall a metal rack held office supplies—bundles of typing paper, boxes of staples and tape, a bag of rubber bands, smaller boxes of ballpoint pens. An old computer collected dust. At the far end, a gray metal locker, like you'd find in any schoolhouse, nestled against the wall. A piece of white tape with EVIDENCE printed in black block letters slashed across the front. An unfastened padlock hung from the loop. Not exactly secure.

"This where you store evidence, I take it," Ray said.

Munson nodded. "Not that we ever really have any. It's empty most of the time."

"Unless someone like Billy Wayne shows up," Pancake said.

"True," Clark said.

Back into the hallway. Past an interrogation room and to a door at the end. Clark pushed through it. Ray and Pancake followed. The lockup. Three cells, the doors to each standing open. Two were unoccupied; the other revealed a man lying on his side, twisted into a sheet.

"Angus," Clark said. "Didn't the chief tell you it was time to mosey on home?"

The man disentangled his legs and swung to a seated position. His hair looked like an explosion, his eyes red, his face creased with bedsheet imprints. "What time is it?"

"Time to go."

He fastened on a pair of sandals and stood. Not easily. Swaying. He gained his balance and forked his fingers through his hair. "Okay, okay, I can tell when I'm not welcome." He gave a toothy smile and nodded to Ray as he staggered past. "See you guys this evening, I suspect." And he was gone.

"Angus Whitehead," Clark said. "He spends more time here than I do."

"And he gets breakfast in bed," Pancake said.

Clark nodded. "Peter does feed him well."

"I meant to ask earlier," Ray said. "Who does your autopsies?"

"Adrian McGill. He's the pathologist over at the hospital."

"So you don't farm them out?" Pancake asked.

"Most of the small towns around here do, but we're lucky. McGill worked for more than a decade down in Dade County. At the coroner's office. So, he knows his stuff."

"Why'd he come here?" Ray asked.

"His wife," Clark said. "She hated the big city. Traffic, crime, noise. Wanted to come here. A slower pace of life. And truth be told, McGill was ready. Wanted to return to hospital work. So he runs the hospital lab. And does autopsies for us."

"Which is like never," Munson added.

"I take it he'd be the one that handled all the evidence from Billy Wayne's killings?"

"He did," Munson said. "Did the autopsies. Collected the DNA and sent samples up to the folks in Jacksonville."

"They did the work on that," Clark said. "We aren't that sophisticated."

"Makes sense," Ray said. "Running a DNA lab isn't an inexpensive proposition."

Munson nodded. "Way beyond our budget."

"So, he retained all the evidence over at the hospital?"

Clark shook his head. "Not long term. Just until he finished his report and sent things up north. Everything then came back over here for storage. We kept it all until Billy Wayne was sentenced, then dumped it."

"Wouldn't be much need for it after that," Pancake said. He gave Ray a glance.

They finished the tour. Ray thanked them both for their time.

"No problem," Clark said. "You need anything else, just give us a shout."

"Will do."

Clark headed to his office while Munson walked Ray and Pancake out. Once on the sidewalk out front, Ray looked up and down the street.

"This is a nice town," Ray said. "I like it. Pleasant. Most folks we've met seem happy."

"It's a great place." Munson scratched an ear. "'Course, I'm biased. I grew up here." He smiled. "Let me ask you something."

"Fire away."

"I meant to ask earlier, but it slipped my mind. Were you guys cops before doing the P.I. thing?"

Ray shook his head. "Pancake was a bum." He looked at Pancake and smiled. "Mostly hung around my son's bar."

"Nice place to hang," Pancake said. "Good food, better drinks, and you should see the chicks that motor in and out." He opened his palms. "I've hung out at worse bars."

Munson laughed. "Sounds like my kind of place." He looked at Ray. "And you?"

"I was military for quite a few years."

"What branch?"

"Marines."

"Not to mention special forces, intelligence, that sort of thing," Pancake said.

"Oh?"

"Let's just say I did a lot of crap I can't talk about."

"What led you to the P.I. world?"

"Needed to make a living," Ray said with a smile.

"I hear you." Munson shoved his hands in his pockets and rocked slightly on his heels. He looked up the street, gaze unfocused. "I've been considering doing the same thing."

"Really?"

"Well, like you heard, this job don't pay all that much."

"A common problem," Pancake said. "Especially in small towns."

Munson looked back at him. "But I can never pull the trigger on that deal. First off, I'm not sure I'd have the patience for it. But mostly I'd be abandoning Chief Morgan." A quick nod. "And he's a great boss. Better guy."

"Seemed that way," Ray said.

"And Frank. I wouldn't leave unless he went with me, and that ain't going to happen."

"He likes the low pay?" Ray asked, smiling.

"Loves the job, for sure." He sighed. "Maybe he would've a few years ago, but since Sara's death, he hasn't been all that ambitious."

"What do you mean?"

Munson glanced back toward the station's entry door. "Not sure I can put it in words." He looked down toward his feet as if considering what to say. "It's just that her death took the wind out of his sails. Hasn't recovered yet." Another glance up the street. "Not sure he ever will." A slight headshake. "I guess Frank and I'll be here until they carry us out on our shields." He smiled. "Being a P.I. is a good dream, though."

"Not much of a dream," Pancake said. "Mostly it's boring and tedious."

Ray laughed. "Punctuated by moments of terror."

CHAPTER TWENTY-ONE

"THANKS FOR TALKING with us," Nicole said.

Peter offered a thin smile. "If I said I had some reservations about reliving everything, I wouldn't be lying."

We were in his office. Nicole and I sat facing him across his desk. He sank into a worn fake-leather swivel chair, Charlaine standing beside him.

"We understand," Nicole said. "If at any time you want to call a halt to this or want us to leave, just say so."

Peter shifted in his chair. "So, how does this all work?"

"We want to ask a few questions. Sort of preliminary things, and to make sure you're comfortable with our questions. Then, if that works out, we'll put together a script of sorts and bring in a film crew and do a real interview. Is that okay?"

Peter gave a half nod. "What do you want to know?"

"Tell us about you and Loretta. How you met, when you were married? Those kinds of things." She glanced at Charlaine. "We want to get to know her. And each of you, too."

Peter leaned his elbows on the desktop, his chin resting on his clasped hands. "We met when we were ten. Nothing special. At that age she was just a girl." He smiled. "It was a couple of more years before I found girls interesting." Now, he opened his hands, palms up. "It was at her birthday party. She had pigtails and a missing front tooth."

"Sounds attractive," I said with a smile.

He smiled, looked away as if thinking of something. "Not then. But later, when we were thirteen, she somehow became beautiful."

"That's how it usually happens," I said.

"She was the most beautiful girl I'd ever seen." He rubbed the side of his nose. "And I thought that every day of her life."

"She was," Charlaine said. "And the best sister anyone could have."

Nicole nodded. "From the pictures I've seen of her, you two look a lot alike."

Charlaine smiled. "Many people thought we were twins. But she was nearly a year older."

I looked back at Peter. "When did you and Loretta get married?"

"When we turned eighteen." He hooked a thumb over his shoulder. "Right down there by the marina. It's where everyone around here gets married, it seems. I was working for my dad. He opened the bakery and ran it until he got sick. I took over then. Loretta began working here even before we got married." He glanced toward the window. His eyes moistened. "Mom and Dad loved her." He looked back at us. "Everyone did."

Charlaine laid a hand on his shoulder, gave a quick squeeze.

"Tell us about that night," Nicole said. "When you discovered Loretta."

Another deep breath, and a slow exhale through puffed-out cheeks. "Worst day of my life. Nothing else was even close. Not even burying my parents." He pressed a knuckle into the corner of one eye. "I was at an Elk's meeting. In Panama City. Got home late." He stared down at the desktop. "I almost didn't go. It'd been a busy day and I was tired, but I'm the treasurer and was set to deliver our annual financial report. But for that, I might not have gone." He sniffed. "Things might've worked out differently."

"When you got home, did anything seem out of place?" I asked. "When you first got there?"

"Actually, yes. There were no lights on. Usually we left a lamp on in the living room. But everything was dark. My first thought was that maybe the bulb had burned out. Or maybe she forgot to turn it on." He picked up a paper clip, examined it, and laid it aside. "I figured she was already asleep so I went to the kitchen and had a bowl of ice cream." He smiled. "She always gave me grief about that." He sighed. "Then I went to our room. And found her."

"What did you see?" I asked.

"The room was dark, of course. But I immediately knew something was wrong. She wasn't under the covers. The comforter was on the floor and she was laying on the sheets. Then, I saw the ropes." He shook his head. "It was so odd, I couldn't make sense of it. It seemed like I stood there forever, trying to sort it out." Another sigh. "When I touched her shoulder, trying to wake her, it felt cold. That's when I knew."

"What did you do then?" I asked.

"I shook her. Called her name. Considered trying CPR, but I knew she was gone. I flicked on the light. That's when I saw the bruises around her neck. I called the police."

"Was anything disturbed?" Nicole asked. "Out of place or anything like that?"

He shook his head. "Not really. Frank Clark was there in a few minutes. Then Munson and Chief Morgan. They found the back door was unlocked. Which also made no sense. Loretta always kept things locked when I wasn't there." He looked past us, focusing on nothing. "I figured she forgot. But, later, I learned Billy Wayne was pretty good at finding his way inside houses."

"Peter called me," Charlaine said. "He was distraught. No, more than that. I thought he was . . ." She hesitated. "I don't know what I thought. He couldn't talk. Babbling and gasping, and—well, I came right over." She again squeezed his shoulder. "He was outside. Sitting on the front stoop. Staring at the sky." Her face screwed down as if holding back tears. "It was awful."

"I can only imagine," Nicole said.

"He managed to get the story out." She looked down at him. "I wanted to go inside. See for myself. Not that I didn't believe him, but I felt she needed me." She sniffed. "Sounds silly, I know."

"No, it doesn't," Nicole said. "It makes perfect sense."

Charlaine nodded, face scrunched even more tightly. "But, Peter wouldn't let me."

"I didn't want her seeing her sister like that. And have to live with that image." Peter reached up and patted the hand on his shoulder. "Truth is, Charlaine was my rock. Without her being there, I would've really lost it." He shook his head. "More so than I did."

"You were my rock," Charlaine said.

"Sounds like you two were close," I said.

"All three of us were," Charlaine said. "When I lost my husband—cancer—Peter and Sara were right by my side."

Family tragedies. Every family has them. Some more than others. I flashed on when I lost my mom. Worst day ever. And looking at Peter and Charlaine, I saw the same anguish on their faces. Hell, I felt it filling the room. My chest hurt.

"You and your sister were tight?" Nicole asked.

"We were," Charlaine said. "I think being less than a year apart had a lot to do with it. The way our birthdays worked out, we started school together. Same grade all the way through. She was always the oldest in our class, and I was the youngest." She sighed. "She took care of me."

Peter nodded. "She took care of both of us. It was her nature."

"When did you learn that Loretta's murder was connected to the others?" I asked.

"Maybe two or three weeks," Peter said. "I forget exactly. Chief Morgan called me and said the crime lab up in Jacksonville had made the connection. Stunned doesn't quite cover it. I mean, a serial killer? Here in Pine Key? In my own home?" He looked at me. "You know, you see this stuff on TV. Read about it in the paper. But you never think something like this would come into your own life."

Isn't that the truth? Bad things always happen to someone else. Usually far away. More like a movie or a novel. Not real. When such tragedies drop in your lap, it's always a shock. My impression was that Peter was still struggling with that. He looked like an injured soul. And they say time heals all. What a lie.

"But it did," Peter continued. "And nothing's been right since that night." He glanced up at Charlaine. "But we're working on it." He gave a weak smile.

"We are," she said.

"When did you step in and help with the bakery?" I asked her.

"Immediately. Wasn't even a question."

Peter nodded. "That's true. Sold her business right then and there."

"My husband and I owned a motel just up the street here. The Piney Woods. I ran it after his death, but my heart wasn't in it anymore. So, I sold it and I've been here ever since."

"Couldn't have kept this place afloat without her," Peter said. "Not even sure I could've kept myself afloat. Especially early on. I was a mess. We both were, but somehow we managed."

"It always comes back to family, doesn't it?" I said.

"Sure does." Another glance toward Charlaine. "Charlaine is so much like Loretta. Same graciousness. Same pleasant way of handling the customers."

Tears welled in Charlaine's eyes, but she remained silent.

Peter folded his hands before him on the desk. "It's funny, I have to remind myself sometimes that she's not Loretta." He sighed. "I even make the mistake of calling her Loretta sometimes. Even after all these years."

Charlaine sniffed back tears. "It's true. He does." She wiped the back of her hand across her nose. "And the truth is, I like that. In an odd way, it keeps her alive."

CHAPTER TWENTY-TWO

"How'd it go today?" Chief Charlie Morgan asked Clark and Munson over his desk.

Clark shrugged. Munson shrugged.

"Nothing unusual?" Morgan asked.

"I showed them the crime scenes." Munson glanced at Clark. "Stopped by your place briefly. Hope that's okay."

Morgan nodded. "Sure."

"I mean, we didn't go inside or anything, but I went through each of the scenes with them. Told them what we found. How we handled them. That sort of thing."

Morgan nodded.

"They seem curious about any of them?" Clark asked. "Ask any questions that seemed out of place?"

"No," Munson said. "Not really. Why?"

"I don't know. It just always gives me pause when someone comes along later and looks into what we do."

"We did it by the book," Munson said. "Like always."

"I know," Clark said. "But no investigation's perfect. I'd hate for them to second-guess us."

"You mean like Tommy Lee Kovac?" Morgan said.

Clark nodded. "Except Tommy Lee's a moron. These guys don't impress me as that."

"Didn't seem that way to me, either," Munson said. "But we don't really know them. They could simply be the digging-dirt-on-a-wayward-spouse type."

"They aren't," Clark said. "They're the real thing."

"And you know this how?" Munson asked.

"I looked into them," Clark said. "On the internet. Called a guy I know in Pensacola. With the PD up there. He says Ray Longly is smart and tough. Said he handled a lot of complex cases. Bank and insurance fraud, embezzling, even took on Victor Borkov's empire." He shrugged. "And won."

"I heard about that," Munson said. "Big shoot-out. Right?"

Clark nodded. "Yep. Anyway, all I'm saying is that I'm not sure how I feel about a couple of hotshot P.I.s sniffing around."

Morgan stared at him. "My impression, from my talk with Jake and Nicole, was that all they wanted was to get a feel for how all this affected the community. I didn't sense anything else."

"And that's probably the case," Clark said. "I just never liked anyone looking over my shoulder."

"Anyway," Munson continued. "They seemed—I guess the word is concerned. More interested in the victims and the families than Billy Wayne."

Morgan stacked several loose pages on his desk as he studied Clark. "You okay?"

Clark gave a one-shouldered shrug. "Sure. Why?"

"Thought maybe reliving all this might be difficult. Dredging up old memories. Opening old wounds."

"There's some truth to that," Clark said. "But, I'm doing okay." He looked past Morgan, toward the window that faced Main Street, not focused on anything as far as Morgan could tell. "It's not like I don't think about it every day anyway."

"I want to show you something that might help," Morgan said. He pointed toward his computer. Clark and Munson moved behind him so they could see the screen. "You're not the only one that does research." He worked the mouse until he found what he was looking for in his browser history. The homepage for Regency Global Productions appeared. Banners down the left side showed graphics for some of RGP's major productions.

"This is Nicole Jamison's uncle's company. Charles Balfour."

Munson leaned toward the screen. "Wow. He's done all those movies? I've seen most of them."

"So has everyone else. Charles Balfour is a heavy weight out there in LA. Won a bunch of Oscars and Emmys."

"Impressive."

"But that's not what I wanted to show you," Morgan said.

Morgan clicked a badge titled "Future Productions." The page listed thirty or more projects. Divided into groups: Post-Production, In Production, and Development Stage. Morgan pointed to the final list.

"These are the things they're exploring." There were thirteen items listed. "Check out number eleven."

"*Aftermath*," Clark said. "That's the project they're working on here."

"It is." Morgan leaned back in his chair. "Looks legit to me. Does that waylay any of your anxieties?"

"Some," Clark said. He hooked a thumb in his belt. "Maybe this'll be good for the town. Maybe we can finally put the Billy Wayne Baker chapter behind us."

"Once and for all," Munson added. "We are way overdue for burying the past."

"Those're my thoughts, too," Morgan said.

CHAPTER TWENTY-THREE

NICOLE AND I left Swift's Bakery and headed up The Boardwalk toward Woody's where we planned to meet Ray and Pancake. Nicole hooked her arm in mine, my other hand occupied with a white bag of bear claws for Pancake. I knew better than to return empty-handed. Never hear the end of it. Peter wouldn't let me pay for them, even when I insisted. He'd have none of it. So I shoved a ten in the tip jar.

"What do you think?" Nicole asked.

"About Peter and Charlaine? I think they like each other."

"Maybe more than like."

That had been my impression and I told Nicole that.

"Makes sense though," she said. "She and her sister are so much alike—at least it seems that way—so I'd think the attraction would be natural."

"They do act like a married couple."

"Actually, I'm surprised they aren't. I mean, they have a long history together, both lost Loretta, Charlaine her spouse a few years ago, work together every day."

"Maybe neither is ready," I said. "Or maybe this community would find that odd."

"Maybe."

"You don't think so, though," I said. Not a question.

"Not really. They're obviously a big part of the community."

"Not to mention turning out all those wonderful goodies."

"I bet half the population drops in there at least once a day."

"My point exactly," I said.

"Which means the town would probably celebrate with them if they ever do."

"I suspect you're right."

"Why would you ever doubt that? Of course I am."

"Even the blind dog finds the bone every now and then."

She unhooked her arm and elbowed my ribs.

"What was that for?" I rubbed the side of my chest.

"Just making a comment. With an exclamation point."

"Message received."

"But, was it understood?" She laughed.

I started to say something stupendously clever, maybe stupidly clever, but, to use another cliché, probably better to let sleeping dogs lie.

We found Ray and Pancake at a deck table beneath an umbrella. Ray had a Dew, Pancake motoring through a plate of fried calamari. I tossed the bag to Pancake.

"Compliments of Peter Swift."

"He's a good man." Pancake tugged out one of the bear claws. He took a bite and followed it with a forked mass of squid tentacles. Not exactly a combination I'd choose, but Pancake treated food like a war zone. Scorched earth.

"Mighty fine," he said.

Pancake's face looked a lot better. Even compared to this morning. He had always healed quickly. Even when we were kids. I think it was from the dirt he rubbed on every bump and scrape. Really. It works.

We sat. "How'd the morning go?" Ray asked.

"Good," I said.

"Tell me about it."

I went through our conversation with Clark in "the box." The details of the night Sara Clark had been murdered. Clark finding his wife.

"That jibes with what Munson said," Pancake said.

Ray nodded. "What was your take on Clark? Was he telling the truth? Was he really torn up about his wife's death?"

"I don't know." I shrugged. "I'm not exactly a psychologist."

"But you know people," Ray said. "You own a bar. You deal with people every day. People of all types. I'd say that qualifies you to judge people. That's why I wanted you to take the first run at him."

Did Ray say that? Was he actually seeking my opinion? Was he mellowing? That didn't seem possible. Maybe I misunderstood him. I glanced at Nicole. She gave me a half smile. She'd heard it, too. I felt like the world had reversed its spin.

"I'm not sure," I said. "Either he's really damaged from his wife's death, or he's an excellent actor."

"How so?" Ray asked.

"He seemed very matter of fact. Almost as if he was reporting something that happened to someone else. Like a cop would. And maybe that's it. He was in cop mode with us. But, I will say that he did, at times, look like he was in pain. And had been for a while."

Ray looked at Nicole. "That your take?"

"It is. I think his anguish was real." She looked at me. "It seemed to me that he really misses her." She shrugged. "But, like Jake, I'm no psychologist either."

"But you know acting. Was he?"

"Maybe. Hard to tell. Sometimes he seemed distant, almost like he was reading a script. But at other times he appeared sad."

Ray nodded. "That meshes with my impression of him. Seemed very matter of fact. Seemed to accept Pancake and I as consultants and not investigators."

"It did seem to me that he and his wife had a good marriage," Nicole said. "At least, he seems to miss her."

"But does he miss her because Billy Wayne killed her, or because he did something stupid and only later did the finality of it hit him?" Ray said. "He wouldn't be the first killer to later regret his actions. All the negative shit builds up, you think you have a solution you can live with, then afterwards realize it was all a big mistake. That the negatives weren't all that negative. That the positives were much more important. But, by then, it's too late. What was done can't be rewound." He shrugged. "Happens all the time."

"I suppose," I said.

"Sound like neither of you could get a good read with him," Pancake said. He tugged a second bear claw from the bag and took a bite. "Means he's either a good cop, or a good killer."

That was the question. Did Frank Clark kill his wife, or was he just another of Billy Wayne Baker's collateral victims?

"What about you guys?" Nicole asked. "Anything new?"

"It was interesting," Ray said.

"In what way?" I asked.

"How you guys doing today?"

I looked up to see owner Betty Lou Thompson standing there.

"I see you had a chat with Peter Swift." She nodded toward the bear claw Pancake held. "Just what a growing boy needs." She laughed.

"That's me," Pancake said.

"Did the names I gave you help?"

"Sure did," I said. "We talked with everyone except Tommy Lee Kovac. I called but got his voice mail."

Betty Lou looked out toward the Gulf. "He had a charter this morning." She glanced at her watch. "Should be back before long." She looked at us. "What can I get you for lunch?"

We ordered. Three of us had fish tacos. Pancake went for pork. A rack of baby backs and a side of fries.

"Have that up in ten," she said and walked away.

"Interesting in what way?" I asked Ray, returning to our conversation.

"Chief Morgan's a good man. Probably a good cop. Clark and Munson seem like a tight pair. My impression is they run a pretty good shop."

There was more, I was sure.

Ray continued. "Except they aren't too keen on security."

"Ain't that the truth," Pancake said.

"Their evidence lockup is little more than a school locker."

"And it ain't locked," Pancake added.

"Really?" I asked. "That means that someone besides Frank Clark could have gotten to the evidence?"

"Sure does."

"Even that dude," Pancake said. "What was his name?"

"Angus Whitehead," Ray said. He looked at me. "The town drunk, it seems."

"Yeah. We met him briefly. Seemed harmless."

"Probably is. From what we saw, he spends many a night there. In an open cell so he can leave whenever he sobers up."

"And it's right near the closet where the evidence locker is," Pancake said.

"So, Angus could be the killer?" Nicole asked.

Ray smiled. "He didn't seem the type. Or capable, I imagine."

Nicole smiled. "Didn't seem like a killer to me either."

Ray took a sip of Dew. "The point is that he could get in the evidence locker completely unnoticed. Means a bunch of other folks could, too."

I sighed. "That doesn't make this any easier."

"My money's still on Clark," Ray added. "He would be the one that knew how to plant the evidence. Then would be in a position to find it as he worked the scene."

"And the one that most likely had a motive to kill his wife," I said.

"Where would that leave us with Noleen Kovac?" Nicole asked.

Ray gave a shrug. "That's the tough one. I still don't see a connection between her and Clark. Either Frank or Sara."

"Maybe Billy Wayne's lying about two not being his," Nicole said. "Maybe it's only one."

Ray shook his head. "I don't see that. It's a package deal. Either he's lying about both or he's telling the truth. It doesn't make sense otherwise."

"Probably so," Nicole said.

Ray looked at Nicole and me. "How'd your visit with Peter go?"

"We had a good talk with both Peter and Charlaine," Nicole said. "Really nice pair."

I started the say something about the conversation Nicole and I had had on our walk over, but what was there to say? We didn't really know them. Didn't know squat about their relationship. Besides, our speculations weren't relevant. Instead, I said, "They are both still dealing with Loretta's death."

"Losing a wife, or a sister, is a real kick in the head," Pancake added.

By the time we finished lunch and the table was cleared, and Pancake was halfway through a large slice of peach pie and massive scoop of vanilla ice cream, Betty Lou reappeared.

"Looks like Tommy Lee's back," she said.

She pointed toward the marina. I followed her finger. I saw a lanky man shaking hands with a couple of guys, who then grabbed the handles of an orange and white cooler and carried it up the dock. The man, who I took to be Tommy Lee, jumped into his boat and began sorting through gear.

"Maybe we'll stroll down there and have a chat," Pancake said.

She nodded. "Be careful with him. Boy's got a temper on him." She gave a quick nod and walked away.

CHAPTER TWENTY-FOUR

PANCAKE AND I walked to the end of the dock where Tommy Lee's white fishing rig was moored, its two blue plastic bumpers tapping against the wood, which creaked and popped beneath Pancake's feet. Weather-worn, the dock could use some refurbishment, at least a few coats of marine sealer. Something else the town likely didn't have the budget for. Blue script on the boat's side read: FISHY BUSINESS.

Ray had earlier decided that Pancake and I should handle this chat. Me to ask the question; Pancake to keep Tommy Lee's temper in check. In case it went that way. He felt that if we all went, Tommy Lee might feel ganged up on. Might get his hackles up from the get-go. And if he did go ballistic, he didn't want Nicole there. She countered that she was acing her Krav Maga classes and could take care of herself. Ray laughed, saying he had no doubt, but he didn't relent.

The rods had been cleaned and stored in a rack along one side, and three shiny reels sat on the rear transom. Tommy Lee was wiping down the rear seats as we walked up.

"Tommy Lee?" I asked.

He straightened, turned toward us. "Who wants to know?"

He was lean, hard, a guy who worked for a living. His deeply tanned muscular arms hung from a sweat-stained gray tee shirt. A rose tattoo on one forearm.

"I'm Jake. This is Pancake."

Tommy Lee cocked his head to one side as he examined Pancake. "What kind of name if that?"

"Mine," Pancake said.

"Looks like you scraped you face there," Tommy Lee said.

"Bicycle, asphalt."

Tommy Lee nodded and smiled. "You the ones doing that film thing I heard about?"

"We are."

"I figured you'd get around to coming by sooner or later."

"We'd like to talk to you about your sister."

He looked at me, hesitated, and then said, "I guess that'd be all right." He tossed the rag he'd been using into a bucket of dingy water. "Get you guys a beer?"

"That'd be good," Pancake said.

"Come on board."

He disappeared below deck and returned with three long-necked PBRs. We cracked them open and sat on the rear bench seat, Tommy Lee hiking a hip up on the gunwale.

"Nice boat," I said. It was. Shiny, clean, new. Looked to be fully tricked out for fishing.

"Thanks." He waved his bottle. "I like it."

"Looks new."

"I've had it a couple of years. But I keep it in good order. My charters want everything up to snuff."

"How long you been in the business?" Pancake asked.

"Six, seven years. I worked for a guy for a couple of years then got my own boat" He looked toward the bow. "It wasn't as big or as functional as this one. Traded it in for this one." He took a slug of beer. "Let me up my charter fees quite a bit."

"Business good?" I asked.

"Sure is. Fishing is popular around here." He smiled. "Always has been."

I nodded.

"So, you want to talk about my sister?"

"We do," I said. "Tell us about her."

"What's to tell? Other than she got killed by that Baker guy."

"Her and several others," I said.

"I don't rightly give a rat shit about the others. But my sister was something else again."

"I take it you two were close?" I asked.

He took a long slug of beer. "Sure were. She was two years older. Taught me a lot growing up. Even helped me with school." He shrugged. "I wasn't the best student. She was. Straight A's. Really good with numbers, which is why she worked over at the bank."

"What happened that day? From your perspective."

He looked out toward the water. "The day before, I'd dropped by the bank to make a deposit. I didn't have no morning charter the next day so we arranged to meet for breakfast. We didn't do that often enough. With work and all." His gaze fell. "But she didn't show." He shook his head. "And that ain't like her. Her word you could take as solid." Another slug of beer. "I called. No answer either at home or on her cell."

"That unusual?" I asked.

"Sure was. I knew, right then and there, that something was out of sorts. 'Course I never expected what I found when I went over there." He looked back toward the water, his gaze unfocused.

"Which was?"

"She was in her room. All stretched out. Roped up. Dead."

"Any signs of a struggle? Or of a break-in, stuff like that?"

He shook his head. "Nope. The door was unlocked. The back one. I went through the front—with my key—so I didn't know that until I looked around." He picked something from one leg of his jeans and tossed it in the water. "But there weren't no busted windows or jimmied doors or anything like that. Fact is, except for her, everything looked normal."

"Was she good about locking up?" Pancake asked.

"Yeah. Not always. But definitely after Loretta Swift got herself killed."

"You called the cops then?"

"Sure did. For what that's worth."

"Want to explain?" I asked.

"Look, I ain't got no beef with them. Not really. I mean, I've rubbed up against them from time to time." He gave a half smile. "Not without reason. But you'd think they'd have done more. I mean, we'd had one murder here. A couple of months earlier. And in pretty short order, we knew it was Billy Wayne Baker. I'd think they'd have been on some kind of alert. More patrols. Whatever."

"Maybe they simply didn't have the manpower," I said. "From what I've seen, it's a small department."

"True that. But, we don't have killings around here neither. Seems they shoulda done more."

"You know Billy Wayne only had one victim in each of the other towns?" I said.

"And we had three. Lucky us."

"What I'm saying is that they probably figured Billy Wayne had done his deed and moved on. Like the earlier ones."

"You sound like Chief Morgan."

"Tommy Lee," I said, "I'm not making excuses for them, just stating the facts."

"Yeah, well, facts ain't gonna help Noleen none, are they?"

"No." I shook my head.

"So what is it you guys are actually doing? Trying to make a hero of Billy Wayne? I've already seen a lifetime of that shit."

"No, actually the opposite," I said.

He cocked his head again. His eyes darkened. "What the hell does that mean?"

"The documentary we're putting together isn't about Billy Wayne. It's about Billy Wayne's victims. And their families and friends. How he impacted such a quiet and pleasant town."

Tommy Lee seemed to search for a response, but apparently couldn't find one, so I went on.

"We want to tell Noleen's story. Your story. The story of this community. We think the victims are more important than the killer."

"That a fact?"

"Sure is."

He nodded. "Okay. You've heard my story. Now what?"

"This is preliminary right now. We're gathering the facts. The plan would be to come back and do a video interview with you. If that's okay."

He examined his beer bottle, ran a thumb around the lip. "I think that'd be good." He looked at me. "I want everyone out there to know what a good person my sister was. Know she didn't deserve this."

"That's the story we want to tell."

He nodded.

"I know you had some harsh words for the cops after all this," I said. "Organized a protest of some type?"

He took another slug of beer. "Like I said, they should've done more. And done it sooner."

"We also heard that you and Frank Clark and Terry Munson were friends."

"So?"

"I'm just wondering how they took all this. You being angry with the department?"

He stared at me for a few seconds before responding. "We were good friends. Back in school. And after. Me, and Terry, and Frank. Frank was always the serious one. Me and Terry just had fun. Chased women." He gave a half smile. "Even dated the same ones from time to time. But then he and Frank got busy being cops and me with my fishing charters and we all seemed to have less time to hang out."

"Life does get in the way."

Tommy Lee nodded. "I guess you'd say we're still friends. I mean, we still end up drinking together from time to time. Just less often than we did."

"So neither of them got too out of joint with your comments about their work? Or the department's work?"

"I think they understood. Leastwise they said they did." He scratched his arm. "Eventually. They was pretty pissed early on. Especially Frank. As I said, he was more serious about stuff than me or Terry."

"Friends do forgive and forget," Pancake said.

"That's the truth." He worked the bottle's label with a thumbnail. "It was Sara Clark's murder that fixed all that. For me, anyway. I figured if they couldn't protect one of their own then maybe I was being a shade too harsh." He shrugged. "'Course, that didn't bring Noleen back."

"We know she wasn't married," I asked. "Did she date anyone regularly?"

"No. She went out now and again. Nothing regular though. She was more married to her job." His head bobbed. "I used to tell her to get out more. Do stuff. But she preferred to work, read books, and watch movies on cable."

"What do you think?" I asked Pancake as we walked back up the dock.

"I think he's a hardworking man who lost his sister and got pissed at the cops. Probably the world in general, too."

"I think he still is."

"Yep. Just less so."

CHAPTER TWENTY-FIVE

ALL HOPE ABANDON ye who enter here.

According to Dante's *Divine Comedy*, that was inscribed over the gates to hell.

See, I did pay attention in school. Sometimes. At least I remembered that.

Probably because I dated an English major for a while. She quoted things like that all the time. Liked to show off. Then again, she had a lot to be proud of. Another story, another time.

Abandoning hope was exactly the way I felt when I reentered the gates of the Union Correctional Institute. If hell existed, this would be a good location for its portal. Nothing good resided inside these walls. The same smells, inmate shouts, and no-nonsense attitude of the guards that had greeted me on my previous visit did so again. When was I here last? Only a few days, but it seemed much longer.

This visit was for a second sit-down with Billy Wayne Baker. Last night Ray, Pancake, Nicole, and I sat down in Ray's room and went over everything we knew. The consensus was that we were on the right track. Nowhere but Pine Key would anyone have a reasonable chance to stage a murder, much less two, as Billy Wayne's work. And Frank Clark was the center of our focus. He had access to Billy Wayne's DNA, each of the crime scenes, and all the evidence collected. It would've been a snap for him to transfer DNA to otherwise clean bedsheets.

What we didn't know was why he would kill his wife. Spousal murder was common so maybe something was going on behind closed doors that no one else knew about. Not like that was rare either. Family and marital secrets. Okay, so far so good. But then, why kill Noleen Kovac? Pancake offered that it might have simply been to muddy the water. Make it less likely anyone would focus on Sara Clark's murder as an anomaly but rather view it as another murder along Billy Wayne's trail. And with his DNA at the scene, Billy Wayne's protestations of innocence would fall on deaf ears. Unless, Billy Wayne had an ironclad alibi for the one or both killings. That would simply have been a risk Clark had to take. Still, if that's how it played out, it was a clever move on Clark's part. And ballsy.

Which brought up another thing that had been bothering me. The timeline. I discussed it with Ray and Pancake earlier while we waited for the go-ahead from the warden on my visit.

"If we assume Billy Wayne only did five of the murders and the final two here in Pine Key are Clark's work, then Clark got lucky."

"How so?" Ray asked.

"Look at the timeline. There were months, in one case a year, between killings."

"The so-called cooling-off period," Pancake said.

"Exactly. Except for number six. Misty Abbott. She was killed only twenty-four hours after Sara Clark. That breaks the pattern."

"Makes it more likely he didn't do Sara Clark."

"But, my point is that Clark's agenda and Billy Wayne's were divorced from each other. Obviously, neither knew the other's plans. Had Billy Wayne struck one day earlier, or Clark one day later, there would have been two killings the same night, at essentially the same time, in different locations. Clark's plans would have gone up in smoke."

"Timing is everything," Pancake said. "Luck helps, too."

"Billy Wayne had luck," Ray said. "Right from his first killing. Apparently, Clark did, too."

"True."

"But they didn't happen on the same night," Ray said. "So, it's a moot point."

"Except for the cooling-off period," I said. "I need to ask Billy Wayne about that. He told me that with the final murder, Della Gibson, he felt antsy—I think that was the word he used—almost immediately. That's why he stayed in Lynn Haven. He felt the need to go hunting again."

"That happens," Ray said. "Many of these killers accelerate their activities right before they get caught. As if the need is getting out of hand and becoming less controllable."

"But," I said, "there were four months between Misty Abbott, number six, and Della Gibson, his final victim."

"Good point," Ray said.

The same disinterested guard, Rafael Lopez, took my belongings and directed me to the same hard bench as before. As I sat there, waiting for my escort, I thought about that conversation again. And a ton of other stuff about Billy Wayne's world. And Frank Clark's.

One question that reared its head was, if Noleen's murder wasn't to create confusion and blur the focus, why kill her? Was there some connection between Frank Clark and Noleen Kovac? An affair? Possible, always possible, but we had absolutely no evidence of that. And to be honest, that wasn't my take on Clark. For one thing, he's the only guy I ever met who didn't undress Nicole with his eyes. So I didn't see him as a player.

Which was why I was here to see Billy Wayne. As Pancake put it, we were getting ready to break some eggs and make an omelet. He of the food metaphors. Always part of his take on everything. But he was right. We were on the doorstep of digging into the private lives of some of Pine Key's citizens. Frank Clark and each of the victims' friends and family at least. Asking questions that sounded less like a benign documentary than an intrusive investigation. A fine line to walk. Breaking eggs.

So, Ray suggested it would be nice to chat with Billy Wayne beforehand. Maybe now that we had refined our focus, he'd come clean. Let us know we were on the right track before we started breaking those eggs.

I wasn't optimistic. Billy Wayne had been adamant about revealing nothing. But maybe, just maybe, if we had come to this threshold on our own, without Billy Wayne's help, he'd feel more comfortable with at least confirming that we were pointed in the right direction.

Truth was that I was sure we were. With or without Billy Wayne's input. Nothing else made sense. But, if Billy Wayne confirmed that, we'd all feel better.

Ray thought he and I should go in together, but I felt if we did that, Billy Wayne would shut down. He might take it as an intimidation tactic. Something I believed he would resist. Not sure why I felt that, but I did. It was something in his eyes. For sure, Billy Wayne couldn't stand up to a physical confrontation, too small for that, but he had that look. That hard gaze that said he could take whatever you offered and not only persevere but grind you down mentally.

Yet, I also felt Billy Wayne had bided his time, waiting to tell his story, and now we offered that chance. He just might see us as his last chance. Or at least his only chance for the foreseeable future. I hoped so anyway.

I was glad to see my escort was once again Marcus McKinney. I wondered if anyone there got days off.

"You back for more?" McKinney asked.

"Seems so."

"People will start to talk." He laughed. "You and Billy Wayne an item."

I followed him through an iron door and along a corridor.

"Oh, we're an item, all right."

Another laugh.

"Well, I'll say you look less wide-eyed than last time."

"Must be getting used to the place."

"Hmmm." He shook his head. "Ain't no getting used to this place."

"How long you been here?" I asked.

"Four years. A little more."

"How do you do it? I mean, dealing with all this?"

He stopped and turned toward me. "You put on blinders. Look straight ahead. Focus on the job. Don't think about the kind of people you have to hang with every day." He shrugged and gave a half smile. "And I'm talking about the other guards." He started walking again, shot a look over his shoulder, "The inmates are another thing altogether."

He unlocked and pushed open a door that led to another corridor, the interview cubicles along one side. He stopped near one, indicating with a wave of his hand that this is where I should wait for Billy Wayne.

"We do have some bad dudes in here," he said.

"Like Billy Wayne?"

"Truth is, he's one of the easy ones. Never tries to paint outside the lines. Does what he's told." He shrugged. "Can't say that for most of the others."

He left, saying he'd be just outside to take me back when I finished.

Two minutes later Billy Wayne appeared beyond the glass. We each picked up our handsets.

"Didn't expect to see you so soon," Billy Wayne said. "You guys are quick."

"We try."

"So, what's the story?"

"Need to ask you a couple of things."

"And I need to hear you tell me you have proof of what really happened."

"We're working on that."

Billy Wayne took the handset from his ear, held it against his chest, and stared at me. His index finger gave the handset a couple of taps before he lifted it back into position. "If you haven't solved the puzzle, why're you here?"

Here goes. Be cool. Ray's catchall for don't screw it up.

"We've been down in Pine Key the last few days," I said.

"And?"

"I was hoping you'd tell me that's where we should be looking."

"I see."

"Look, Billy Wayne, we want to believe you."

"You should. I haven't lied about any of it."

"We focused on Pine Key because of the three victims there. Because it made no sense to look elsewhere. The logistics of planting evidence anywhere else is simply too impossible to believe. And we think Frank Clark is the likely suspect. He had access for sure."

"So, why're you here?"

"For you to confirm we're in the right place. On the right track."

He shook his head. "Didn't I say from the beginning that you'd have to do this without my involvement?"

"You did. But now that we know all the players down there and have someone to look at, things are going to change. We've stayed off the radar. Been very friendly. In return, the folks down there, even the police department, have been helpful. Even welcoming. But now we're entering a new phase. We'll make some waves. Stir things up. We don't want to go there unless we're dead solid on the right track."

Billy Wayne stared but said nothing.

"Okay, let me ask you this. You told me last time that after the murder of Della Gibson, you were restless. Didn't want to go back to Tallahassee. Felt the need to hunt. Remember that?"

"I do."

"Did you ever feel that after any of the other killings? Like you needed more?"

He seemed to consider that for a minute. "Can't say I did."

That definitely put Frank Clark in play.

"Do you think Frank Clark is the bad guy here?"

Still, Billy Wayne didn't respond.

"Okay, here's our thinking. We eliminated Loretta Swift. She was the first victim in Pine Key. No one would've had any evidence to plant before her. So that one's on you."

I studied his face. Nothing. Billy Wayne would make a good poker player.

"So the other two there are in play. Let's say Clark is the bad guy. He could've controlled the investigations, controlled the evidence, planted it. It would have been easy for him. He was at ground zero. But what we're having trouble with is . . . why? I get him killing his wife. Maybe. Marriages do fall apart and end up with one spouse dead. And friends and neighbors are often shocked. Didn't know there were problems brewing. Okay, I get that. But what about Noleen Kovac? The other victim down there. I don't see any connection between her and Clark."

"What do you want me to say?"

"Do you know of any such connection?"

"Me? I don't know any of the folks down there. Don't know who's fucking who. Who's backstabbing who. Nothing. I was simply in and out and . . ." He stopped. Shook his head. "I think I've said enough on that subject."

"You have," I said. I gave him a nod. "That's all I needed to know."

He raised an eyebrow. "So, what now? What's your next move?"

"Haven't figured that out yet. Just wanted to make sure we were on firm ground before shaking things up. And now I am."

"I didn't say a word."

"And I didn't hear anything." I smiled.

Billy Wayne smiled. "Guess you better get to work."

CHAPTER TWENTY-SIX

"Why don't you do something useful?" Nicole said.

"Like what?"

"Go play with Pancake."

We were in our room. Fresh from a brief chat with Ray about my visit to Billy Wayne's world, followed by Nicole's invitation to an extended shower. Oh, yeah. She does love water—showers, jacuzzies, hot tubs. And she isn't even an Aquarian.

"So, after you've had your way, you want to toss me aside?"

"It's what we girls do."

"I feel so used."

"You'll get over it." She rolled out of bed. "Tonight. If you're lucky." She laughed.

"What are you going to do?" I asked.

"Wash my hair."

"Your hair's fine."

"Jake, go play. I'm sure Pancake is up for it."

"He's up for anything that involves food and alcohol."

"My point."

That's how I ended up motoring down the crowded Boardwalk. Actually, following Pancake as he parted the waters. He was good at that. And he appeared to be on a mission. Must be hungry. Big shock. We, of course, headed to Woody's. Ray had some calls to make and said he'd join us later.

I had opted for jeans and a cabernet-colored RGP shirt; Pancake jeans and bright green shirt. With his red hair glowing in the late-afternoon sun, he looked like a giant leprechaun. I told him so. He grunted, saying that's what he was going for. He added, "Women love that look."

Which for Pancake was true. To emphasize that point, when we climbed the stairs and entered Woody's, Laurie Mae, owner Betty Lou's daughter, greeted us. She locked her arm with Pancake's and led him to a table on the deck. I veered toward the bar, where I saw Angus Whitehead had planted himself on a stool. Looked like he was well into a day of drinking. It occurred to me that he might have an unusual take on the whole Billy Wayne Baker ordeal. Since he apparently spent so much time sleeping in the jail, he might have picked up something useful. If he was capable of picking up on anything. In his usual anesthetized state that might be wishful thinking. But, why not ask? I climbed on the stool next to Angus.

"How's it going?" I asked.

He looked at me and blinked as if clearing his eyes. Then, a flash of recognition. "You're the guy I saw over at the police station."

"Guilty," I said.

"You that Hollywood dude? One that's making that movie?"

"You might say that. I'm Jake Longly."

"I'm Angus."

We shook hands.

"I know," I said.

"You do?"

I smiled. "You're some kind of celebrity around here. At least over at the police station."

He laughed and slapped a knee. "That I am."

The bartender swiped a towel across the bar and asked, "What can I get you?"

"Blantons on the rocks. And whatever my friend is having."

"Got it. One Blantons and one gin with lime."

"Thanks," Angus said.

"My pleasure."

"I hear you guys are doing some film thing on Billy Wayne Baker. That true?"

"Actually, it's more about what Billy Wayne did to this community."

Angus shook his head. "He sure did a number." His eyebrows gave a couple of bounces. "Enough to drive a man to drink." He drained the drink before him.

The bartender replaced it and slid my bourbon toward me.

"Want to join me and my friend at a table?" I nodded toward Pancake, sitting at a table on the deck, chatting with Laurie Mae.

"Really?" Angus said.

"Really."

I waved a hand toward the bartender and indicated we were moving. He eased us away with a nod.

I introduced Pancake.

"I saw you over at the police station, too," Angus said. "When was that?" He didn't wait for an answer. "Don't matter. One day's like the other." He gave a head bob and a lopsided grin. "Pancake, huh? Ain't never knowed anyone by that name."

"Me either," Pancake said.

"What happened to your face?" Angus asked Pancake.

"Alcohol and a bicycle."

Angus laughed, slapped his leg again. "Been there. 'Course I broke my nose." He wagged his head. "You'd think I'd have learned, but truth be told, I've done that twice." Another laugh. "That was wine. I stay away from wine now."

"Remind me not to ride bikes with you two," I said.

Angus looked at me. "It just now come to me. Jake Longly. You that baseball player?"

"Long time ago."

"I remember. Texas Rangers." He shook his head. "My brain works that way. I forget stuff. Then I remember it. You were good."

"I had a couple of okay years."

Laurie Mae returned with a bourbon for Pancake. "Get you guys anything to eat?"

Angus and I declined. Not so Pancake.

"Nachos," Pancake said. "Maybe some calamari."

She headed toward the kitchen.

"What's your take on Billy Wayne Baker?" I asked Angus.

"Pure evil is what that boy was. As pure as ever can be."

I nodded.

"I mean sneaking in here and killing all those folks." He took a slug of gin.

"You knew the victims, I'm sure."

"Sure did." He scratched an ear. "'Course I know everyone around here." He laughed. "Comes from spending so much time here at Woody's. Everybody comes in here."

"This your favorite watering hole?" Pancake asked.

"One of them, that's for sure." He cupped his glass of gin like it was a treasure. "But, yeah, I knew all the victims. I guess I knew Loretta Swift best."

"She and Peter seemed to take care of you," I said. "Whenever you end up crashing over at the jail."

He nodded and smiled. "That's a fact."

"You spend a lot of time there?" I asked. "At the jail?"

"Well, it beats driving home. Not that it's that far, but I ain't usually in no condition to operate a motor vehicle."

"I bet Chief Morgan appreciates that," I said.

"He's a good man. And he don't mind me hanging around. Most times, leastwise." He gave a half shake of his head. "Can't say the same for Clark and Munson."

"How so?" I asked.

"Oh, they're all right, I suspect. But they do get all bent out of shape sometimes." He scratched an ear. "Aren't very nice about asking me to leave." He smiled. "But the chief likes me. I think he considers me sort of a mascot." Another laugh, another leg slap.

"How often do you end up there?"

"Three, four nights a week. Some afternoons, too."

"Oh?"

"If I drink lunch, I sometimes need a nap before happy hour." He laughed and slapped his knee yet again. I guessed that was his signature move. Bet he had the bruises to prove it.

"Bet that doesn't sit well with Frank Clark and Terry Munson," I said.

"Sure don't. Sometimes they'll roust me early in the morning. Tell me the jail ain't no motel. Like I don't know that." He shook his head. "And I like to sleep in."

I smiled. "Maybe they need the space."

"For what? Ain't never no one there except me." He rubbed one side of his nose. "They just like to flash their badges. Their asses, too."

I laughed.

"Like the night they brought those three girls in," Angus said. "The ones that were shoplifting. Seemed to me they might've had more on their mind than messing with me."

"What happened?" Pancake asked.

"I was in there sleeping. I'd had a late lunch, or was it an early dinner? Anyway, I got tanked and went over there and napped. They brought those girls in. They told me to get out." He looked out toward the marina. "Guess they didn't want me around them. Acting like I was some dirt ball or something."

"Maybe the girls were uncomfortable."

"Don't see why. I'm pretty harmless." He gave me a grin. "Most the time. Anyway, they wasn't very nice about it."

"So you left?" I asked.

"Sure did." He shrugged. "Didn't want to bite the hand that feeds me. Places that let you wander in and sleep aren't all that easy to come by."

"Smart move," I said.

"They was in a pissy mood. In fact"—he hesitated, stared at the floor—"was that the same night?" He gave a quick head shake. "Sometimes I get things mixed up." He looked at me. "My memory ain't always the best."

"So what happened?" Pancake asked.

"When?" Angus' face wore a confused look.

"You said something else happened that night."

"See? That's what I mean." Then his eyes narrowed and his brow furrowed as if he were thinking back to that night. Then he nodded. "Yeah, come to think of it, I do believe it was the same night." He paused, started to say more, but before a single word came out, he straightened his shoulders, looking toward the restaurant's entrance. His head dropped. "I probably shouldn't be talking about nothing."

I followed his gaze. Clark and Munson walked in. They saw us and came our way.

"Please tell me you guys aren't feeding Angus alcohol," Clark said.

"I think he's feeding himself," Pancake said.

Angus raised his glass. "My favorite food group."

Munson tilted his head toward Angus. "I guess we'll see you later tonight."

"Nope." Angus shook his head. "Pizza night. With my mom." He glanced at me. "She's eighty-three. Still lives by herself. I go over once a week, bring pizza, and we watch old movies. She loves Tracy and Hepburn. So, I'll probably crash over there."

"Care to join us?" I asked them.

Munson shook his head. "No. Thanks though. I'm meeting someone."

"Another time."

"I'll sit a spell," Clark said.

"See you later," Munson said and walked away.

Clark dragged a chair out and sat.

Angus drained his drink and stood. "I hate to leave you boys but I got to get over to the pizza place. It's been a pleasure." His head gave a couple of bobs. "You guys can buy me drinks anytime." He laughed and waved over his shoulder as he weaved away.

"He's a character," I said.

"Oh yeah," Clark said. "He's all that."

Laurie Mae appeared. "Get you anything?" she asked Clark.

"Iced tea." He glanced at me. "I got the duty tonight."

Pancake and I decided on anther round.

"Thanks for today," I said to Clark. "We appreciate you guys being so open with us."

He shrugged. "Hope it helps some."

"It does."

I saw Munson climb on a barstool next to a thin brunette. Clark followed my gaze.

"Terry's got a date tonight."

"I hear he's a bit of a ladies' man."

"Been that way since high school. Women love him." Clark looked at me. "Sort of reminds me of you. I suspect you've had good-looking women after you your whole life."

Pancake laughed. "You don't know the half of it. Of course, with Nicole, he's punching way above his weight."

"My friend," I said.

Clark laughed.

The drinks arrived. Clark stirred in a couple of packs of sugar and took a gulp.

"Can I ask you something?" Clark said. "About Billy Wayne?"

"Sure."

"Back a couple of years. When he confessed and got packed off to Raiford. I heard from a prosecutor up there that he had made waves about not doing some of the murders. One or two. I forget." He looked at me. "You guys hear anything like that?"

Was he fishing? Worried about us being on his turf? Maybe uncovering his misdeeds?

"No," I said.

Pancake nodded his agreement. "Who would believe him anyway? Not to mention, he did confess to all the murders."

"He sort of had to," Clark said. "He did leave his DNA everywhere."

"That makes any denial on his part moot, I would think," I said.

"Sure does." Clark sighed. "I just wondered if any of your research uncovered anything like that?"

"No. And that's not what we really care about. Our film isn't about him. It's about this town and the people here." I looked at him. "It's your story we want to tell."

Clark nodded. "Good. This town don't want to hear much more about Billy Wayne." He drained his tea. "Guess I better get to my rounds." He stood. "Make sure everyone's behaving themselves."

CHAPTER TWENTY-SEVEN

NICOLE AND RAY showed up a little before six thirty. She looked stunning. She wore black tights with just a hint of a gray geometric pattern and a red RGP shirt. Her hair freshly washed and parted down the middle framed her face like two silk curtains. She attracted even more than her usual attention. Ray looked like Ray, his shirt slate gray.

Munson and his date had left shortly after Clark while Pancake had spent the past half hour flirting with Laurie Mae, even setting up a date for after she got off at ten. He also skeletonized a rack of ribs. This after demolishing the nachos and calamari he had ordered earlier. I got maybe three chips and one wad of squiggly legs. Both were good. Pancake obviously agreed. Though his food filter is suspect. He loves everything. Just so there's a lot of it.

We had also knocked back a few more bourbons. I had a nice warm buzz going. Nicole obviously saw the signs, as she laid a hand on my arm when she sat and said, "Looks like we're having a fun evening."

I raised an eyebrow. "Have a couple of those margaritas and it'll be epic."

"I'll make a note of that."

Pancake's love of all things food was underlined when Betty Lou took our orders. Pancake went for the barbecued chicken, potato salad, beans, and cornbread. The rest of us had fish tacos.

Betty Lou soon returned with our drinks, including Nicole's large salt-rimmed margarita. As she passed them around, she asked, "How's everything going?"

"Fine," I said.

"You talked with any of the folks I gave you?"

"All of them," I said.

"Good." She placed the final drink on the table in front of Ray and clamped the tray against her side with one arm. "I got a couple of more that might help."

Nicole pulled a notepad from her purse. "Fire."

"Whitney Wilkins. She works over at the bakery. She can give you some insight into Peter and Charlaine."

"We met her briefly when we were over there," Nicole said as she scribbled down the name. "Are they an item? Peter and Charlaine?"

Betty Lou smiled. "Not that I know. But they damn sure should be. Neither of them has anyone and Charlaine's so much like her sister. To my eye they'd be a natural." She shook her head. "But what do I know?"

"Probably a lot," Nicole said. "And from what little I saw of them, I agree with you." She winked at Betty Lou. "I got the impression there's something going on there."

"Lordy, I hope so." She gave a hearty laugh. When it settled, she continued with her list. "Then you could chat with Sally Foster. Lives next door to the Clarks. She probably knew Sara better than anyone." She watched as Nicole wrote down the name. "And maybe Patti Ryan over at the bank. She and Noleen were good friends." A busboy came by and took the service tray from her. "That's about all I can think of now."

"This helps," Nicole said.

Betty Lou smiled, gave a quick nod, and walked away.

After dinner, we took the stairs down to the water-side gazebo. With the bourbons and cigars Betty Lou foisted on us. With little resistance on our part.

The gazebo had become our office of sorts. Seemed like we often found our way here. And why not? It was comfortable, more or less private this time of night, and had a great view of the boat-filled harbor, now cast in soft moonlight.

We barely got our cigars lit when Ray jumped right in.

"Sounds like Billy Wayne confirmed we're on the right track," he said.

"As close as he could without coming right out with it," I said. "But we really knew that already."

Which was true. None of the other killings offered any reasonable opportunity to stage two murders. The geography alone made that close to impossible. What I had really hoped to get from Billy Wayne was who he thought did the staging. But, again, logic only pointed in one direction—Frank Clark. The old motive, means, and opportunity triad.

"We had an interesting encounter with Frank Clark," I said.

"When?" Ray asked.

"Just before you guys got here. He sat with us for a few minutes. He asked if we knew anything about Billy Wayne denying any of the murders."

"He did?"

"Sure did," Pancake said.

"What did you tell him?" Ray asked.

"That we haven't heard anything like that," I said.

"Good." Ray took several puffs from his cigar and waved away the smoke cloud. "You think he was fishing? Trying to see what we knew?"

"That was my impression. He didn't look nervous or anything like that, but it did seem to be out of the blue."

"Maybe he's starting to regret us being here."

"You think he might shut us down?" Nicole asked. "Stop cooperating?"

Ray seemed to give that some thought. "He might. Wouldn't be smart on his part though. Better to keep us close, I'd think."

"Like the Godfather," Nicole said. "Friends close and enemies closer."

"Exactly," Ray said. He took a sip of bourbon. "But we have a problem."

"Which is?" I asked.

"Every case has a linchpin. Where things intersect. Where the motives and the murders mesh tightly." Another sip of bourbon. "Our problem is that we have no connection between Frank Clark and Noleen Kovac. If we're going to buy into Clark being the killer, we need to find that connection."

I took a sip of whiskey, laid my cigar on the edge of the table. "To be honest, I haven't seen or heard anything that suggested that he and his wife weren't a solid couple. No hint of trouble."

"Closed doors and all," Pancake said. "It's out there. We just haven't found it yet."

"Maybe," I said.

"Got to be, if he's the killer."

"Which brings us back to Noleen Kovac," Ray said. "Clark having marriage trouble? Killing his wife? I get that. But why Kovac?"

"A cover?" I said. "Like Pancake said before."

Ray looked at Pancake. "Go on."

Pancake nodded to me. "I'll let Jake take it."

"Pancake and I talked about it earlier. Our thinking is this. Let's say Clark wanted his wife dead? Money, girlfriend, for whatever reason. Billy Wayne comes along. He sees an opportunity. A good cover. Loretta Swift's murder offers DNA evidence. Exactly what he needs to stage Sara's murder as one of Billy Wayne's."

"And no matter how much Billy Wayne denied it," Pancake said, "after he was caught, of course, no one would believe him. DNA doesn't lie."

"If Clark only killed his wife," I said, "and if the killer was caught and denied doing it, there could be some scrutiny of Sara Clark's murder. Remember, the FBI was involved so Clark might not've been able to keep it in house. But throw in Noleen Kovac and things are more complex. Less focus on Clark."

"You're saying Clark selected Noleen at random?" Ray asked. "As random as things can be in a town this size? But at least someone he had no history with. Other than small-town cop and citizen."

"Just throwing out ideas," I said. "But wouldn't two murders, one with little connection to Clark, deflect some of the attention that might be directed his way?"

"Sure would," Ray said. He pointed his cigar at me. "That's a clever idea."

"It was Pancake's idea," I said. "But, let's say that's true. How do we approach this? Without raising anyone's hackles?"

"We're going to have to do exactly that," Ray said. "Don't see any way around it. We need to ask questions that might make some folks uncomfortable. Even question our purpose for being here."

"Tricky," I said.

"Sure is. But be cool and it'll work out."

I shrugged. Be cool. Ray-speak for saying little but gathering a lot. No small task here.

Ray continued. "You and Nicole hit up the folks Betty Lou told us about. Pancake and I are meeting with the pathologist tomorrow. The one that did the autopsies. Then we'll begin getting deeper into Frank Clark's world and see what we can find on Noleen Kovac."

"Sounds good."

"Oh," I said. "We, Pancake and I, just had a chat with Angus Whitehead."

"I met him," Ray said.

"He was telling us about something that happened at the station the night the shoplifters were brought in."

"Same night Sara Clark was murdered," Ray said.

I nodded. "Apparently, when the three girls showed up, they tossed him out. Clark and Munson. Said they weren't very nice about it. More so than usual." I glanced at Pancake. "I think he said they treated him like a dirt ball."

Pancake nodded.

"They had a lot on their plate that night," Ray said. "Even before the murder was discovered. The fight on The Boardwalk, the shop-lifters, the car accident on the bridge. Don't you think they'd find Angus particularly annoying under those circumstances?"

"Sure. But he said something else happened."

"What?"

"Clark and Munson showed up about that time. He got nervous, clammed up, and left."

Ray considered that. "Any idea what he might be referring to?"

I shook my head. "No. But, whatever it was, it was enough for him to remember something happened. With Angus it could be anything. His brain isn't the most functional."

"Maybe revisit him at some time," Ray said. "Can't hurt."

"Next time I see him," I said. "Which shouldn't be too long. I think he's at Woody's on a daily basis."

"What's your take on him?" Ray asked.

"Seems to be a happy drunk." I looked at Pancake, who nodded agreement. "A pleasant enough guy. I suspect he has a fairly good relationship with the police. Morgan and Clark for sure. And probably even with Munson though he said he was sometimes a dick."

Ray smiled. "At least he doesn't seem to have worn out his welcome over there. They tolerate him using the jail as a B and B."

CHAPTER TWENTY-EIGHT

THE NEXT MORNING, Nicole and I decided to go for a walk. Get some fresh Gulf air and a little exercise. Sure beat Krav Maga classes. Much safer, and infinitely less painful.

Our first stop was the reception desk downstairs to see where the best hiking trails were. A trim, neatly dressed middle-aged woman with chin-length dark hair, streaked with gray, smiled and looked at us over half glasses that rode low on her nose.

"You must be Jake and Nicole," she said.

"We are."

"I'm Louise Phillips. The owner. You met my daughter Monica when you checked in."

"Yes. She was very nice."

"She better be." Louise laughed. "She's the one who told me about you. Handsome and gorgeous were the words she used." Another laugh.

"Yes, Jake is gorgeous," Nicole said.

She's funny. She really is.

Louise thought so, too. "She told me about the film you guys are doing. On Billy Wayne Baker."

"Not exactly on Billy Wayne," Nicole said.

"Monica told me. And, I have to say, I like the approach you're taking."

"Thanks. Our goal is to tell this town's story."

"It's quite a tale."

"I'm sure you knew the victims," I said.

"Very well. Especially Loretta Swift. She and I went way back."

"I'm sorry."

Louise gave a brief nod. "Still miss her. She could light up a room."

"That's what we hear," Nicole said.

"And Sara Clark?" I asked. "I understand she was into a lot of things around here."

"That's a fact. She seemed to volunteer for everything. And she always did a good job."

"Everyone says she and Frank had a great marriage. Sort of pillars of the community."

She sighed. "That's true. Her murder damned near killed Frank." She slid the sign-in ledger book to one side and flattened her palms on the counter. "They were married a long time. One of those couples you just knew were made for each other. 'Course you could say the same for Peter and Loretta."

"We heard that, too," I said.

"Were Loretta and Sara friends?" Nicole asked.

"Absolutely. Peter and Loretta always took goodies over to the police station. Every morning. Sara was often there. Frank practically lived there. So, yeah, the two couples got along very well."

"What about Noleen Kovac? She part of that group?"

"I don't think so. I mean everyone here knows everyone else. It's a small and tight community. But Noleen wasn't that close to either Loretta or Sara. That's my impression anyway." She slid her glasses off her nose and let them dangle from the old chain that wrapped her neck. "Of course, the Clarks, the police department, too, for that matter, did their banking over where Noleen worked." She smiled. "We do, too."

"I talked with Tommy Lee," I said. "He felt Noleen was a loner. Kept to herself."

"That's true. I'd see her around from time to time, but she didn't go to many of the community events. Except for the annual Pine Key Fishing Regatta. The Farmers and Merchants Bank where she worked is one of the event sponsors."

"Tommy Lee also said she didn't date much or see anyone on a regular basis."

"I don't really know but I wouldn't be surprised if that's true."

"Sounds like the town lost three very special women," Nicole said.

"We did. None of them will ever be replaced."

Nicole laid a hand on the counter. "I think we'd like to get you on camera when we get into production."

"Me? Whatever for?"

Nicole smiled. "You're a part of this community. You knew the victims. You know the town. You also have a finger on the pulse of what visitors say and think when they come here. All of that is important to the story we want to tell."

Louise gave a nod. "Anything I can do to help."

"Besides, you'd look good on camera."

Louise laughed. "I don't know about that."

"I do," Nicole said. "It's my job to know those things. You'll be great."

We left Louise to her workday and headed down The Boardwalk. Louise had said that once we cleared town, heading south, the walk was quiet and peaceful. The wooden walkway ended at a dirt and gravel trail that wound through some scrub brush and trees before opening along the coast, where it melted into a sandy pathway that snaked through the dunes and followed the shoreline a good ten feet above the beach. We passed a few other walkers, each nodding and saying, "morning," and a young couple throwing a stick into the water, their yellow lab retrieving it and splashing back toward them as if retuning it were a life-and-death matter.

Louise was right. The walk was pleasant, with expansive views over the Gulf. Beat the hell out of Krav Maga classes. Easier for sure. I opened and closed my fists a few times. They actually felt normal.

"You miss it, don't you?" Nicole asked.

"Miss what?"

"Our classes."

"Yeah. Like I miss jock itch."

"Colorful."

"Trying to be funny."

She slapped my butt. "Keep working at it. You'll get there."

Thirty minutes out, we turned back toward town. I saw a boat churning out into deep water. Fishing rig for sure. I wondered if it was Tommy Lee Kovac, taking a charter group out for a day of wetting lines. Too far to tell.

"Isn't this great?" Nicole said.

"Sure is."

It did have all the makings of a prefect morning. Until that old "man plans; God laughs" business reared its ugly head. In the form of a phone call. I checked my caller ID. Tammy. My ex. My insane ex. I punched it over to voice mail and kept walking.

Two minutes later another call. Another dump to voice mail. Ninety seconds later another.

"You might as well talk to her," Nicole said. "She won't give up."

Over the months I had known Nicole, she had gotten to know Tammy. Sort of. Enough to know that Tammy's major flaw was that she lived in Tammyville. A place brimming with drama. Tammy possessed some deep-seated and inexplicable need to drag me into her psychosis. I mean, we were divorced. And she was married to Walter the wonder attorney.

I answered.

"Jake, why are you ignoring my calls?"

"What do you want?"

"It's Walter."

The aforementioned mega-buck wonder attorney. Part of his mega-bucks came from my wallet. He handled our divorce. Not exactly handled. More like manipulated, engineered, whatever term works best for me getting a proctoscope and Tammy getting a big check. But then, he was now stuck with her, so I got off light.

"I guess it wouldn't do any good if I said I wasn't interested."

Nicole laughed. Even she saw that wasn't going anywhere.

"Is that Nicole?"

"It is."

"I can't believe she's still with you. Guess you haven't had time to cheat on her yet."

"Or a reason."

"You're such an ass."

"I am. Is that why you called? To forward that little tidbit?"

"No. It's Walter."

"So you said."

"He's having trouble peeing."

I expected a lot of crazy shit from Tammy. Voice of experience here. But this took the cake.

"Okay. What am I supposed to do about that?"

"What if it's prostate cancer? Or something like that?"

"He's surviving you. I don't think a little prostate problem will derail Walter."

"Jesus, Jake. Show a little compassion. A little empathy for what I'm going through."

"You? It's Walter's prostate."

I could feel the heat through the line. Almost hear her teeth grinding. It's the small pleasures that make life fun. But thankfully, she couldn't think of anything to say so I continued.

"I'm not a doctor. You do know that?"

Laughter burst through the line. "You a doctor? That's a hoot."

"It is. So why are you asking for my medical opinion?"

"I'm not. Walter's seeing his urologist this morning. I just thought you'd be a little sympathetic. I should've known better."

She hung up. I returned my phone to my pocket.

"That sounded like fun," Nicole said.

"Sort of like a prostate infection." I smiled. "An incurable one."

We ended our walk at Swift's Bakery. Why not? Whitney Wilkins manned the counter. She looked up and smiled as we came in.

"Welcome back," she said.

"Thanks," Nicole said. "Smells good in here. As usual."

"Just took a fresh batch of cinnamon rolls out." She nodded toward the tray on the counter behind her.

We ordered a pair and two coffees.

"Where's Peter and Charlaine?" I asked.

"He's on a supply run up to Panama City. Charlaine took some stuff over to the police station. Oh, and the mayor's office. Mayor Olsen has some budget meeting with the city council this morning and she always serves pastries for those things."

"To soften them up?" Nicole asked.

"Absolutely."

She handed us each a plate with a massive cinnamon roll, dripping with icing.

"Looks good," I said.

"Take a seat and I'll get some coffee."

We did.

She settled two cups on the table and filled them. "Anything else?"

Nicole swiped a finger through the icing and licked it. "Hmmm. Wonderful."

Whitney smiled. "We try."

"Can I ask you something?" Nicole said.

"Sure."

"It's personal."

"Oh?"

"About Peter and Charlaine? Anything there?"

She hesitated and then said, "Why'd you ask that?"

"She's nosey," I said.

"I am. But the last time we were here, I got a vibe. And, we've talked to several people around town. Many of them think Peter and Charlaine would make a good couple."

Whitney smiled. She glanced toward the door, then lowered her head slightly, her voice dropping. "I do, too."

"Maybe you can make that happen," Nicole said.

"I'm working on it. They're just not quite ready yet." She shrugged. "But, if you ask me, I think it'll work out. They're perfect for each other."

The front door opened. I looked up. Pancake.

"I'm hungry," he announced.

Of course.

"You came to the right place," Whitney said.

"I thought you and Ray had a meeting this morning?" I asked.

"Headed that way," Pancake said. "But can't do that on an empty stomach." He looked at my plate, then up to Whitney. "I'll take three of those."

"What? Nothing for Ray?" I asked.

"He can forage for himself."

CHAPTER TWENTY-NINE

RAY PARKED IN front of the Pine Key Hospital just as Pancake polished off his third cinnamon roll.

"You get enough to eat?" Ray asked.

"For now." Pancake licked his fingers and wiped them with the wad of napkins Whitney had stuffed in the bag. "Don't want to talk about autopsies and stuff on an empty stomach."

"Is your stomach ever empty?"

"Not if I can help it."

The white stucco building sat in a wooded area two blocks north of downtown. Brown block lettering over the entry portico indicated it was the Pine Key Medical Center. Not exactly what Ray would consider a true medical center, too small, but it appeared to be clean and pleasant. He and Pancake had done their research. The hospital had eighty beds, including a six-bed ICU, four surgical suites, an emergency department, and ten beds devoted to rehab services.

They had also delved into Dr. Adrian McGill, the pathologist. The guy who performed the autopsies on the three Pine Key victims. Everything they found echoed what Clark and Munson had told them earlier. Dr. McGill had trained in Pensacola and then Jackson Memorial Hospital/University of Miami Medical Center in Miami, was board certified in clinical pathology, and had indeed spent ten years working in the Miami/Dade County Medical Examiner's Office, which was located on the Jackson Memorial campus. He relocated to Pine Key nearly ten years ago.

Ray held the door for a nurse pushing a wheelchair, the passenger a woman, cradling a newborn. A young man, loaded down with overstuffed plastic bags, trailed them. He looked bewildered. Ray gave him a smile. Poor kid had no idea how life was going to change. Ray remembered when Jake came home from the hospital. He wasn't ready. His wife wasn't ready. But they managed. At least Jake had been what they called "a good baby." Meaning he ate well, slept a lot, and didn't raise too many ruckuses. That came later. The teen years when Jake pushed the envelope to the breaking point. Pancake had helped him push.

Dr. McGill sat behind his desk, microscope before him, a tray of stained slides near his right hand. He looked to be the fifty-seven years his bio had stated, his hair thinning and graying, a mustache-goatee combination, also gray, enveloping his mouth. He wore green surgical scrubs. He looked up when they entered.

"Dr. McGill?" Ray asked.

"You must be Ray Longly," McGill said as he stood.

"I am." They shook hands. "This is Pancake."

"Never heard that name before."

"Me, either. But it works."

McGill had no reply for a second or two but then said, "Please. Sit." They did.

"Looks like your injury is healing well," he said to Pancake. He smiled. "Betty Lou Thompson told me about it."

"She seems to get around," Ray said.

"She does. She also told me about the film you're working on. Sounds interesting."

"It is."

"I understand you're going to focus on the victims, not Billy Wayne Baker."

"That's true," Ray said. "Everyone knows Billy Wayne's story, what he did, but no one knows what the victims' families and friends went through."

"An admirable endeavor." He gave a slow nod. "I understand Charles Balfour is producing it."

Ray nodded. "Also true."

"How on earth did you get someone like him onboard? I mean, he's a big deal."

"He is. But the concept came from his niece, Nicole Jamison. She dates my son, Jake."

"Ah. So that's your connection," McGill said. "But why do they need to involve a P.I. firm?"

Ray smiled. "We're what they call technical consultants. Pancake and I are trying to nail down all the police and forensic work. To help clarify and explain things. Give it perspective."

"Makes sense. Anyway, Chief Morgan called, said I should talk with you. Apparently, you guys impressed him. No easy task." He smiled.

"He's an impressive guy himself."

McGill nodded his agreement, then opened the right-hand drawer of his desk. Three folders appeared. "I pulled my records on the cases." He laid them on his desk, tapping them with an index finger. "To help my feeble memory." Another smile. "So, what can I help you with?"

"What we know is that each victim was killed at home. Bound and then strangled. Manually. And there were no real signs of a struggle in any of them."

"That's true."

"So none of them resisted? Fought back?"

"I, of course, read all the crime-scene reports and none of them indicated any kind of struggle," McGill said. "I also visited each scene and that was also my impression. In the autopsy examinations, other than the wrist and ankle ligature bruises and abrasions I saw in all three, the closest thing would be some contusions on the right upper arm of Noleen Kovac. In a finger and thumb pattern as if someone had grabbed her there."

"So, maybe she thought about resisting?" Pancake asked.

"Maybe. Morgan thinks—and from what I later read about Billy Wayne—he used a knife to force compliance. Then he tied his victims in a four-point manner and had his way." He slid the files an inch or two to the left.

"So, the MO was consistent?" Ray asked. "In each of the three? No deviations that you saw?"

McGill nodded. "The scenes were more or less mirror images of each other. Right down the line. Same restraints, same manual strangulation marks, same DNA."

"We talked with a prosecutor. Up in Jacksonville. He felt Billy Wayne must have had an accomplice." A total lie. But he wasn't sure how else to generate the discussion he wanted to have.

"Why would he think that?"

"He felt that the lack of any struggle meant the victim must have been overpowered. Or intimidated, into not resisting."

McGill seemed to give that some thought but then slowly shook his head. "I don't buy it. If by overpowered he means held down, that didn't happen. There was no evidence of any blunt force trauma, no bruises that suggested manual restraint, and no defensive wounds. Except for the ligature bruising and the arm contusions I mentioned in the Kovac situation, there were no signs of any of that. At least in the three cases I examined. Maybe he saw something different in the others."

"No," Ray said. "The others were similar to the ones you handled."

"Who is this guy? The prosecutor?"

"Can't say. It was a private conversation. Privileged, so to speak. As is this one."

"I understand."

"Just so we're clear," Ray said, "you saw no signs of a struggle or resistance from the victims? And the MO in each suggested a single, and the same, assailant?"

"That's my opinion."

"And nothing about any of these gave you pause?"

"No." He stared at Ray for a few seconds and then said, "I mean, could Billy Wayne have had someone with him? Someone who held a gun or something like that? Sure, it's possible. But I have no evidence that indicated that."

"We don't either," Ray said.

"Good. I'd hate to think I messed something up."

"You didn't."

"I heard through the grapevine, a couple of years ago now, back around the time Billy Wayne finally confessed, that he'd said he didn't kill everyone he was charged with. But, I can tell you right here, right now, he did these three. His DNA was there. No doubt. And, of course, he did confess to all the killings."

"He did. Let me ask you about the DNA. You took the samples from the bedsheets in each case. Right?"

"Yes. There was no vaginal DNA in any of the victims."

"That seems to be his MO after the first victim. So, after you collected it, what happened?"

"We, for obvious reasons, don't do DNA testing here. I collected the samples and sent them up to the state lab. They did the work."

"Samples, or the sheets? What was sent?"

"Just the samples I collected. Swabs. The sheets went back to the police department. They held them after that."

"That's what they told us," Ray said. "They kept them locked down until the case was finalized and Billy Wayne packed off to prison. Then they destroyed them."

McGill nodded. "Pretty standard."

"We'll get out of your hair and leave you to your work," Ray said.

McGill smiled. "It's never ending, it seems."

Ray stood. "Thanks for taking the time to talk with us."

McGill stood. They shook hands. "Hope it was helpful."

"It was. I have to say, I'm impressed. From everything I've seen, you, Chief Morgan and his crew, everyone, did a bang-up job. Under difficult circumstances."

"We try," McGill said. "First of all, having this happen here in Pine Key, and then having the FBI breathing down our necks didn't make it any easier."

Ray laughed. "You all seemed to have weathered it well."

CHAPTER THIRTY

AFTER NICOLE AND I finished our breakfast and our chat with Whitney, we walked outside. The sky was clear and clean. Cleaner than me. Each of the cinnamon rolls Whitney had whipped up contained a pound of butter and a cup of sugar. Maybe more. My hands and face felt sticky and greasy. Even a half-dozen napkins didn't help. I started to suggest another shower, but then we'd be late for our meeting with Patti Ryan. Probably would've been worth it, but I knew Nicole wouldn't go for it, so instead I said, "Going to be a nice day."

She licked a finger. "I feel like I need a shower."

Really?

She licked another finger. "But we have a meeting and a shower with you always takes time."

"Oh?"

"That thing of yours always gets in the way."

"What thing?"

She bumped her hip against mine. "I'll show you later."

"Lucky me."

"Yes. Lucky you." Another hip bump.

But, we opted for the shower anyway, thinking we should be a little more presentable before we visited with Patti Ryan at the bank.

It wasn't as much fun as it could have been. Nicole was all business. Quick shower, tan slacks, a lemon yellow RGP shirt, and she was good to go. I opted for jeans and white shirt with a black logo.

We left the hotel under a few clouds but an otherwise pleasant-looking day. A soft breeze came off the Gulf and the day's expected ninety-degree temp was still a few hours away.

"Get your game face on," Nicole said. "We have work to do."

She, the loyal and dedicated Longly Investigations soldier.

A block up Elm Street, we found the Pine Key Farmers and Merchants Bank. A low red-brick structure with a sloping green metal roof, darker green window shutters, and a pair of white columns flanking the entry. Inside, the typical bank hushed silence reigned. To the left a long counter, topped with a glass partition, interrupted by four teller windows. Customers stood before two of them. Toward the rear were four desks, two occupied, one by someone I recognized as Patti Ryan. She looked a few years older than her photo on the bank's website. Today, she wore a white blouse beneath a gray jacket, glasses dangling from a black neck cord. She smiled as we approached.

"Ms. Ryan?" I said.

"You must be Jake and Nicole."

We shook hands and sat facing her.

"Please," she continued, "call me Patti."

"Thanks for seeing us, Patti," Nicole said.

"My pleasure."

Nicole had called earlier to set up the appointment. She had gone over the project and explained why we wanted to meet with her.

"As I mentioned on the phone," Nicole said, "we want to talk about Noleen Kovac."

Patti folded her hands before her. "What do you want to know?"

"Everything." Nicole smiled. "Anything. What was she like?"

"Smart. Hard worker. Definitely dedicated to the bank. And one of the sweetest people I've ever known."

"That's what we hear."

"Her death was a huge shock. I mean, of all people." She sighed. "That's true of all the women that were murdered, of course. Each of them was good people. But, Noleen was part of our family here."

"How long did you know her?" I asked.

"Years and years. At least a dozen."

"Were you close?"

She nodded. "She often came for dinner at the house, or out to restaurants, with my husband and me."

"We heard she wasn't big on social activities."

Patti smiled. "That's true. I used to chide her about it. But she did get involved in a few things. She and I belonged to a book club. We worked together on the annual Fishing Regatta. But, true, she liked staying home and reading." Her eyes moistened. "Lord, I miss her."

"Are you okay?" Nicole asked. "We don't want to cause any discomfort."

Patti smiled, dabbed a tear from the corner of one eye with a knuckle. "That's kind of you to say." She sniffed. "I'm just being a ninny." She opened a desk drawer and removed a tissue, swiping both eyes. "You'd think after all this time I wouldn't do this. But it still hurts."

Nicole shifted forward slightly in her chair. "Time never heals as well as they say."

Patti nodded. "Ain't it so." She sighed. "Okay, I'm together again. What else can I tell you?"

"We know Noleen wasn't married, and the people we talked to said she rarely dated," Nicole asked. "From what you've said, I suspect that's your assessment, too?"

Patti nodded. "No, she never married. Never found the right guy. Back a few years, four or five, she had a fairly long-term relationship with a guy named Adam. Nice guy. He worked in a bank, too. In Panama City. They met at a Chamber of Commerce event up there."

"How long did they date?"

"A couple of years. I thought they were the perfect couple."

"What happened?" Nicole asked.

"His bank moved him to a branch up in North Carolina. Charlotte, I think. A good career move for him, but the distance proved too much. They saw less and less of each other so, as with most long-distance relationships, it didn't last."

"How did she handle that?"

"At first, not well, but she got over it and moved on. I heard he did, too. Got married."

"She date anyone local?" I asked. "Anyone we should talk with about her?"

"A few. But, like I said, not many and not often."

I nodded.

"She did go out with Detective Munson a couple of times. You might talk with him."

"Terry Munson?"

"Yep. But then he's dated about everyone in town." She laughed. "Even asked me out a couple of times. Back before I was married."

"So, nothing serious?" Nicole asked. "Between Noleen and him?"

"Oh, no. Just a couple of dates. A few years back. Terry isn't a one-girl kind of guy."

"We heard that, too," I said.

"He's our local playboy." She smiled. "But Noleen knew that. I think she went out with him just for kicks. She knew nothing serious would come of it."

"I take it that's why you turned him down?" Nicole asked.

"Exactly. Plus, he isn't my type."

"Did they part on good terms?" I asked. "He and Noleen?"

"They did. We would still see him out and about. At a bar or restaurant. Sometimes with someone, sometimes flying solo. He'd always stop by and say hello to us, to Noleen." She paused as if considering something. "I think Noleen liked him okay. But, as I said, no future there."

"So, he didn't break her heart or anything like that?"

"No. Noleen wasn't easily swept off her feet. She was more grounded. Terry was all about the moment."

"And then he had to investigate her murder."

Patti nodded. "Sure did. I talked with him a couple of times."

"How'd he take it?" I asked. "Since they'd at least dated, did he seem uncomfortable?"

"Maybe. He was definitely concerned. I got the impression he took it personally. But, both he and Frank Clark are like that. They do a good job and seem to take everything around here personally."

"In my experience, a lot of small-town cops think that way," I said.

"I guess that's true. Not like big cities. In places like this, everyone knows everyone. Whether they dated or not." Another sigh. "My impression is that both Detective Munson and Detective Clark feel like this is their town and they're responsible for keeping things in order. Keeping everyone safe." She shook her head. "They definitely took Billy Wayne Baker personally."

"Makes sense."

"I remember running into Frank Clark once," Patti said. "A few months after the death of his wife. He was sitting in McGee's, having breakfast by himself. I sat with him for a few minutes. He was sad, stressed. Said he felt responsible for her death. In fact, for all three victims. Said they should have done more. I told him he was being too hard on himself. I asked him exactly what he thought they could have done." She looked at me. "He couldn't come up with a single thing. Not one." She shook her head. "I wouldn't have that job on a bet. Being a cop. The way I see it, you're damned if you do and damned if you don't."

Was that ever the truth. Tracking the bad guys versus invasion of privacy. Excessive force versus not protecting the citizenry. Strictly enforcing the law versus letting law-abiding folks bend the lines a little. Often making snap decisions, life-and-death ones, on dark streets, inside someone's home, anywhere and everywhere things go awry. And, getting second-guessed at every turn. Damned if they do and damned if they don't just about covered it.

"What about Noleen's brother?" I asked. "I understand he was critical of the police."

Patti smiled. "Critical would be the polite way to say it. He was furious. Basically tried to instigate a palace revolt."

"Detectives Clark and Munson told us about that," I said. "Said they understood but were somewhat surprised because they had been friends."

"That's true. Tommy Lee, Clark, and Munson go way back."

"Sounds to me like he and Noleen were close," Nicole said. "That could explain his reaction."

"That was always my take on it. I mean, he and Noleen had the usual sibling stuff, but they were indeed close. She was the big sister. Helped him out a lot."

"You mean financially?" I asked.

"No. Tommy Lee runs a successful business. He can take care of himself that way. Just being there for him. Advising him."

I nodded.

"When their parents died a few years ago, an auto accident up near Gainesville, coming back from a football game, they inherited a fairly large sum. So, neither Noleen nor Tommy Lee had financial problems."

"The parents had a sizable estate?"

"Sizable enough. Plus the house. They sold that almost immediately. Neither wanted to keep it, or live in it, for sure. So, they sold it and put the funds in the trust."

"A trust?" Nicole asked.

"Yeah. I handled it for them. It was shared. Equally. Noleen was the executor."

"Why her? Why not both?"

Patti smiled. "Their parents thought Noleen was more mature and had better money sense. And that's true."

"Money can be evil," I said. "No problems between them?"

Patti shook her head. "No. Like I said, each of them was doing fine without it." She hesitated for a couple of seconds. "Well, maybe except for the boat deal."

I looked at her and waited.

"Tommy Lee wanted to take some of his share to get a bigger boat. For his charter business. Noleen discouraged him. She felt that he had a good boat and that the charter business could be shaky. I agreed with her. She asked me to talk with him and I did. I told him that things like maintenance expenses, competition, the seasonal nature of the business, not to mention the rising insurance costs, could become problematic. Anyway, Noleen encouraged him to keep that money safe for a rainy day rather than expand his business." She shrugged. "Of course, after Noleen's death, he inherited all the money and bought the boat anyway."

"We saw it," I said. "Looks nice."

Patti shrugged.

"How much money are we talking about here?" Nicole asked.

Patti smiled. "You know I can't talk about that. Besides, I don't know. Not anymore. Tommy Lee moved all his accounts to a competitor shortly after Noleen's death."

CHAPTER THIRTY-ONE

ONCE OUTSIDE THE bank, I called Ray. Told him of our conversation. "Interesting," was his only response, but added that he and Pancake would look into Tommy Lee's finances. I didn't ask how. I knew. Pancake was going phishing. And hacking. And spoofing. Or was it spiffing? I could never keep all the techno-babble straight.

Earlier, as we walked to the bank, Nicole had called Sally Foster, Frank Clark's next-door neighbor, asking her if she was willing and had time to chat. Sure. She was off and would be home most of the day. In and out. To call before we headed over. Nicole did and we got the green light. As Nicole pulled into the drive, Sally Foster pushed open the front door.

The house was a small craftsman style, white with charcoal trim and a pair of dormer windows interrupting the roofline. Flowers filled the brick-lined planting areas to each side of the entry stoop. She beckoned us inside and we gathered in her living room. Two large multi-paned front windows made the room feel light and comfortable. Nicole and I sank into an overstuffed white sofa, Sally sat to our right in a plum-colored wingback chair. She offered coffee, but we declined.

On the coffee table I saw a collection of a half dozen snow globes. I picked up one. It was a Florida beach scene with two palm trees, a blue sky, and a yellow sun. I shook it. The "snow" swirled and then slowly settled over the trees and beach. Cool.

Nicole flashed me a look. Like a mom disciplining a five-year-old. I put the globe down. I never get to have fun.

"Sara gave me that one," Sally said. "I love it."

"It's cool," I said. "Snow in Florida."

Sally smiled. "It does happen. Rarely." She leaned back in her chair. "Betty Lou called me yesterday and said you might be coming by. She told me about your project."

"We'll have to thank her," Nicole said.

Sally smiled. "She does have her finger on the pulse on everything around here."

"And she's a funny lady," I said.

"She is. And a very decent soul."

"Thanks for seeing us," Nicole said.

"Your documentary sounds like something we could use. Not just this town, but everyone. I'm tired of Billy Wayne Baker being some kind of cult hero." She sighed. "Particularly with the younger crowd."

"He's not alone," I said. "Seems like the killers get all the ink. And TV coverage. Bundy, Gacy, Dahmer. It's a universal disease."

Sally smiled. "Hopefully, this will put an end to that."

"Probably not," Nicole said. "But maybe it'll make a dent."

"So, what can I tell you?" Sally asked.

"Betty Lou said you were close to Frank and Sara Clark."

"Oh, yes. My late husband and I considered them our closest friends. More than simply neighbors. And after my husband passed, Sara and Frank were lifesavers."

"Sorry about your loss," Nicole said.

"We were married twelve years when he got cancer. Lung. Took him in less than six months. It was an awful time."

"I suspect so," I said. "I lost my mom the same way."

Sally looked at me. "It's so sad. To watch them simply disappear. Eaten alive."

I remembered it well. Mom under ninety pounds before she passed. Not to mention the pain. Deep, dehumanizing, uncontrollable pain. Took all hope for a graceful exit off the table.

"Sara was my anchor," Sally continued. "Wouldn't let me drown in self pity. Made me saddle up and move on. At a time when giving up, crawling into bed, seemed the only option."

"That's what friends do," Nicole said.

"We became even closer after that."

"What about Frank?" I asked. "How did he handle Sara's death?"

"He was distraught. Sad. I had to be his anchor. Of sorts, anyway. We sat and talked many times. He managed to do his job, but his enthusiasm faded. I could see it. I'm sure the folks down at the police station could, too."

"You must have helped," Nicole said. "He seems like he's back at it full speed."

Sally smiled. "I hope so. But, the truth is, Frank is a tough guy. Always was. The kind that soldier on and do what's necessary. I think he would've landed on his feet anyway."

"Unlike what you and I went through," I said, "Sara's death was sudden, unexpected. I'm not sure which is worse."

She released a long, slow sigh. "Me, either."

"From everything we've heard, they were a perfect couple," Nicole said.

Sally gave a short laugh. "Not perfect. Frank worked too much. Drank more than Sara would've liked. But, overall, they were solid."

"But no real problems?" I asked.

"Nothing important. The usual couple stuff."

I saw her glance at Nicole. A look. Like she might have something else to say but couldn't—or wouldn't. I searched for some reasonable way to continue this thread without seeming too curious. I got nothing.

My cell buzzed. I pulled it from my pocket and glanced at the screen. For once, and only once, I was glad to see it was Tammy. She had a knack for calling at the exact worst time. Like when we were in New Orleans in the middle of a standoff with Tony Guidry and his crew. This could have been one of those, but right now, it was a welcome escape strategy. I felt leaving the two of them alone, for some girl talk, would be a good move. Never thought I'd think this, but God bless Tammy.

"Excuse me," I said. "I need to take this."

I walked outside.

* * *

Nicole waited until Jake pulled the front door closed. "And?" she asked.

"And what?"

"I got the impression you had more to say."

"No. Not really."

"No or not really?" Nicole smiled.

"I can't." She shook her head. "It wouldn't be right."

Nicole scooted to the edge of the sofa, leaning forward, resting her elbows on her knees. "It's just us. This goes nowhere else."

"You're doing a story on the victims and the families. How could it not go further?"

"It won't. I promise." Nicole looked down at the carpet for a beat and then back up to Sally. "Something's on your mind. Something that's heavy. I can see it. Something you've never told anyone before. Am I right?"

Tears gathered in Sally's eyes. She looked at the carpet, her head rotating slowly back and forth. "I can't. I just can't."

Nicole decided to roll the dice. She slid from the sofa, dropping to her knees before Sally. She grasped the woman's hands. Cold, trembling. She gave them a soft squeeze. "Whatever it is, it's eating you up. I can feel it. And it'll keep eating until you let it out."

Sally fought back tears. Not successfully. She said nothing for a full two minutes. Nicole could sense her internal struggle. She wanted to talk. Some secret that was obviously a heavy burden, evidenced by the slump of her shoulders, the sadness that etched her face, the tear trails that marked her cheeks.

Sally let out another long sigh. "Sara was seeing someone."

"As in an affair?"

Sally nodded.

"Who?"

Sally extricated her hands from Nicole's grip and shook her head. "I can't say."

"Again, can't or won't?"

Sally looked toward the front window. Nicole followed her gaze. Jake stood in the front yard, phone to his ear, an exasperated look on his face. One she had seen before. Tammy. She buried her smile.

Sally closed her eyes and rubbed both temples. Nicole held her breath, waited, letting Sally mentally play it out. Which way would she go? Open up or shut down? Nicole was hoping for the former but got the later.

"I can't," Sally said. "In fact, I've already said too much." Tears welled in her eyes. "I shouldn't have told you about Sara. It's not fair to her."

Nicole rose from her knees and returned to the sofa. "Did she tell you about the affair? Tell you who it was?"

"Yes, and no." She shrugged. "She did tell me she was seeing someone. She was very guilty about it. But she never said with who."

"So, you don't know?"

Sally hesitated. As if still wrestling with what to tell and what to keep hidden. "I can't say."

"You know," Nicole said. It wasn't a question.

Sally shook her head.

Nicole glanced across the living room toward the dining room window that faced the Clarks' home. "You saw him. Coming and going. Didn't you?"

Sally hesitated, then nodded.

"But you can't tell me who it was?"

Sally shook her head.

"Afraid of the backlash?" Nicole said. "Creating a stir?"

Another hesitation, then Sally said, "It would at least do that." Her gaze again dropped. "And for no real purpose. Talking about the past won't bring her back."

"Did Frank know?"

"No. Sara was sure of that."

Nicole struggled with whether to press Sally for more or back off and let it go for now. She felt that knowing was critical, but if she continued, Sally might feel cornered, or threatened. Which was better? Press on or leave the door open for another time? Finally, she said, "You can relax. Your secret's safe."

The front door swung open. Jake came in. Sally's shoulders jerked to attention and she wiped tears from her eyes with the back of one hand.

"What'd I miss?" Jake asked.

Nicole glanced at Sally. "We were just talking about how much she missed Sara." Nicole stood. "Sally, thanks for talking with us."

Sally stood. "I'm glad you came by." She laid a hand on Nicole's arm. "Gave me a chance to tell someone what a good person Sara was."

* * *

After we climbed in the car, I asked, "What was that about?"

"What?"

"Something went on in there after I left."

"You're not only cute, you're smart."

I shook my head as she fired up her Mercedes. "Are you going to tell me?"

"Sara was having an affair."

CHAPTER THIRTY-TWO

"WHAT DO YOU mean she was having an affair?" Pancake asked.

We were sitting at our de facto office—the gazebo near the marina.

"You know," Nicole said. "Boy, girl, clothes off, in bed. I'll draw you a diagram." She laughed.

"You're funny." Pancake looked at me. "She's funny, Jake." Then back to Nicole. "In a mean and evil sort of way."

"I told you," I said. "You just didn't believe me."

He bounced an eyebrow at Nicole. "But I do want to see your etchings."

"Speaking of affairs," Nicole said. "How about you and Laurie Mae?"

"Nice girl." He smiled.

"And? What did you guys do last night?"

"Went down the road here to a bar. Country music, beer, cowboy and cowgirl types."

"And?" Nicole wasn't going to let him off the hook that easily.

Pancake smiled. "Nice girl."

Ray jumped in, bringing the conversation back on point. "Who was Sara Clark seeing?"

"She wouldn't say," Nicole said.

"She say why she wouldn't tell?"

Nicole shrugged. "Small town. Dead friend's reputation. Expose someone else's infidelities. Create a stir where it's better to let things lie. Probably all those reasons."

Ray clasped his hands before him on the table. "How'd she find out?"

"Sara told her," Nicole said. "She was guilty and needed to tell someone. She and Sally were very close. Sara never told her with who, but Sally saw him, coming and going."

"So to speak," Pancake said.

Nicole smiled. "True."

"So, she knows who the guy is?" Ray asked

"Yes. But she wouldn't tell me more than that."

"Did she think Frank knew?" I asked.

"She said no, she didn't think so."

"But she's not sure?" Ray asked.

Nicole shook her head. "I doubt she could be sure."

"If he did, it would be a motive for murder," I said.

"Damn straight," Pancake agreed.

"Maybe you can chat with her again," Ray said. "After she's had time to think about things."

"I was thinking the same thing," Nicole said. "That's why I didn't press her harder."

"That's because you're smart." Ray smiled.

Nicole gave a mock bow.

Ray jerked his head toward Pancake. "Tell them what you uncovered today."

Pancake pulled some pages from a file folder and slid them toward me. The header said it was from Pine Key Farmers and

Merchants Bank. The one where Noleen Kovac had worked. Where she and her brother, Tommy Lee, had their accounts. The first two pages showed a listing of Noleen's accounts and balances. From back when she was alive. The third showed the same for Tommy Lee. And the final three showed an accounting of their joint trust.

"It looks like Noleen and Tommy Lee did business there for many years," Pancake said. "The entire time she worked there. The trust was set up over four years ago. By the parents shortly before they died." Pancake slid that page to one side and tapped it with his index finger. "You can see the original amount was just north of three hundred K."

"That's adult money," I said.

"True. And it didn't sit dormant. Noleen was the principal trustee and she made several investments—stocks, bonds, that sort of thing. Looks like she knew what she was doing because over a couple of years she made the two of them another sixty thousand."

"No withdrawals?" Nicole asked.

"None."

"That goes along with what Patti Ryan over at the bank told us," I said. "Tommy Lee wanted to use some, but Noleen discouraged him. Patti, too, for that matter."

"Well, his patience paid off," Pancake said. "Now, if you look at the bottom of each page, the accounts were zeroed out. Tommy Lee found another bank and moved everything there." He removed pages from another folder. "He transferred everything to Commerce National. After Noleen's death."

I examined the pages. Tommy Lee had set up three accounts. Personal checking and savings—where most of the trust money ended up—and a business account under Kovac's Charters. The balances in each were healthy.

"Shortly after getting the inheritance stuff worked out and after moving the money to his new bank, Tommy Lee transferred a hundred K to his business account and traded his old boat for the new one."

"Could be a motive for murder," I said. "If we assume the sister was blocking the money going to him—and as executor I assume she could do that—then taking her out of the picture leaves Tommy Lee free to do as he pleases."

"That's a hefty motive for sure," Pancake said.

"So, what're we saying?" I asked. "That Clark killed his wife and Tommy Lee killed his sister?"

"Maybe," Pancake said.

"But, they both have alibis," Nicole said. "Tommy Lee was out on the water when Noleen was killed and Clark was on a bridge with a load of witnesses when his wife was murdered. At least, that's what he said."

"We could ask him again," Ray said. "Make sure. If we can do it without creating suspicion."

"I might have another way," Pancake said. "I ran across a newspaper article about that accident. We could chat with the reporter. I forget her name, but she works for the local paper. She was there. That'd give us an independent corroboration of Clark's alibi."

"That's not really the problem," I said. "In both murders, Billy Wayne's DNA was present. Right? So, Clark I get, but how would Tommy Lee frame Billy Wayne? He had no access to the evidence."

"He does know Frank Clark," Pancake said.

"That well?" Nicole asked.

"They do go way back," I said.

"But way back and well enough to help him frame someone for murder are two different things," she said.

I couldn't argue with that. It was a big leap. Not impossible, but without some other connection, unlikely. "Maybe he paid Clark to help him?"

Pancake shook his head. "Didn't see anything like that. No big cash withdrawals. And these things are usually handled that way. Ten, twenty thousand disappears and someone ends up dead." He scratched his chin. "Nothing like that in any of these records."

"Maybe he had a cash stash at home?" I said.

"Like in a coffee can?" Nicole asked.

"Funny. I suspect a lot of his business is cash. Tips and things like that for sure. If he wanted to keep that income off the books, he'd avoid putting it in the bank."

Pancake nodded. "Probably not a coffee can, but maybe a home safe."

Ray gathered up the documents, scanning each. "There's some truth in that. Over a few years, he could've easily accumulated several thousand. And, when he needed it, it was right there." He squared the pages and placed them on the table. "But that doesn't feel right to me." We all looked at him. "I don't see Clark potentially trashing his career, or his life, for a few grand."

"Maybe it wasn't money," I said.

"How so?" Ray asked.

"What if Clark helped Tommy Lee with his problem in exchange for Tommy Lee helping him? Clark supplies the DNA and Tommy Lee does the killings? For himself and for Clark?"

"Interesting."

"I'm just thinking out loud," I said.

"That's actually clever," Ray said.

Did he say that? Did I hear him correctly? Ray saying I had a brilliant idea. Well, not all the way to brilliant, but clever is a huge step.

"That wouldn't require moving any money around," Pancake said.

"But it requires a conspiracy between Clark and Tommy Lee," Ray said. "And if Tommy Lee did do both murders, his alibi would have to be trashed. We'd have to show he wasn't on the water the night his sister was killed." Ray sighed. "And he'd need to be available for Sara Clark's murder."

"But if he did," I said, "Clark could easily plant the DNA when he worked the scene."

Ray nodded. "Very easily."

"*Strangers on a Train*," Nicole said.

"What?" I asked.

"The Hitchcock movie. Two strangers decide to kill each other's wives."

"Good movie," Pancake said. "Based on the Patricia Highsmith novel."

"Yes," Nicole said. "Raymond Chandler did the screenplay."

Pancake nodded. "Starred Farley Granger and Robert Walker."

How'd they know all this? I barely remembered the movie. And I would've never pulled Farley Granger out of my ass.

"You're thinking Clark and Tommy Lee might have cooked something like that up?" Ray asked.

Nicole gave a one-shouldered shrug. "I'm saying it's happened before. At least in a movie."

Ray tapped a finger on the table. "Since both apparently have alibis for when their wife or sister were murdered, they could have done exactly that. Clark takes care of Tommy Lee's problem and Tommy Lee takes care of Clark's wife. Clark supplies the DNA in both cases." He shook his head. "Not sure I buy it, but then again, I've seen stranger stuff."

"How could we prove that?" I asked.

"First step would be to check out alibis," Ray said. "If they did something like that, and, again, I'm not saying I completely buy into it, they would each need alibis for the time of the murders."

"And the other one would have to be off the grid, so to speak," I said.

"Exactly," Ray said. "The questions then become, what were Clark's and Tommy Lee's alibis for the murders? Where were they when the wife and sister were killed? Were their alibis solid?"

"Clark was working a shoplifting and then an auto accident when his wife was killed," Pancake said. "Chief Morgan and Munson both confirmed that. Maybe that reporter will, too. Tommy Lee was out on a night charter when his sister was murdered. So he says."

"But, where was Tommy Lee when Sara was murdered?" Nicole asked. "And Clark when Noleen was?"

"There you go," Ray said. "That's what we should focus on. The key is doing it without pinging anyone's radar."

"Especially Clark's," I said.

"So, we know where Clark was the night his wife was murdered," Nicole said. "At least it seems so. But where was he the night Noleen was killed?"

"That could be a trickier question," Ray said.

"What about Tommy Lee?" I asked. "How do we check out his alibi? And find out where he was the night Sara was killed?"

"We need to see his schedule book," Pancake said.

"And how are we going to do that?"

"I bet he runs his business out of his home. At least, he doesn't have an office or anything like that so I suspect that's the case."

"Okay, so?" I asked.

"We need to take a look-see," Pancake said.

"What? Break into his house?"

Pancake smiled, nodded toward Ray. "Ain't like we never did it before."

"Why do I think that could get messy?" I asked.

"Oh, ye of little faith," Pancake said. "I got me an idea. Sit tight. I'll be back."

I watched as he walked toward the marina and down the dock. Tommy Lee's boat sat at the end, Tommy Lee onboard, working.

CHAPTER THIRTY-THREE

"How's it going?" Pancake asked.

Tommy Lee looked up. He was flushing out his bait tank, his tee shirt wet, hands grimy. "Oh, hey."

"Looks like you're prepping to head out."

"Got a charter later today."

"Business must be good."

"It's the busy season. Got to make hay while the sun shines." Tommy Lee wiped his hands on a stained, light-blue towel, then used it to swipe sweat from his face. "How about a beer?"

"Sounds good."

"Come on board."

Pancake sat on the rear seat. Tommy Lee stepped below and returned with a pair on PBR longnecks. He handed one to Pancake and then twisted the cap off his. He took a couple of gulps, then rolled the bottle across his forehead. "Hot as a bitch today."

"Sure is." Pancake opened his bottle and downed half of it in a series of gulps. "Good. Thanks."

"Looks like your face is healing okay," Tommy Lee said. "Can't hardly see it now."

"Amazing what rubbing a little dirt on it will do."

"Ain't that the truth. So, how's your film stuff going?"

"Fine. Slow, but fine." He waved a hand. "I like your boat."

"Yeah, she's a good one."

"I think you said you picked it up a couple of years ago. Right?"

Tommy Lee nodded. "Got a good deal. Couldn't turn it down."

"Still looks brand new."

"Got to take care of your equipment. Folks expect a comfortable ride." He smiled. "And lots of fish."

"I suspect you know all the best spots."

"That I do." Tommy Lee climbed into one of the fishing chairs, swiveled it toward Pancake, gently rocking it back and forth. "Like today. Got a couple of guys from over in Orlando. I'm taking them out late today. Do a little evening fishing." He pointed south. "Maybe a dozen miles that way's an excellent cove. Always good luck there." He smiled. "A very few others know about it."

"I worked on a fishing boat once," Pancake said.

"Really?"

"Back in high school. Summer job. It was actually a shrimp boat." Another slug of beer. "Hard work. Kept me in shape for football."

Tommy Lee laughed. "It'll do that." He opened one hand and looked at his palm. "Rough on the hands though."

"I remember it well."

"Too bad you guys aren't from here. I could use another hand. I got one guy who's pretty reliable. Not always available though. Otherwise I have to grab whatever yahoo I can find. Mostly kids. Not very experienced. Or interested. Kids seem to be lazy now' days." He scratched an ear. "Truth is that sometimes I think I do better with just me."

"Lot of work."

"True. That's why an experienced hand would be a good thing."

Pancake leaned back, the longneck scissored between two fingers, dangling. "I'm probably too soft for that now."

"You don't look soft to me," Tommy Lee said.

"I do visit the gym. Lift a little." Pancake opened one hand, inspecting it. "But this P.I. work isn't all that manual. Makes your hands soft, for sure."

"What exactly do you guys do? I mean, what does a P.I. do?"

"Not this consulting stuff. This is a first for us. Mostly we look into cheating spouses, bank shenanigans, some criminal investigations for defense attorneys. That sort of stuff."

"Not sure I could do that."

Pancake smiled. "It does take a certain attitude. Of course, rummaging around in folks' dirty laundry often makes you want to take a shower."

"That's my point."

"What do you charge for a charter?" Pancake asked.

"Depends on how many, and how long."

"What if we wanted to hire you? The four of us. A half day."

"Two grand."

"Sounds good. We might want to do that. If you have the time."

"Wouldn't be for a couple of days, but we could make that happen."

"You have an office? A secretary? How would we set it up?"

"No office. No secretary. Just me. I run everything out of my home." He tilted the bottle toward Pancake. "I probably won't get back before maybe ten tonight. Call me first thing tomorrow morning. I'll check my schedule and we'll set it up."

"Sounds good." Pancake stood. "Good luck tonight."

Tommy Lee nodded.

"Thanks for the beer. I owe you one."

"No problem."

Pancake stepped off the boat. "Call you tomorrow."

CHAPTER THIRTY-FOUR

THE REPORTER FOR the *Pine Key Breeze*, the local twice-weekly newspaper, turned out to be Gloria Whitt. Based on her list of credits, she seemed to be their primary contributor. Mostly stories on local happenings. Things like restaurant reviews, social and fund-raising events, city council meetings, human interest pieces, as well as local crime reports. She had a broad range, it seemed. Pancake had located the article she wrote about the accident on the bridge that Clark and Munson had investigated the night Sara Clark was murdered. It contained quotes from each detective, indicating they had indeed been there. But for how long?

Ray dispatched Nicole and me to talk with Gloria while he and Pancake continued their snooping into Tommy Lee and Frank Clark. Was there a connection between the two? If so, what?

The newspaper's office occupied half of a low, white clapboard duplex on Main Street, practically across the street from Woody's. Nicole and I found Gloria inside, sitting at a corner desk, facing her computer. She wore a lemon blouse beneath a dark blue cardigan, buttoned, sleeves pushed up to her elbows. Very sedate and professional. Incongruously, purple streaks highlighted her short, light brown hair, and a row of multi-colored ear studs lined the arch of her right ear. A Bluetooth device clung to the left one, its short microphone extending along her cheek. She spoke and typed at the same time. She glanced up as we approached, briefly raised a finger, and went on with what she was doing. We hung back and waited. When she completed the call, she returned her gaze to us.

"You're the ones that're making that documentary?" she asked.

"That's right," Nicole said.

"Actually, I've been looking for you two."

"You have?"

"Yeah. I wanted to do a piece on you and what you're doing. I think our readers would like that."

"That would be nice," Nicole said.

"If you have the time, it won't take but a few minutes. Does that work?"

"Perfectly," Nicole said.

For the next ten minutes we answered her questions. Who we were, what Regency Global Productions was all about and what their interest in the story was, what the slant of the production would be, things like that. She typed away as we talked. She interrupted her questioning twice to answer incoming calls, telling each she'd get back to them as soon as possible. Her multitasking skills were impressive.

Finally, she said, "This is good stuff. I'll get something ready for the next edition." She looked at me, then Nicole. "How rude of me. Here I am babbling on about my work when I'm sure you didn't come in here for that."

"Seems to me that you're pretty good at what you do," I said.

She laughed. "I try. And I do love it." She unclipped the earpiece and rested it on the desktop. Its blue light pulsed slowly. "So, what can I do for you?"

"We're doing research for the documentary," Nicole said. "Trying to get a better feel for how the murders affected the town. We thought that if anyone knew, it would be you."

"Tore it up. As simple as that." She sighed. "Things are better now, but we're not near back to normal."

"Hopefully, the documentary will offer some healing."

"From what you said, I suspect that'll be the case." One sleeve of her sweater had drifted downward and she shoved it back up to her elbow. "How can I help?"

"We read your articles on the killings," I said. "Very good reporting."

"Thanks."

"I particularly liked the interview you did with Detective Clark," Nicole said.

"That was a tough one. Frank's a good guy. Sara's murder did a number on him." She looked down and shook her head. "We sat down the next day. He was still shell shocked, I think. It was a tough interview."

"It read like that."

"I mean, coming home, finding your wife strangled? Does it get any worse?"

"No," I said. "I don't think it does."

"We talked with him," Nicole said. "He told us it had been a strange day already. Some shoplifters, then a big accident out on the bridge. Then, finding Sara."

"In fact," I said, "we read the article you did on that accident."

"It was a mess. Fortunately, there were no major injuries, but the three cars that tangled jammed up the traffic. Took nearly three hours to get things back to normal."

"You were there all that time?"

"Mostly. Actually helped push a couple of the cars off the roadway." She laughed. "The life of a reporter."

"That's what Clark said. Said he was tied up there for a couple of hours. Investigating the accident, getting the traffic moving."

She gave a quick nod. "He and Terry Munson were both there."

"The entire time?"

She glanced toward the ceiling, as if recalling the incident. "Yeah. I talked with both of them." She looked at me. "Why?"

"Clark told us he was, even today, wishing he hadn't been there," I said. "That maybe if he'd been home, Sara would be alive."

She offered a grim half smile. "He beat himself up over that. I talked with him a few times. Not just for the article but here and there when our paths crossed. Which they do frequently. He knows all the juicy stuff on any criminal activity around here. Which means stolen bikes and knocked-over trash cans." She laughed. "Teenagers being teenagers. Anyway, I told him over and over that there was no way he could've known so it wasn't his fault." She pursed her lips and gave a slight headshake. "But guilt can be irrational."

"That's the truth," I said.

"So, yeah, they were there. Along with a couple of dozen volunteers."

"Volunteers?" Nicole asked.

"The stranded motorists got out to help. Also, a few folks who'd heard about the pileup came out to help. Small towns stick together."

"I'm sure Clark and Munson appreciated the help," I said.

"They did." She hesitated, smiled. "In fact, I remember that, as soon as we got the bridge open, they had to hightail it back to the station and deal with those shoplifters. They barely made it back before the parents showed up to retrieve them. Drove up from Mexico Beach, if I remember correctly."

"That's what Clark told us," I said. "And, I understand the girls had to come back for several weekends of community service."

Another laugh. "Sure did. Which I thought was a good lesson for them. I did a piece on that, too. Talked with the parents. They were definitely onboard with the punishment."

"Bet that ended their shoplifting careers," I said.

She shrugged. "You ask me, maybe for two of them. The third, she was actually the youngest of the three, I don't think so."

"Really?"

"She had an attitude. One that said her life wasn't going to go so well." Another shrug. "Not overly repentant. I remember her father. Single parent. Nice guy but passive. Way overmatched by his daughter. I felt sorry for him. I suspected the daughter would butt heads with the law again before too long. Seemed to be her nature. But, that was just my take. I could be wrong."

"I bet you have a pretty good handle on people," Nicole said. "Reporters usually do."

"Maybe. I sure hope so." She laughed. "My mother always said I was too naive and trusting for my own good. She's still amazed I make a living at this."

CHAPTER THIRTY-FIVE

WE LEFT GLORIA Whitt to her work. Before we had taken a dozen steps away from her desk, she had replaced the earpiece and busied herself with returning calls. I waved from the door. She nodded.

I called Ray. He and Pancake were at Woody's. Said it was happy hour and Pancake was hungry. Shocking.

We found them at a deck table, Ray with a Corona, Pancake with PBR and a platter of fried calamari that looked like a pack of pit bulls had marched through it. Only remnants remained.

Pancake pushed the plate away. "I would've saved you some, but I didn't."

Nicole punched his shoulder and then sat next to him. "Would've been disappointed if you had."

"They have more," he said.

He waved a hand. Laurie Mae headed our way. I noticed she more or less nestled up against Pancake. Hip to his shoulder.

"Welcome," she said. "Something to drink?"

Nicole ordered her usual. A sixteen-ouncer. This one black raspberry. Me a Maker's Mark on the rocks.

"I'll have another," Pancake said. "And maybe some nachos."

"Love a man with an appetite." Laurie Mae smiled. Her gaze held Pancake's for a couple of seconds. "Anything for anyone else?"

Shrimp tacos all around. Laurie Mae motored toward the kitchen, waylaid briefly by a table that ordered another round of drinks.

"She likes you," Nicole said.

Pancake spread his hands open. "Why wouldn't she?"

Nicole laughed. "Can't think of a single reason why not."

"Let's get caught up," Ray said. He nodded toward me.

"Gloria Whitt, the reporter, remembered the night well. Even that the three shoplifters had been arrested that night."

"Good memory," Ray said.

"She's sharp." I glanced at Nicole, who nodded her agreement. "Even if her mother doesn't think so."

Ray gave me a quizzical look.

"Something she said. Apparently, her mother thinks she's naive. Regardless, she said both Clark and Munson were there for several hours. Then they both returned to the station in time to talk with the girls' parents."

"Which means if the ME was right about Sara Clark's time of death, Clark had a pretty solid alibi." He glanced at Pancake. "Wonder if Tommy Lee can say the same."

"So, you're buying into that they might've exchanged murders?" I asked.

Ray took a slug from his beer. "Not buying into anything. Not rejecting it either."

Pancake pointed toward the marina. I looked that way. Backlit by the late afternoon sunlight, Tommy Lee stood on the dock, waiting for three men to board his boat. I didn't see a mate so assumed Tommy Lee was making the run solo.

"Looks like Tommy Lee's charter is ready to go," Pancake said. "I suspect we'll know his schedule pretty soon."

"You're actually going to break into his house?" I asked.

He leaned back, folding his thick arms over his thicker chest. "Unless you got another plan?"

I didn't.

"He runs his business from his home so everything we need should be there. Not only if he was indeed out on the water the night his sister was murdered, but also where he might've been the night of Sara Clark's killing."

I now saw Tommy Lee's boat crank up and pull away from the dock, the reflected sunlight burnishing its wake.

"Nicole and I'll scrape together the bail money," I said.

"You're funny," Pancake said. "Ain't he funny, Ray?" Ray nodded. "Not as funny as Nicole, but funny."

"We'll need you guys to stay here." Ray waved a hand. "Somewhere around here. Keep an eye out and let us know if Tommy Lee comes back early for some reason."

"I suspect he'll be gone for a few hours," I said.

"Likely." Ray gave a nod. "But contingencies must be covered."

So Ray.

CHAPTER THIRTY-SIX

RAY AND PANCAKE tugged on latex gloves as they crossed Tommy Lee's backyard. Dark and quiet. Getting in proved easy. No alarm. Cheesy-ass lock. Took Ray all of thirty seconds to click open the rear door and they were inside. No alarm system to deal with.

Ray and Pancake had returned to the hotel, changed into dark clothes, and waited for darkness. They decided to walk over to Tommy Lee's place. Only a half a dozen blocks from Main Street. Seemed everything in Pine Key was near Main Street. Walking meant no vehicle to keep up with and allowed for escape into the trees behind Tommy Lee's property if necessary. You just never knew.

The door opened into a small kitchen, a few dirty dishes piled in the sink, but otherwise neat and well ordered. Beyond was a dining room, large living room, and a hallway that led to three bedrooms. One had been converted into an office. On the desk sat an iMac and Tommy Lee's schedule ledger. Green canvas cover, "2018" in block print on the front. Inside were weekly pages, most days filled with charters, each with neat block printing that gave the name of the customer, their addresses and contact info, and credit card numbers. Today's clients were under the name Scott Hansen from Orlando.

Ray tugged open the left-side drawers, finding a stack of similar books. 2017 was blue, 2016 red. Ray flipped open the latter. He thumbed to February and the date Tommy Lee's sister, Noleen, drew her last breath. Morning and then an evening charter. Guy named Wayne Ripley. Tampa address. Ray snapped a picture of the page with his phone. Then on to March and the night Sara Clark was killed. Morning charter, afternoon and evening free. He grabbed another image.

"He was out on the water the night his sister went down," Ray said.

"But free for Sara Clark," Pancake said.

"How convenient."

Pancake grunted.

In the lower right drawer, a small metal box yielded a stack of bills. Ray counted them. Just north of $1,300.

"Boy had cash," Pancake said.

"Probably not enough to hire a killer," Ray said.

"Maybe he spent that a couple of years ago."

Ray searched the other drawers, finding the usual office stuff, a couple of paperbacks, a stack of business cards.

And then struck gold.

In the middle drawer. Flip phone. No doubt a burner.

"Got a phone here," Ray said. He held it up.

"What'd he do with it? Play street hockey?"

It had definitely seen better days. Scratched, dented, the alignment of the two halves slightly off.

"He does work on a boat."

"Maybe he used it for a bobber," Pancake said.

Ray opened it. The screen was cracked but it lit up.

"At least it works." Ray immediately checked the call history. Well, well. Only one number was registered. Two calls in the past four days. One outgoing, one incoming. Before those nothing since early 2016. Total of eighteen calls, from late January until the last day of March.

Pancake, looking over his shoulder, said, "Isn't that interesting?"

Ray closed the phone. "Lots of communication around the final two murders here in Pine Key."

"Conspiracies require conversation," Pancake said. "And then there's the new ones. Started the day after we arrived."

"Someone's nervous."

"Gotta admit, I was skeptical about that, but this changes my mind."

"Sure does." Ray looked at the phone, turned it over in his hand. "What do you think we should do?"

"Take the fucking thing."

"If he misses it, it'll let him know something is up."

"A little pressure never hurts. Maybe he'll do something stupid." Ray nodded.

"Either way, we can track the other number," Pancake said.

"Probably another burner."

"That'd be my bet."

Ray slipped the phone in his pocket. They searched the other rooms, finding nothing of interest. Back in the kitchen, Ray said, "Let's go."

They worked their way into the trees that lined the rear of the property and circled behind Tommy Lee's neighbor before reaching a cross street. They turned toward town.

"Maybe we should simply make a call," Pancake said. "See who answers."

"Right after we try to track down the owner."

"Won't be able to. Maybe when and where the phone was purchased, but unless we get lucky, that'll be it."

"Let's hope for luck."

They made it only a half block down Elm when car lights washed over them. They moved to the shoulder, no curb here, just mowed grass. The car stopped beside them. The passenger window slid down.

Frank Clark.

"How you guys doing?" Clark asked.

Ray walked to the window, bending down. "Out for a walk."

Clark nodded. "Nice night for it."

Ray glanced up the street. "Nice little community you have here. Everything is so neat and well kept."

"That's true. Folks do take pride in their homes."

"What about you?" Ray asked. "Making your patrols?"

"Yep." Clark scratched one ear. "Nothing ever happens, but I do love driving around after the town has settled in for the night. Quiet and peaceful."

Ray gave a soft laugh. "I suspect that's true."

"Give you a lift?"

"No. Thanks. We're enjoying the evening."

Clark hesitated, gave a nod. "Take care." He drove away, turning left at the next street.

"Think he knew we were here?" Pancake asked.

"Maybe. More likely it's just what he said. Routine patrol."

Ray's phone chirped. Incoming text from Jake: APPROACHING DOCK.

Tommy Lee was back.

CHAPTER THIRTY-SEVEN

NICOLE AND I had returned to the hotel with Ray and Pancake. Nicole grabbed a sweater and we headed to Woody's while Ray and Pancake planned their assault on all things Tommy Lee. We put on our casual, no-worries personas, briefly chatted with Betty Lou, and then returned to the gazebo. After an hour my butt went to sleep from sitting so long. We wandered along the piers, inspecting the boats. Everything from sailboats, to small runabouts, to fully rigged fishing boats—like Tommy Lee's. Around sunset, we relocated to the gazebo, which afforded us a direct view of the marina and the Gulf. Each time a boat appeared, and there were only three that did so, our collective heart rates went up until we saw it wasn't Tommy Lee. Around nine, Betty Lou came down the stairs and walked toward us, a tower of glasses in one hand, a bottle of bourbon in the other.

"Mind if I join you?" she asked.

"Looks like you have the right ticket," Nicole said, nodding at the bourbon.

"That ain't all." She reached into her jacket pocket and pulled out half a dozen cigars.

"Betty Lou, you're the best," I said.

She laughed. "That I am."

She unstacked the glasses and poured a generous portion in three of them. "Where's Ray and Pancake?" she asked.

I glanced at Nicole. "Working. Computer stuff."

"They'll be here soon," Nicole said.

"Laurie Mae sure seems taken with Pancake," Betty Lou said.

"I think it's mutual," I said.

"Seems like a nice guy."

"He is," I said. "Known him all my life."

"Good to know."

Nicole looked at her. "Don't worry. Pancake's one of the good guys. Whatever happens between them, he'll treat her right."

Betty Lou gave a nod.

"And if he doesn't," Nicole said, "I'll kick his ass."

That drew one of Betty Lou's wonderful laughs.

We each lit a cigar.

Betty Lou took a couple of puffs, leaned back in her chair. "I love nights like this."

"What's not to like," Nicole said.

"It's why I live here." She puffed her cigar. "And why I ain't never lived anywhere else." She shrugged. "Too old and too entrenched to move." A sip of whiskey, a lick of her lips. "Not that I ever would,"

"Reminds me of Gulf Shores," I said. "Only smaller and quieter."

"It is that." She tilted her glass toward the Gulf. "Here comes Tommy Lee back in."

I looked that way. In the darkness I could only see the faint hint of a wake, a boat for sure, but no way I could identify it. "How do you know it's him?"

"By the sound." She clamped her cigar between her teeth. It bobbed as she spoke. "I know every boat here. They're all a little different. Tommy Lee's got that big old motor. Hard to miss him."

I pulled out my phone and shot a text to Ray. Two words: APPROACHING DOCK. He immediately replied: BE THERE IN 5. I sent back: GAZEBO.

I glanced at Nicole. "Ray and Pancake are on the way."

"Good." Betty Lou smiled. "I hate for those other glasses and cigars to go to waste."

They didn't. Ray and Pancake arrived. So did Laurie Mae. Over the next hour we finished off the cigars and killed the bottle of whiskey. It was nearing ten thirty.

Ray stood. "As usual, it's been a pleasure." He looked at Pancake. "But we have some work to do."

"This time of night?" Betty Lou asked.

Ray smiled. "We manage to work odd hours."

Pancake gave Laurie Mae a hug. "This'll only take an hour. Tops. Want to hit that bar again after that?"

She smiled. "You bet. I'll meet you there."

"Unless Dad has a curfew for us." Pancake nodded toward Ray.

"You and Jake never heeded curfews when you were kids," Ray said. "Don't see any reason you would now."

We said our goodnights to Betty Lou, thanking her for the goodies, helped ferry the empty glasses and whiskey bottle up to the restaurant, and headed back to the hotel. We gathered in Ray's room.

Ray discussed the cash Tommy Lee had on hand, and what it might, or might not, mean. The consensus was that it was simply business as usual for Tommy Lee. Wouldn't be remnants of any payments to Clark as that would've been two years ago. Then, Pancake worked his laptop, while Ray made a couple of calls.

"Okay, we got it," Ray said. "Both phones were purchased together. January 2016. A mom-and-pop store in Panama City. Cash. No record of the buyer."

"How do you know that?" I asked.

Ray gave a half smile. "Just have to know the right people to call."

Of course.

"Means they can't be traced," Pancake said.

"Figures," I said.

"And after two years there won't be any security videos at the store," Ray said. "Even if they have such a system." He gave a quick nod. "But all is not lost. This phone only has one number stored and has only ever called or received calls from that number."

"The other phone?" Nicole asked.

"Exactly," Ray said. "Which means these phones are incestuously linked."

"Makes a murder swap that much more likely," Pancake said.

"Are we saying that Tommy Lee and whoever has the other phone are in league with each other?" Nicole asked. "Killed for each other?"

Ray nodded. "Looks that way. Look at the timeline. The phones were purchased in January. A month after Loretta Swift was murdered and a month before Noleen Kovac's killing."

"You're thinking Tommy Lee and Frank Clark planned this after they saw an opportunity to blame both killings on Billy Wayne?" I asked.

"That'd be my guess," Ray said. "Look at it from their point of view. Tommy Lee wants all the inheritance, but his sister's in the way. Frank Clark knows his wife is cheating and wants out of the marriage. Maybe even exact some form of revenge." Ray opened his hands, palms up. "Old story. Greed and revenge."

"How do we prove that?" Nicole asked.

"By finding the other phone," Ray said.

"What about fingerprints?"

Ray shook his head. "Odds are the two cells were only in the same place shortly after they were purchased. That was two years ago.

And from the looks of this one, it's been through a lot. No way it would've held prints that long."

"Maybe we can find out who might've been up in Panama City the day they were purchased," I said.

"Could've been Tommy Lee," Ray said. "I checked his schedule book, and he had no charters that day."

"What about Frank Clark?" Nicole asked.

Ray sighed. "Don't see a way we can get to his work schedule without exposing our agenda."

"And creating backlash," Pancake said.

"So, the key is discovering who has the other phone," I said. "How are we going to do that?"

"Let's start by making a call," Pancake said.

"To who?" I asked.

Pancake raised an eyebrow. "To whoever answers."

He picked up the burner.

"You sure?" I asked. "Won't that put them on notice?"

"And shake his tree," Ray said. "I like that." He gave Pancake a go-ahead nod.

Pancake turned on the speaker function, held up a finger to silence everyone, and made the call, the phone now lying flat on his palm. Took five rings before an answer came.

"What's up?" The voice crackled and fuzzed, barely audible. As if the speaker had been damaged somewhere along the line. Made sense from the look of it.

Each of us held our breath.

"Tommy Lee? What's going on?"

Silence.

"Tommy Lee?"

Pancake disconnected the call. "Anybody recognize that voice?"

I shook my head. "Don't see how. It was so broken up and raspy."

"It was male," Ray said. "That's about all I could tell."

The burner rang. Even the ring crackled. Pancake again activated the speaker and clicked the answer button.

"Tommy Lee?" The same voice.

No response.

"What the hell is going on?" Pause. "Quit fucking around." Another pause. "What the hell is wrong with you? This isn't funny."

We waited him out. His breathing, now ramped up a notch, hissed and popped through the speaker. The call ended.

Pancake closed the phone.

"Now we wait and see if that puts a few ripples in the pond," Ray said.

CHAPTER THIRTY-EIGHT

WHAT THE HELL was that about? Why would Tommy Lee call at this hour? Why would he call at all? Why wouldn't he talk? Maybe the mic was out on his phone. They were cheap, after all. And two years old. Actually, more. But they had worked fine a few days ago. Could be Tommy Lee hadn't charged it in a while. No, that couldn't be it or it wouldn't have worked at all.

This wasn't a dead mic or battery.

It all felt wrong. Sounded wrong. Someone was there, listening, waiting. He had no doubts there.

Answering had been a mistake. But how was he to know? Only Tommy Lee had access to the phone, or even knew it existed. When it buzzed, vibrating the drawer in his bedside table, he simply reached for it, flipped it open, thinking Tommy Lee had urgent news. Or a problem.

Why did he say anything? Why not answer and wait for Tommy Lee to speak? But, no, he had to open his mouth. Shit, he'd even used Tommy Lee's name.

And then called back.

Stupid.

He'd only gotten home an hour ago, been asleep for a half hour, max. Just enough to fall into a deep dreamless trough. Where the brain didn't function very quickly. If he'd been awake he might've handled it better.

Too late to backtrack now. What was done was done. But what did it mean?

He swung out of bed, feet on the floor. He could blame it on being asleep, brain fuzzy, not thinking clearly, but what difference did that make? He'd fucked up.

Or was he making too much of this? Could be a faulty phone. Could be Tommy Lee dialed by accident. Maybe a pocket dial. Not likely on the old clamshell type. And even if that was possible, why did Tommy Lee answer when he returned the call? And say nothing.

Fuck, fuck, fuck.

The big question, the scary question, was if Tommy Lee wasn't the caller, who was? Was it someone who could recognize his voice? Even worse, had Tommy Lee flipped on him? Had someone dug up the phone, learned what they had done? Leaned on Tommy Lee? He wasn't the smartest guy. Or the toughest. Under pressure he would fold. He knew that from the beginning. But, to get done what needed doing, he'd needed Tommy Lee.

The plan had been perfect. Not a single flaw. Only he and Tommy Lee knew who did what, when, and how. A fact that had been buried for over two years now.

Something had changed. He felt it in his gut, and his gut was never wrong.

Now, his gut spoke to him. Only one real possibility. Those two private investigators. That's what had changed. He knew about Ray Longly. Smart guy. Thorough guy from what he had learned. And he was here, roaming all over town. Talking, asking questions. Had he uncovered something? Had he cracked Tommy Lee? That guy with him, Pancake, looked like he could crack anyone. Literally.

He massaged his temples. What to do?

He walked to the bathroom and splashed water on his face. Looked in the mirror. Was that fear he saw? That ramped up his pulse, now pounding behind his eyes?

There was a single truth in play here. Secrets, dark secrets, can only be kept by a single person. Anyone else with that knowledge was a liability. Simple as that. A liability that must be eliminated.

He had to see Tommy Lee. Face-to-face. Gauge what's what. And, if necessary, fix it.

Unless it was a trap. Tommy Lee spills his guts, makes the call, sets the snare. But, if so, why didn't he say anything? Wouldn't he have said that he needed to talk? That something big had changed?

He saw no perfect answer here. Anything he did, or didn't do, could come back on him.

Driving over and knocking on Tommy Lee's door wasn't an option. If it was a trap, he could walk himself right into prison. The irony? He could end up in Raiford with Billy Wayne Baker.

Jesus, what a clusterfuck.

He dressed in all black, grabbed his backup weapon, a .38 snub nose. Purchased for cash, no records, at that gun show up in Pensacola. Years ago. Numbers filed off. Untraceable.

He melted into the trees behind his home and circled the town's perimeter. Staying in the shadows, he made his way the six blocks to Tommy Lee's.

He squatted beneath a scrub pine, surveying the situation, letting his pulse settle. The house was dark. Mostly. A slight glow fell through the kitchen window. The light coming from deeper in the house. The living room where he knew Tommy Lee always left a lamp on at night. No shadows, no movement.

He pulled the gun from his jacket pocket, took a deep breath, and hesitated. What would he find inside? Tommy Lee, his phone on the fritz, giving up, going to bed, now sound asleep? Or a welcoming committee?

The back door was unlocked. Apparently, Tommy Lee wasn't very security conscious. Hell, no one in town was. Maybe they were for a while after Billy Wayne showed up, but old habits have a way of seeping back in.

The kitchen, dining room, and living room were quiet. The hall empty, another small night-light in the bathroom to his right. Tommy Lee's room dark, and the man himself sprawled facedown on his bed, wearing only boxers, covers mostly kicked to the floor.

He tapped Tommy Lee's leg with the .38's muzzle. He stirred. He tapped again and Tommy Lee rolled over, eyes squinted, confusion on his face.

"What's going on?" Tommy Lee asked. His voice thick with sleep.

"That's what I want to ask you."

"What?" He swung his legs off the bed and sat up. "What are you doing here?"

"Where's your phone? The burner?"

Tommy Lee rubbed his eyes. "What are you talking about?"

"The phone. Where is it?"

Tommy Lee reached for the bedside lamp.

"No lights."

"What the hell is going on?" He started to stand.

He pushed the barrel into Tommy Lee's chest. "Sit."

"What the fuck are you doing? Have you lost your mind?"

"Did you call?"

"What? No."

"Someone did. So, I ask again, where is the other fucking phone?"

"In my office."

"Show me."

He followed Tommy Lee down the hall, where a search of his desk drawers found nothing. Floor beneath his desk, filing cabinets, closet. Each pulled open and examined. Still nothing.

Tommy Lee dropped into the chair behind his desk. "It was in this middle drawer. I swear."

"And now it's not."

"That doesn't make any sense."

"What makes sense is that someone else has it. Someone who called me. Someone who must know what it means."

"Who?"

"That's what I'm asking you. Who did you tell?"

"No one. Jesus, why would I?"

That actually made sense. Didn't change things though. "Who had access to your house?"

"No one."

"Someone did."

Tommy Lee shook his head. "Tell me what happened?"

"I don't have time."

He raised the gun.

CHAPTER THIRTY-NINE

"So why do you think something's wrong?" Chief Morgan asked Roy Polk.

"Like I told you on the phone, he didn't show up this morning. Ain't like him. He's got two charters today. The first was at seven thirty. Three guys." Roy shook his head, his long stringy hair pulled back in a ponytail wagging with the movement. "And they ain't none too happy."

It was near nine now.

Morgan knew Roy. Had for years. Did all sorts of odd jobs. Mainly on Tommy Lee's boat for the last couple of years. Plus construction, yard work, anything requiring muscle and sweat. Hard worker as far as Morgan could tell. Never had any run-ins with the law, for sure.

Morgan never knew Roy to be an alarmist, usually the opposite, a relaxed, unhurried attitude. But, right now, Roy wore healthy concern creases across his brow.

"Maybe he slept in?" Morgan said.

"Ain't like him to do that. Besides, I banged on his door pretty good." He glanced toward the house. "Figured that'd wake him up if he was in there."

"He say he had anywhere to go? Last night or this morning?"

Another headshake from Roy. "Not that I know. He had a night charter last night. I couldn't make it, and I guess the other guys he uses as deck hands couldn't neither, so he went out on his own."

"I take it he came back from that?"

"Yep. His boat's at the dock. Just like always. We was supposed to meet there about six thirty. So we could get it ready. When he didn't show, I went ahead and got it all set up. Then seven thirty rolled around, and no Tommy Lee. I called a few times but got no answer. By eight I was worried and by eight thirty, I sent the customers back to their hotel. Said I'd call when I knew something. That's when I came here."

Morgan stood at the curb, near Roy's red pickup, now eyeing Tommy Lee's house. "You go inside?"

"Nope. I wouldn't walk into a man's house without an invite." He rubbed his nose with an index finger. "I tried the front door. Figured I'd stick my head in and give him a shout. It was locked. I peeked 'round back, thinking maybe he was out there doing something. Nope. His truck's there in the drive." He pointed that way.

Morgan nodded. "You wait here. I'll take a look."

The front door was indeed locked and Morgan saw no one through the front window. Everything seemed normal. Nothing out of place. He circled toward the back, checking the windows along the way. Dining room, kitchen empty. The rear door was unlocked.

"Tommy Lee," he shouted after cracking open the door. "It's Chief Morgan. You here?"

Silence.

He shouldered his way in, pulling his service weapon. He wasn't sure why he felt the need to have the gun in his hand, but its weight afforded a degree of comfort. There was something in the air. Like low-level electricity. Sweat gathered on his forehead, upper lip.

He went room to room, kept yelling Tommy Lee's name. Dining room, living room, first bedroom, all empty, orderly in a lived-in fashion.

Tommy Lee's room. Bed messed up. Slept in. No Tommy Lee. Next room. Tommy Lee's office. That's where he found him. Slumped in the chair behind his desk. Left eye gone, back of his head blown out. Blood and brain matter peppered the wall and curtains behind.

Morgan froze. Even his breathing stopped. A trickle of sweat eased down his cheek. He took a ragged breath and began visually sorting through the scene before him.

No weapon. No signs of a struggle. Tommy Lee had been shot sitting right there in his chair. He circled the desk, careful to avoid the bloodstains. He touched Tommy Lee's forearm. Cold. He'd been dead awhile.

Now he took in the remainder of the scene. Desk drawers pulled out. A few papers on the floor. Over the blood. Tossed after Tommy Lee was shot. Closet stood open. Two banker-type boxes lay overturned, contents on the floor. More papers.

He retraced his steps. Now, he saw that the sofa cushions were disheveled as if someone had lifted them and not replaced them properly. Cabinet beneath the TV open. A disturbed row of DVDs. A couple had fallen to the carpet.

In Tommy Lee's bedroom, the bedside drawer yawned. Inside, a pair of readers, a paperback, a bottle of aspirin, another of Benadryl. The closet door stood open, a few clothes on the floor, shoes lined along the top shelf. Disarrayed, one shoe on the floor.

He returned to Tommy Lee's office. He stood in the middle of the room, facing Tommy Lee's corpse, and began taking a visual and mental inventory of all he saw. Studying the details. You never knew what might be important, and he wanted to cement it in his mind before he called in the troops.

"What the hell?"

Morgan turned to see Roy Polk standing there. All bug-eyed.

"I thought I told you to wait outside."

"You did. But you was gone kinda long and I thought maybe you needed help."

"Go on now. This ain't something you need to see."

Polk hesitated, his gaze falling over the scene one last time. He turned and left.

Morgan walked back into the living room. Stood for a minute. What the hell? Only one conclusion. Whoever shot Tommy Lee was looking for something.

He made two calls. Frank Clark, telling him to round up Munson and get over there. Pathologist Dr. Adrian McGill.

CHAPTER FORTY

IT WAS NEAR ten thirty. Ray leaned on The Boardwalk railing, paper coffee cup he had picked up at Swift's Bakery in his hand, staring out toward the marina. The sky was clear, not a single cloud visible, but the day was already beginning to heat up. He could feel it on his back as the sun just topped the buildings and began lighting up The Boardwalk.

Pancake stood next to him, gnawing on the ham and cheese croissant he'd chosen from Swift's counter. They'd had breakfast only an hour earlier, over at McGee's, but the big guy never passed up food. One of the many things he loved about Pancake. And envied. But he could never eat like the big old redhead. Not physically possible. Not to mention he'd need an entire new wardrobe.

They'd been talking about the cell phones. Neither doubted that they provided proof positive of some sort of murder conspiracy. Nothing else made sense.

Some might say it could merely be a coincidence. But Ray knew better. Serendipity wasn't in play here. If it ever really was. There were no true coincidences. Not in human behavior. There was always a glue that held seemingly disparate events together. In this case, the glue was the cell phone and neither he nor Pancake doubted it married Tommy Lee Kovac to Frank Clark.

The facts were that the phones were purchased after the murder of Loretta Swift and used around the time of the Noleen Kovac and Sara Clark killings. Then nothing. Until now. Why now, after two years? Only one thing had changed. They had arrived and begun asking questions.

Someone was panicked. Or two someones. Clark and Tommy Lee.

He had to admit that their scheme was nearly perfect. Brilliant, in fact. Perfect alibis, perfect evidence. Neat and clean. No one to ask questions.

Except for Billy Wayne Baker. Had he simply faded away in prison, or had Jason Levy not reached out to him, become his benefactor, the plan would have worked. Clark and Tommy Lee would have skated. God bless Billy Wayne's little sociopathic soul.

Now the problem was how to shake them from the tree. Prove the other phone was indeed possessed by Frank Clark. Of course, if Clark were smart, he'd destroy it. Deny he ever had it. It'd be his word against Tommy Lee's. A battle Clark would easily win. He was the cop, the aggrieved husband; Tommy Lee the man with a hard-on for the police department. No contest.

He smiled. It was beginning to look as though Nicole had been right. This sure smelled like a murder exchange. Just like in the movies. The more he knew of her, the more clever she seemed. Maybe some of it would rub off on Jake. Probably not.

He looked down to where she and Jake stood. Near the wharf. Jake with a cup of coffee, Nicole with her head resting against his shoulder. Was she the one? The one that would finally make Jake grow up? He could only hope.

He had to admit, grudgingly so, that he held a certain degree of admiration for Jake sticking to his own life choices. Even if he couldn't understand them. Lord knows, he'd tried to guide Jake into the business. His business. But, at every turn, Jake had refused. Maddening, but then again, hadn't he raised him to think for himself, be his own man? File that under unintended consequences.

Truth was, Jake would be a very effective P.I. Sure, parts of the job were high-tech, the kinds of things Pancake could do in his sleep, but mostly it was getting people to talk. To tell their stories, and their secrets. Jake knew people. No doubt about that. And people liked him. Tall, handsome, with an easy, laid-back attitude, folks seemed to warm to him quickly. Feel at ease. For a P.I., that's gold.

"Been looking for you guys."

Ray turned. Chief Charlie Morgan walked up.

"You found us."

"Yeah, Louise Phillips over at the Tidewater said you guys had headed this way."

"Good police work." Ray smiled. "So, what's up?"

Morgan looked up and down The Boardwalk. Already getting crowded. "Let's take it over to my office."

"Sounds serious," Pancake said.

"Sure is."

Ray nodded. "Let's go."

He called to Jake and Nicole. When they turned and looked that way, he waved them up. The foursome then followed Morgan to the police station.

As they walked, Pancake leaned toward him and whispered, "How do you read this?"

"Don't know. But he doesn't look happy."

Pancake grunted. "Don't walk happy either."

Which was true. Morgan's strides were long, purposeful. As if he wanted to get down to business.

"You think he stumbled on why we're really here?" Pancake asked. "Maybe got word from someone up in Raiford? One of the guards?"

"That'd mean Billy Wayne was talking out of school. My read on him is that's not likely."

Another grunt. "I suspect we'll know in a hot minute."

When they entered the police station, they ran into Angus Whitehead, standing in the lobby, tucking in his shirt, shoving his tangled hair back from his face.

"Hey there," Angus said.

Ray nodded.

"Angus, you still here?" Morgan asked. "I told you two hours ago it was time to hit the road."

Angus humped his shoulders. "Guess I nodded off." He grinned at Ray. "Too much to drink last night."

"Which is every night for you," Morgan said.

Angus' head bobbed. "True that." He grinned. "Man's got to have a hobby. Mine involves whiskey." He headed toward the door, waving over his shoulder. "I 'spect I'll see you this evening, Chief." And he was out the door.

Morgan turned down the hall toward his office, Pancake following. Ray waited, stopping Jake and Nicole.

"Now that I think about it, it's probably best if Pancake and I handle this."

"What's going on?" Jake asked.

"Don't know. But I'm picking up an odd vibe."

Jake stepped toward him. Lowered his voice. "You think our cover is blown?"

"Pancake asked the same thing." Ray glanced toward the entrance, shook his head. "Feels like more than that."

"Okay. Nicole and I'll go have a chat with Angus. The conversation Pancake and I had with him the other day left some unanswered questions."

"Sounds good."

When Ray entered Morgan's office, Frank Clark and Terry Munson were there, standing beside Morgan's desk. Morgan had settled in his chair. Pancake and Ray sat facing the trio. Ray studied them. Not a smile to be seen.

"What's this about?" Ray asked Morgan.

"I understand you two were over near Tommy Lee's place last night."

Ray looked at Clark. "Like we told Detective Clark, we were out for a walk."

"You didn't go by Tommy Lee's place?"

"We don't even know where he lives."

Morgan seemed to consider that for a few seconds. "I see. But you do know him? Met him?"

"Sure," Pancake said. "In fact, I talked with him yesterday. Down on the dock. He was getting ready to head out."

"What'd you talk about?" Clark asked.

"A charter. We were going to call him this morning and set up a trip."

"Is that the last time you saw him?" Morgan asked.

"No," Ray said. "We saw him come in last night. Maybe nine or so."

Morgan glanced at Clark, back to Ray. "Saw him where?"

"We were down by the marina. He came in with a group of fishermen."

"You talk to him then?"

Ray shook his head. "We figured he'd be busy closing down his boat, cleaning it up, all that. Didn't want to interfere with the man's work. Setting up a charter could wait until today."

"You didn't happen to drop by his place last night? Later?"

"Am I missing something here?" Ray asked.

"Exactly where were you when you saw Tommy Lee last night?" Munson asked. "And who were you with?"

Ray leaned forward. "This is starting to sound like an interrogation."

Morgan shrugged. "That's because it is."

"About what?" Ray asked.

"Tommy Lee got himself killed last night," Clark said.

"What?" Pancake said.

"Just what I said. Someone shot him in the head. Cold-blooded."

The phone call, Ray thought. Whoever answered did indeed get spooked. Had to clean house. He held Clark's gaze. "What does that have to do with us?"

Clark smiled. "You were there. Maybe a block from Tommy Lee's house."

"So were you."

Clark's smile evaporated. "Want to give us your timeline last night?"

"Do you?"

"Look, we've welcomed you here," Munson said. "Even helped you with your little project. And then this?"

Ray got it. Munson stepping up. Protecting his partner. Letting Ray know this was a united front. It's what he'd do.

"I fail to see how the two are related," Ray said.

"Who found him?" Pancake asked.

Morgan leaned back in his chair. It creaked under his weight. He nodded to Clark.

"One of his deck hands," Clark said. "Tommy Lee had a charter this morning. Seven thirty. He didn't show so by eight thirty or so he got worried and went over to Tommy Lee's. No answer. Called us."

"Who?" Ray asked. "The deck hand?"

"Guy named Roy Polk," Clark said.

"He a suspect?" Ray asked. "Maybe Tommy Lee and he had issues. Maybe he owed this guy some money?"

"Not likely," Clark said. "But we'll have another chat with him."

"Anybody else on your suspect list?" Pancake asked.

"Besides you two?" Clark said.

"Yeah, besides us."

"We ain't had much time to sniff around yet," Munson said. "Tommy Lee ain't even cold yet."

"So, your timeline?" Morgan injected.

"After we saw Detective Clark on our walk, we went back to the marina. Sat in the gazebo until maybe ten thirty, eleven." He looked at Clark. "We saw Tommy Lee come in. Well after we saw you."

"Who?" Munson asked. "You two, your son, and his girlfriend?"

"And Betty Lou and her daughter. We had whiskey and cigars."

The furrows in Morgan's brow relaxed. Seemed that putting Betty Lou in the mix took some steam out of his expression.

"Then what?" Clark asked.

"Back to the hotel. We had a meeting in my room. Did some computer work, made a couple of phone calls." Ray held Clark's gaze, looking for some reaction. He got nothing. But then, Clark was a cop. Trained to show no reaction. "Went to bed after that."

"Except for me," Pancake said. "I met Laurie Mae. We hung out until two or so."

"What time was he killed?" Ray asked.

Morgan leaned forward, elbows on his desk. "Doctor McGill said his best guess was sometime between ten p.m. and two a.m." He sighed. "Based on the body temp, rigor, and lividity."

"What kind of weapon?" Pancake asked.

Morgan hesitated as if considering the question. "Don't know yet. But, from what I saw, I'd guess a mid caliber. Not a pop gun, not a cannon." He looked at Ray. "I take it you guys have weapons with you?"

"Just one," Ray said. "A Sig Sauer P320. Forty caliber."

Morgan looked at Pancake. "You?

"Nope. Don't need a gun."

That was true. Pancake was a more break-your-head-with-a-fist kind of guy.

"Look," Ray said. "I get it. I know how it works. We're not local. We were apparently in the neighborhood. But, I think you have to ask why? What earthly reason would we have to do anything to Tommy Lee Kovac? We barely knew him."

Morgan's shoulders relaxed. "Been asking myself the same things. Ever since Frank told me he saw you over there."

Ray scooted forward to the edge of his chair. "We didn't. We wouldn't. And we have no idea who did. Or why."

Morgan stirred his desktop with an index finger as if thinking things over. Finally, he glanced at Clark, shrugged, gave a deep sigh. "Don't see no reason to hold you guys. 'Least not yet."

Ray stood. "Then, we'll get out of your hair and let you guys get to work." He locked his gaze on Clark for a beat, then turned toward the door, Pancake following. He stopped in the hall, letting Pancake pass, and looked back toward Morgan. "If we can help in any way, let us know."

Morgan raised an eyebrow. "I think we can handle it."

Ray nodded.

Morgan returned the nod. "Just don't plan on leaving town."

Ray smiled. Morgan obviously liked old Westerns.

CHAPTER FORTY-ONE

BY THE TIME Nicole and I made our way out of the station and to the street, I saw Angus half a block away. Not exactly holding a steady course. Sort of wavering along the sidewalk. We caught up.

"Angus," I said.

He listed to his left and wobbled a step as he tried to apply his brakes. I thought he might fall. He spun and looked at us. Then, smiled. "You scared me."

"Sorry. Mind if we ask you a few questions?"

"About what?"

A woman ushered two kids, boy and girl, maybe four and five, past us, nodding and flashing a brief "morning" as she passed.

"Maybe we can sit somewhere."

Angus looked past me, then across the street. Hesitating, buying time. I got the impression he was headed somewhere. Home? Breakfast? When he rubbed his chin, I saw a slight tremor in his fingers.

"Maybe buy you a drink?"

"It ain't even happy hour yet."

"I guess it is a little early."

He grinned. "I'm just messing with you. Ain't never too early for a drink."

"Then, it's settled," Nicole said. "We'll buy you breakfast. Or lunch. Your choice. Wherever you want."

"Lots of places to choose from." He brushed his hair from his eyes. "Maybe over at McGee's. They make a mean Bloody Mary."

"You like Bloody Marys?" she asked.

"Me? No. I'm a whiskey man." He grinned. "But you look like a Bloody Mary kind of girl."

Nicole laughed. "I've been known to knock back a whiskey or two myself. But, a Bloody Mary sounds good." She hooked arms with Angus. "Let's go."

I followed behind. She got her sway on, making sure her hip bumped Angus from time to time. She was good. Getting him softened up. More likely the opposite. Maybe pliable would be a better word.

At McGee's, we found a small round table near the back. Nicole and I had the Bloody Marys and they were great. Actually, better than that. Angus woofed down ham and eggs and a pair of biscuits and was now working on his third drink.

He swiped his chin and mouth with a napkin. "That was good. Thanks."

"No problem," I said.

"What you want to jaw about?" he asked.

"That night. When the shoplifters were brought in. Clark and Munson tossed you out of your cell. You said they were extra angry."

"They were. And not very nice."

"You also said something else happened."

"I did?"

"Come on, Angus," I said. "You remember."

"I remember he didn't want me around those girls," Angus said. "Like I was some pervert."

"But there's more," I said. "Right?"

His brow wrinkled and he took another gulp of whiskey. Then a slow nod. "Yeah, I remember now. I needed to pee." He glanced at Nicole. "Sorry."

"I'm familiar with the term," she said, smiled.

His head bobbed. "I would've gone back inside, but Clark and Munson weren't in no good mood. I didn't want to chance aggravating them any too much. So, I stepped into the shrubbery. There alongside the station. While I was doing my business, Clark and Munson came out. It was dark so they didn't see me." He stared at the table for a couple of seconds, as if picturing the scene. "Clark went off on a couple of kids skateboarding along the sidewalk. Told them he'd lock them up if they didn't get out of folks' way. Followed them half a block giving them hell the whole way."

"He was under a good deal of stress," Nicole said.

Angus gave a head bob. "I suppose so. Munson, too. While Clark was going all Dirty Harry on the kids, Munson was on the phone giving somebody the business." He leaned back. "He was mad. Like a hornet." He grinned. "I was glad I wasn't the only one he was pissed at."

"How come you remember this?" I asked.

"Well, I was squatting in the bushes, these two all worked up, and ranting. I was afraid if they saw me, I'd be slammed in the slammer for sure." Angus laughed. "I should be a poet." Another laugh. "Besides, I remember all kinds of stuff. Mostly random happenings." He gave a headshake. "Things pop in and out of my head all the time. I remember the oddest stuff." He grinned. "And forget all sorts of stuff, too."

"How far away were you?" I asked.

He shrugged. "Ten, fifteen feet. I sort of ducked down in the shrubbery. Didn't want him to see me. Maybe think I was was eavesdropping." He sat silently.

"And?"

"I couldn't hear him all that good."

"What did you hear?" Nicole asked.

"He was upset, all right. Like he was mad at the person he was talking to." He glanced toward the front of the cafe. "Not just mad but sort of frustrated. He was cussing and all. Like the guy wouldn't listen."

"Guy?" I asked. "He was talking to a guy?"

"Yeah." Angus nodded but then stopped. "Well, I assumed it was a guy."

"Why?" Nicole asked.

"The way he talked. Seemed all pissed off. Curt." He smiled. "I like that word. Anyway, he shouldn't've been talking to no lady that way."

"But, you're not sure?" I asked.

Angus' gaze hit the ceiling above me, his brow knitted. "No. I ain't."

"I take it he didn't use a name or anything like that?" Nicole asked.

"Not that I heard. Or remember."

"Anything else?" I asked.

"Like what?"

"Well, you remembered the event so it must have made an impression. I was just wondering if maybe something else happened."

"I'll tell you what I remember most. I was glad he was mad at someone besides me. And I damn sure didn't want him to know I was squatting in the bushes." He laughed. "I didn't move for a long time. Clark came back up the street, and they climbed in their car and left." He shook his head. "I stayed low for another five minutes in case they might've forgotten something and came back." His shoulders bucked. "That's what I remember most."

CHAPTER FORTY-TWO

"WHAT DO YOU think?" Morgan asked Clark and Munson.

He had Frank Clark's handwritten crime-scene report spread before him on his desk. They had already discussed, and dismissed, Ray and Pancake as viable suspects. Not impossible but extremely improbable was the consensus. Though Clark added that they had the means and opportunity if not clearly the motive. At least, none that any of them could see. So, since they still stood at square one, Morgan steered the inquiry to other possibilities.

Clark slipped off his jacket and finger-hooked it over one shoulder. His other hand rested on the butt of the service weapon that clung to his right hip. "Not sure what to think. The scene, for sure, didn't offer any clues. Unless either of you saw something I missed."

Both Morgan and Munson shook their heads.

"Far as I know, Tommy Lee didn't have any real enemies," Munson said. He stood next to Clark, hands resting on the back of one of the visitors' chairs.

"Roy Polk?" Morgan asked. "Any friction there?"

Clark shook his head. "Not that I've ever heard. We'll have a chat with him, but honestly, I don't see that going anywhere. He and Tommy Lee have been friends a long time." His hand left his weapon and he hooked a thumb in his belt.

"Friends do have issues sometimes," Morgan said. "Anyone else we should be looking at?"

"I'm not entirely ready to give up on Ray Longly," Clark said. "All I do know is that those two, him and his partner, were in the area. Out for an evening stroll. And they don't seem the strolling type."

"I agree," Munson added. "Ray Longly doesn't impress me as a guy who does anything without some purpose."

Morgan's fingers drummed his desk. "I thought we'd already put that to bed." He sighed. "I don't see a good motive. And like they said, they don't even know Tommy Lee."

"My feeling is they know more than they're letting on," Munson said.

"How so?"

Munson shrugged. "Me and Frank talked about this. This whole deal seems a little off. I mean, a documentary? They come in here sniffing around our work." He shook his head. "Never felt comfortable about that."

"Me, either," Clark added. "Nicole Jamison, I get. She's movie people. Even Ray's son, Jake. I'll buy that. But two P.I. types? I don't like it."

Morgan rubbed a finger along his nose. "Anything specific? Anything they've done seem out of bounds?"

Clark and Munson looked at him but said nothing.

"Yeah, I haven't either," Morgan said. "Fact is, everyone I've talked with that had any interaction with any of them said they've been very polite. Professional, friendly."

None of the three said anything for a good half a minute.

"So, what now?" Clark asked.

"Work the case. Like you usually do. Start looking for anyone with a grudge, or issue, even minor, with Tommy Lee. And maybe keep a closer eye on Ray Longly and his sidekick." He shrugged. "Just in case."

Clark nodded and he and Munson left.

Morgan sat back in his chair. His head cocked back, gaze directed at the ceiling. He sorted though his mental files on every conversation he'd had with Ray Longly, with any of the folks he and his crew had talked with. He got nothing.

Okay, so they were researching a documentary on Billy Wayne's victims. To tell their stories. An interesting slant. He'd never seen or even heard of anything quite like that. He liked it, he really did, but was there another agenda at work here? And if so, what was it?

His experience told him that when things don't add up, they don't add up. It was that simple. And to grab the right thread, to unravel the ball of twine, you needed to go back to the beginning.

The trick was finding the beginning.

The simple truth was that everything started when Billy Wayne Baker decided to plant his flag right there in Pine Key. He knew Jake Longly had talked with Billy Wayne. He'd told him as much. Even said Billy Wayne looked too mild, passive to be such a brutal killer. But he was. No doubt there.

But so what if Jake Longly had a chat with Billy Wayne? If the intent was to dig into Billy Wayne's world, it only made sense to talk with him. See what he might share. Maybe give some insight into why Billy Wayne came here. Chose this town. Chose the three victims that Morgan knew so well. Of course, from everything he knew about Billy Wayne, he wasn't the most forthcoming person on the planet.

Something niggled in his brain. Something about Billy Wayne making waves about his confession. He had no details on that. And Billy Wayne did confess to all the killings. Not to mention, he more or less had to. DNA don't lie.

Again, so what? What could any of this possibly have to do with Tommy Lee getting his head blown off?

He leaned forward, thumbed through the small notebook where he kept all his contact info. He found the number he wanted and picked up the phone.

It took a couple of minutes to get Ralph Keaton, the Union Correctional warden, on the line. He'd known Ralph for a few years. They'd first met at a conference up in Tallahassee and had had several conversations during the whole Billy Wayne investigation.

"Chief," Keaton said, "been a long time."

"Sure has."

"How are things down there?"

"The usual. Chasing the bad guys."

Keaton laughed. "When you catch them, send them on up here. I got a spot for them."

"I heard you might be adding a new unit."

"Maybe. If I can get the suits over in Tallahassee to pony up the funds."

"Glad to know I'm not the only one with such problems," Morgan said.

"I get the sense this isn't a social call," Keaton said.

"It is and it isn't."

"What can I do for you?"

Morgan explained the reason for his call. Jake's visits with Billy Wayne. The documentary. The murder of Tommy Lee Kovac. His inability to connect the dots.

"Yeah, I heard about the documentary. Sounded like a good idea to me. That's why I approved Longly's visits."

"You know anything about those conversations?"

Keaton sighed. "Is this off the record?"

"We never talked. And if we did, it was about fishing."

Keaton hesitated. "One of my guards overheard part of it."

"And?"

"Why don't I hook you two up. Better if you get it from him."

"I'd appreciate it."

"His name's Nick Swanson. Good man. He's out in the yard. I'll get him in here and have him give you a call."

"That'd be great."

"Give me fifteen minutes."

The call came twenty minutes later. Swanson told his story. He'd been outside the room but heard bits and pieces. But what he heard was interesting. And very troubling.

CHAPTER FORTY-THREE

"WE'RE GOING TO head out," I said to Angus as Nicole and I stood. "You want another drink?"

"Sure wouldn't say no," Angus said.

"You got it."

Our waitress loitered near one end of the bar, chatting with the bartender, a cup of coffee in her hand. We headed that way.

"Take care of Angus over there." I nodded his way. "Whatever he wants. Put it on here." I handed her a credit card.

"You sure? He can put them away."

I smiled. "That's fine."

She laughed. "Why can't I find a guy like this?" She looked at Nicole. "He's a keeper."

Nicole smiled. "He's not without his faults."

She's funny. She really is.

"Don't they all have them, honey," the waitress said.

She ran the card, leaving the total open. I signed it and we left.

"Did you hear that?" I asked as we walked up the street.

"What?"

"I'm a keeper."

"Never said you weren't." She slapped my butt. "What now?"

"Let's go see Betty Lou. I want her take on Tommy Lee's murder."

"I might want another Bloody Mary," she said. "Or maybe one of those killer margaritas."

"You trying to keep up with Angus?"

"Not sure that's possible."

As we headed down The Boardwalk toward Woody's, I called Ray. "How'd it go with Chief Morgan?" I asked.

"Interesting. I'll bring you up to speed later. Anything with Angus?"

"Not sure. He went on about how Clark and Munson had treated him that night. How Clark went off on some skateboarders and Munson had a rather angry phone conversation with someone."

"Any idea with who?"

"No. And I'm not sure it means anything. Like you said, Clark and Munson were stressed to the max that night. Anyway, we're heading over to talk with Betty Lou," I said. "Get her take on Tommy Lee. You and Pancake come by and we can compare notes."

"Sounds good," Ray said. "But first, me and Pancake are going to see Roy Polk. He's one of Tommy Lee's deck hands."

"Any issues there?"

"I guess we'll see. Later." He disconnected the call.

In the end, Nicole settled on the Bloody Mary. I did, too. Betty Lou ferried them to the table.

"Got a minute?" I asked.

"Sure do." She sat down.

"I guess you heard about Tommy Lee Kovac?"

"Everyone's heard. It's buzzing all over town." She shook her head as she wiped her hands on the bar towel she held before wading it and laying it on the table. "I hope we don't have another Billy Wayne rearing his head."

"I don't think so," I said. "Tell me about Tommy Lee."

"Good man. Worked hard, for sure. Never had no trouble with him. Not in here anyway. I've never heard a bad word about him." She looked out to where Tommy Lee's boat sat idle in its slip. "Hard to believe."

"You have any thoughts on it?" I asked.

"You mean like who could've done it?" She shook her head. "Not a clue."

"He didn't have any issues with anyone?"

"Not that I know."

I smiled. "Somehow, I suspect that if he did, you'd know."

"Probably would." She picked up the towel and blotted at a ketchup stain on her gray shirt. "Truth is, he was a very nice young man. I mean, he had his issues with the police. After his sister's murder. But, I guess that's understandable. And that was years ago. Far as I know, that all blew over."

"That's more or less what he told Pancake."

"Where is the big guy?"

"He and Ray are going to have a sit-down with a guy named Roy Polk."

"Roy? Why?"

"He was supposed to go out with Tommy Lee this morning. It was him that called the police."

"You don't think he had anything to do with this?" Betty Lou asked.

"Do you?"

She hesitated a beat. "No. He and Tommy Lee were tight. Worked together for years."

"No issues?"

Her eyes narrowed. "Mind if I ask what this has to do with your documentary?"

Uh-oh. Not much got by Betty Lou. I searched for an answer.

"Tommy Lee is a collateral victim," Nicole said. "His sister was one of Billy Wayne's victims. We were planning to film him. So, anything that happens to him, related or not, is part of the tragic story."

Betty Lou nodded. "Makes sense." She looked at me. "But to answer your question, Roy more or less depended on Tommy Lee for his livelihood. Don't see how him doing anything like this would be in his best interest."

"That makes sense, too," I said. "Maybe it was a burglary that went wrong. I know Tommy Lee ran his business from his home. Maybe he had money there."

"Could be. I know he didn't care too much for banks. 'Least not the one his sister worked at."

"That's right," I said. "I heard he moved to another one. Maybe he kept a pile of cash at home."

Betty Lou shrugged. "Wouldn't surprise me none. You probably wouldn't believe how many folks 'round here do."

"Not smart."

"No. But they do it anyway."

CHAPTER FORTY-FOUR

ROY POLK LIVED about a mile north of town in an isolated area that was mostly scrub brush and swamp. Only one way in and out. Ray held onto the roof handle as Pancake guided his truck along the uneven gravel road, the truck gyrating, pebbles pinging against the undercarriage. Polk's home proved to be a weather-dulled and dented Airstream, resting on concrete blocks.

Polk was sitting in a plastic lawn chair near the trailer's entrance, a cigarette in one hand, a long-necked beer in the other. He stood when Ray and Pancake stepped from the truck.

Polk was lanky, thin, and wore dark green cargo shorts and a black tee shirt with a faded Jack Daniels logo, both a couple of sizes too large and hanging from his bony shoulders and hips. His stringy brown hair was pulled back into a ponytail.

"Roy Polk?" Ray said, walking toward him.

"Who wants to know?"

He flicked the cigarette to the ground and crushed it with his sandal. Ray noticed there were maybe two dozen other flattened butts. Obviously, Polk's preferred place to relax. Or today, ponder Tommy Lee's murder. An orange plastic pail beside the chair held several empty beer bottles. PBR being Polk's choice.

"I'm Ray Longly. This is Pancake."

"You the ones making that film Tommy Lee told me about?"

"We are."

Polk pulled a partially crushed box of Marlboros from his pants pocket and shook one up. "What brings you out here?"

"Wanted to talk with you about Tommy Lee."

"Already talked with the police." He lipped the cigarette from the pack, before returning it to his pocket.

"We know. But they're looking into his murder. We're more interested in Tommy Lee."

Polk's eyes narrowed. "Why?"

"He tell you what the film we're doing is about?"

"Some." A Zippo appeared. He thumbed up a flame, lit the cigarette, and clacked it closed.

"We're interested in the aftermath of Billy Wayne Baker's killings. How it affected the family and friends of the victims. And since his sister was one of those victims, we had him set to be part of the show."

Polk sighed. "Yeah, he said he was going to be on film."

"He was. But, now, things have obviously changed."

Polk spun the Zippo with his fingers a couple of times, then slid it into his pants pocket. "Sure have."

"I understand you found him?" Ray asked.

"Yep. We had an early charter this morning. He didn't show. Ain't like him. I called and called. Got no answer. Went over to see if he was alright. He didn't answer my knocks. I knew something was off so I called Chief Morgan."

"Did you see him? Tommy Lee?" Pancake asked.

"Sure did. Chief Morgan was in there a while so I went in. Wish I never had." His shoulders dropped and he scuffed the ground with one sandal. "His head was all blowed off." He looked up. "I ain't never seen anything like it."

"How long did you know him?" Ray asked.

"Forever. Since we were kids. Worked with him since he started the business."

"I hear business was good."

"Sure was. He got that new boat a couple of years ago and things moved up after that."

"An upgrade?" Pancake asked. "The boat?"

He nodded. "Could take out parties of six, sometimes more. Better charters, if you know what I mean. Folks from Orlando and Tampa and places like that expect bigger and newer. And they're willing to pay for it."

"So, more money?" Ray said.

"For sure. He made more, I made more. Things were looking good." He took a long drag from the Marlboro, exhaling the smoke upward. "Not sure what I'm going to do now."

"I know Tommy Lee ran his business from his home. Did he keep money there?"

"Some. Most was banked. But I guess he had a couple of grand on hand at any given time." He stuck the cigarette in his mouth. It bobbed as he spoke. "You ask me, that just might be what got him killed."

"What makes you think that?" Ray asked.

"Everything I saw there. At his place. Not just Tommy Lee and all that blood." He shook his head. "But to me, the place looked messed up. Not massively, like turned-over furniture and the like. But drawers, cabinets, closets were open. Stuff pulled out. Even looked like someone had dug beneath the sofa cushions."

"Who knew he kept money there?"

"Far as I know, only me and Tommy Lee. He never talked much about his business." He finished the cigarette and crushed it as he had the other one. "I guess some of the others that helped him from time to time could've known." He sighed. "But I doubt it. Tommy Lee was never very close with any of them."

"How many are we talking about?" Rays asked. "Other crew members?"

"Lately? Only two. But, if he didn't go out alone, which he did a lot, I'd say I went out with him about ninety percent of the other times. He only used the other guys if he needed an extra hand and I was away or sick or something like that."

"Besides money, did he keep anything else valuable there?" Ray asked.

"Not that I know."

"Do you know anyone who would have done this?" Pancake asked.

He shook his head emphatically. "No. Tommy Lee was good people. Never had no trouble with anyone."

"Except the police, I hear," Ray said.

"That was long ago. Right after Noleen was killed." Another sigh. "I sure didn't blame him. Fact of the matter is I agreed with him. I thought the police were dragging their feet." He propped his hands on his hips. "'Course after Frank Clark's wife was murdered, things sort of changed. He figured if Clark couldn't protect his own wife, he could be forgiven for any of his failures. At least to a point."

"So you have no idea who could be responsible for Tommy Lee's murder?"

"I've been sitting here drinking and smoking and asking myself that same question ever since I got back here." He scratched the back of one hand. "It just don't make no sense."

"Can I ask you an odd question?" Ray said.

"Don't see no reason why not."

"What kind of phone did Tommy Lee use?"

He smiled. Sort of. "An iPhone. Latest model. Man, he loved that thing."

"Ever see him with an old flip-type one?"

He tossed Ray a quizzical look. "Not in ten years. Maybe more. No one has those anymore."

Ray nodded. "Like I said, an odd question."

"Tommy Lee liked his gadgets. His phone. The boat's radar." Now he did smile. "He really loved the fish finder. Thought that was about the coolest thing ever."

Ray heard the sound of car tires crunching gravel and turned toward the road. A black sedan pulled in next to Pancake's truck. Clark and Munson stepped out.

"You guys get around," Clark said.

"We were just leaving," Ray said.

"Mind if I ask why you're here?"

"They was talking to me about Tommy Lee," Polk said.

"The documentary," Ray added. "Trying to get a better handle on Tommy Lee." He turned to Polk. "Thanks for your time. You've helped us better understand Tommy Lee."

"Glad to help."

Ray nodded to Clark and Munson and then he and Pancake headed toward the truck. When they got there, Ray saw that Clark had followed them. He turned to face him.

"You stepping on my investigation?" Clark said.

"Wouldn't do that."

Clark stared at him.

"Look," Ray said. "You have a job to do. I respect that. So do we. We aren't really interested in your case. And definitely not trying to interfere. But Tommy Lee is a part of our story. The more we know about him, the better we can make the final product."

"You sure that's all it is?" Clark asked.

"What else could it be?"

"You tell me."

"I just did."

Clark gave a quick nod. "Guess I'll have to take you at your word. For now."

CHAPTER FORTY-FIVE

IT WAS WELL past Pancake's feeding time when he and Ray joined Nicole and me on the deck at Woody's. Nicole was into her second Bloody Mary. I, wisely, stopped at one. We had had a long talk with Betty Lou before she had to get back to work.

"About time to clear out the lunch crowd and prep for the happy hour chaos," she had said. "Got a feeling it'll start early and run late today. What with Tommy Lee's murder on everyone's mind. Stress and alcohol go together." She looked at me. "Maybe I can get Pancake to hang around. To keep order." She laughed.

"He can do that, all right," I said. "When he's not creating the chaos. But if you feed him, he'll never leave."

"Sort of like a stray cat," Nicole said.

That got an even deeper laugh from Betty Lou.

"Thanks for chatting with us," Nicole said

"Chattin's my favorite pastime," Betty Lou said. Then she was gone.

Betty Lou returned when she saw Ray and Pancake arrive. "'Bout time you showed up." She nodded toward Nicole and me. "Been babysitting these two all day."

"I've had that duty with Jake his whole life," Ray said.

"Me, too," Pancake added.

"You guys are funny," I said, then to Pancake, "I think Betty Lou has a job offer for you."

"Doing what?"

"Sort of a bouncer," Betty Lou said. "I'm thinking with the Tommy Lee situation; this evening could be a mite rowdy."

"What's the pay?" Pancake asked.

"Everything on the menu."

"Sure beats what Ray pays." His eyebrows gave a bounce. "I'm in. I'll start with page one and work my way through."

Betty Lou laughed. It crossed my mind that she thought he was kidding. I knew better.

She took our order, only Pancake ordering food, and was off again.

We shared notes. I told of our talk with Angus, and how we left him drinking his way through the day over at McGee's. Ray and Pancake covered their visit to Roy Polk, including Clark and Munson showing up.

Then, Pancake, having devoured calamari, tacos, French fries, and key lime pie, summed everything up.

"What we have here is a murder-swap conspiracy. Don't see it any other way. Clark couldn't have killed his wife, or Tommy Lee his sister. But Tommy Lee was available the night Sara Clark was murdered, and Clark the night Noleen Kovac was killed. According to Munson, Clark had the duty the night Noleen was murdered. Means all the other cops were home, tucked in. He'd have the run of the town. And the next morning, he's the one that answered Tommy Lee's call." He looked at Nicole. "Just like you predicted."

She raised her glass to him and nodded.

Pancake continued. "If you look at everything we have, all the facts we know to be true, it comes down to that."

"So, in the end, Billy Wayne was telling the truth?" I said.

"I think we can safely say that that's the case," Pancake said. "Billy Wayne moved around. Never hit the same place twice. Which is actually pretty smart." He nodded to me. "And from what Jake here said about his second visit up to Raiford, Billy Wayne more or less confirmed that this is where the problem was. Where murders that weren't his took place."

"That was my impression," I said.

"So, old Billy Wayne comes in here to this nice little town, kills Loretta Swift, and goes on his way. Then, Frank Clark gets to thinking. Maybe he can use this to knock off his cheating wife."

"But we don't know that he knew she was cheating," Nicole said.

Pancake shrugged. "Couples know a lot they don't let on. Clark's a cop. Means he's suspicious by nature. Can dig up facts, do surveillance, all kinds of stuff. So, he could've known even if no one knew he was aware of Sara's infidelity. He lets it ride. Lets it fester. Until he sees a chance to fix it." He shrugged. "Maybe things were comfortable in the Clarks' home. Other than her stepping out. Maybe he thought why rock the boat until you can completely capsize it?"

"Makes sense," she said.

"So, he has this all balled up inside him. Until an opportunity presents itself. If his wife is killed and the evidence is planted to drop it in Billy Wayne's lap, that might solve his problem. But, then, thinking like a cop, it might just look too convenient."

"You mean, like he had access to the evidence?" I said. "And he'd be the one doing the investigation?"

"Exactly. He might've pulled it off. Particularly here, where he's a big dog. But the possibility of it all blowing up was real." Pancake looked out toward the Gulf. "And don't forget, this is the Billy Wayne Baker case. The FBI was involved."

"Which could really get tricky," Nicole said.

"Enter Tommy Lee Kovac," Pancake continued. "He and Clark go back. Maybe Clark knew Tommy Lee was having money issues with his sister. Maybe they sat down and hatched a plan. A murder exchange. Each creates an alibi, each does the deed for the other, and Clark is free and clear. No one would question his wife's murder if there was another one. And if his alibi was ironclad. Like working an accident on the bridge. With his partner. Not to mention a newspaper reporter documenting it. Toss in Billy Wayne's DNA at both scenes and the conspiracy is perfect."

"Three murders would stir the mud," Ray said. "Make everything all murky. So much so that Clark wouldn't stand out as a suspect."

Everyone sat quietly for a few minutes, absorbing everything.

"And now, with Billy Wayne bringing us in, and you guys finding the phone, everything is suddenly very shaky," I said.

"And that makes folks with something to hide nervous," Ray said.

"Do you think Clark killed Tommy Lee?" I asked.

"I do," Ray said. "The phone call spooked him. Maybe thinking Tommy Lee was getting all sideways. I mean, why would he call and say nothing? Answer Clark's return call and again say nothing. Was Tommy Lee becoming a liability? Or worse, someone else had the phone. That would kick his anxiety into the stratosphere. Either way, Clark saw everything falling apart. The conspiracy unraveling. So, he needed to find the phone and eliminate the only person who could put him in the middle of this."

"Which is the way all conspiracies end," Pancake said.

"So, we need to find the other phone in Clark's possession to prove all this?" Nicole asked.

"Which won't be easy," Ray said.

"I have a question," I said.

"Go ahead."

"Could the other half of the conspiracy, the guy who answered the phone, be the guy Sara was seeing and not Frank Clark?"

Ray shook his head. "Not likely. Clark's the one who had access to the DNA evidence. And the guy at the scenes where he could plant it. The way I see it, he's ground zero in this entire opera."

That made sense.

"Speak of the devil," Pancake said. He nodded toward the entrance.

I looked that way. Clark and Munson. They saw us and headed our way.

"How'd your talk with Polk go?" Ray asked.

"Fine," Clark said. He offered nothing else. Just stood there. The late afternoon sun highlighted the scowls on each of their faces.

"What can we do for you?" Ray asked.

"Maybe do your job," Clark said. "Work on your documentary but stay out of our business."

"Like I said before, that's not our intention."

"It doesn't smell that way to us," Munson added.

That's when Chief Morgan arrived. He didn't look happy either.

"We need to talk," Morgan said.

"Okay."

Morgan looked around. "Not here."

CHAPTER FORTY-SIX

WE GATHERED IN the gazebo. Our de facto office. I had always considered it private and cozy. It didn't feel that way about now. Nicole, Ray, Pancake, and I sat. Morgan didn't. He leaned against the rail, flanked by Clark and Munson.

It felt like the OK Corral. The Earps and the Clantons squared off in a claustrophobically confined area. I could taste the tension in the air. Problem was that down there in southern Arizona, in the suddenly appropriately named Tombstone, everyone was armed. Here, only Clark and Munson were, something they made painfully obvious, each with a hand resting on a service weapon. At least we had Ray and Pancake on our side. Evened the odds. Sort of. I wished I'd paid more attention at our Krav Maga classes. I hoped Nicole had.

"So, talk," Ray said.

He looked calm. Pancake, too. Me? I thought I might throw up.

Morgan looked at me. "Maybe you should tell us about your visits with Billy Wayne Baker."

"We can't really talk about any of our interviews," Ray said. "It's a privacy issue."

Morgan sighed. "I don't think that posture will help here."

Ray shrugged. "You obviously have something on your mind, so why don't we start there."

Ray and I might have our issues, but one thing I never doubted was his poise. Grace under pressure as he liked to put it. I didn't feel all that graceful.

"I had a chat with the warden up in Raiford," Morgan said. "One of the guards, too. One that overheard Jake's talk with Billy Wayne.

Uh-oh.

"Enlighten us," Ray said.

"Okay, let's play it that way. Seems much of the dialog revolved around Billy Wayne saying he didn't kill a couple of his victims. Said someone else might've done them." His knuckles whitened as he gripped the railing behind him. "Seems he directed you this way."

"Not exactly," I said.

"Then what exactly?"

"He confessed to all the murders," I said. "What's to discuss?"

Morgan came off the rail, widened his stance, scratched an ear. "Makes me think that maybe all this documentary crap was simply a cover for you to come in here and snoop around."

I felt Nicole coil. She squared her shoulders. "The documentary is real."

"If you say so," Clark said.

Her jaw came up. "I do."

Lord, I loved her. She was a warrior of the first order. Of course, pissing off a group of armed cops might not be the best move, but it felt good.

For a brief moment, Morgan looked like he wasn't sure how to handle the standoff. He recovered quickly. Looked at me.

"Is that how you remember your conversations? Billy Wayne denying some of the murders?"

"I'd say Billy Wayne Baker isn't exactly the most reliable source for anything," I said. Did I say that? That was a good answer. I think

Morgan wanted more so I continued. "I was simply gathering background info on his activities. What he confessed to or didn't wasn't part of that."

"What exactly did he say his activities here in Pine Key were?"

"I guess you know that about as well as anyone. Except maybe Billy Wayne."

"What's that supposed to mean?" Munson said.

"Just what I said. Whatever he said he did or did not do would have to be taken with a grain of salt. Don't you think?"

I was on a roll.

"I guess it depends on whether you believed him or not," Morgan said.

"Would you? Believe anything he said?" This was now getting to be fun. I felt poised.

Even better, that seemed to deflate Morgan a notch. Definitely on a roll here. Ray thought so, too. I sensed more than saw a slight smile at the corners of his mouth.

"Have we done anything since we've been here that would make you think we were in Billy Wayne's corner?" Ray asked. "Anything other than working on our film project?"

Morgan glanced up toward The Boardwalk, hesitated a second, then gave a quick nod. "Can't say that you have."

"Then, there you go."

"I just have a nagging feeling that things aren't as they seem."

"Are they ever?" Pancake said.

Morgan shrugged.

"I don't think there's anything we can say to convince you that we're legit," Nicole said. "Except wait and see. Once this project is completed, I think you'll be pleasantly surprised."

Morgan stared at her. "I hope that's the truth."

"It is."

Well, not entirely.

Morgan gave a quick nod and looked at me. "Just so we're clear here, Billy Wayne did or did not say some of the killings here weren't his work?"

I glanced at Ray. He gave me a slight nod.

"No, he didn't." Technically that was true. Though he slipped up, let the truth slip out, Billy Wayne admitted nothing directly. "And, like I said, why would I believe him if he did? He left his DNA at each scene. Hard to deny he was present, don't you think?"

Morgan gave another nod.

I continued. "So, I don't see anything Billy Wayne Baker has to say on his guilt or innocence has any relevance here. Or carries much weight." I hesitated a couple of seconds. "Unless you have any doubts. Know something we don't."

Ta da. That was a great answer. I somehow refrained from standing and taking a bow. Nicole thought it was good, too, as she placed a hand on my arm, giving it a slight squeeze.

"I have no doubts as to Billy Wayne Baker's guilt," Morgan said.

"Then we're all on the same page here."

CHAPTER FORTY-SEVEN

"WHAT'S THAT?" CHIEF Charlie Morgan asked.

"It's a phone," Ray said.

Morgan scowled. "I can see that. But what's it doing on my kitchen table?"

It was now nearing seven in the evening. After the confrontation in the gazebo, Ray, Pancake, Nicole, and I had sat down in Ray's room at the Tidewater and gone over various options on how to move forward with the investigation. Everyone had an opinion but, in the end, we all agreed. Or rather, Ray agreed for us. It was time to bring Morgan inside. Let him know what we knew. Or better, what we suspected.

"It's a pre-paid burner," Ray said. "One of a pair purchased two years ago up in Panama City. January of 2016 to be exact."

"And this means what?" Morgan asked. He maintained an air of casual curiosity, but it was facade. I could see worry gather in his face. Guess he knew we wouldn't be here, in his home, unless it was something intended for his eyes only.

"It was a cash transaction," Ray said. "Small independent phone store. January would put the purchase a month after Loretta Swift's murder and a month before Noleen Kovac and two months before Sara Clark were killed."

A crease now appeared in Morgan's brow. "Okay." He said it slowly. His mental wheels no doubt ramped up.

Ray nodded to Pancake.

"According to its call log, this phone was only ever used to call one number," Pancake said. "The other phone purchased at the same time."

"So the two are married to one another," Ray said.

Pancake continued, "There was a flurry of communications during the months surrounding the murders of Noleen Kovac and Sara Clark, then nothing." Pancake paused. "Until a few days ago."

The crease deepened. Morgan picked up the phone, examined it. "Where'd you get this?"

"From Tommy Lee."

That seemed to knock Morgan back. "He gave it to you?"

Ray shrugged. "Not exactly."

Morgan's face hardened. "You telling me you broke into Tommy Lee's house and stole this?"

Ray shrugged but said nothing.

"Okay, I get it," Morgan said. "But if we're going to talk turkey here, you've got to come clean. This is all off the record."

Ray smiled. "I'm not worried about that." He waved a hand. "It's four against one as to what's said here anyway."

Morgan scowled.

"But, we're here to clear the air. Tell you how we see all this playing out."

Morgan's shoulders sank, as did his head. He suddenly looked older, tired. I suspected his cop's mind knew that what was coming wasn't anything near what he wanted to hear.

"Go ahead," he said with a wave of one hand.

Ray did. He laid it all out. The phones, the timeline, the alibis Tommy Lee and Frank Clark had arranged, Tommy Lee's money motive, Sara Clark's affair, the call to the other phone, the person who answered knowing it was Tommy Lee calling, the murder of Tommy Lee. Then, he sat back and waited.

Morgan said nothing for a full minute. He stared at the phone he still held. Turned it over and over in his hand. His head gave a couple of shakes as if he was absorbing everything bit by bit. His mind trying to put all the pieces together. Probably praying for some other explanation. I could almost feel the pain swelling inside him. Finally, he sighed and looked up.

"Who answered when you called?" Morgan asked.

"Don't know. Male, but that's about it."

"The speaker's fractured," Pancake said. "What we heard was all broken and fuzzy."

Morgan examined the phone. "I take it this thing didn't record the conversation?"

Ray shook his head. "No. It doesn't have that capability."

"Too bad. Maybe I could've recognized the voice."

"Unfortunately, not an option."

"So whoever has this missing phone is the other half of the conspiracy?" Morgan asked. "Along with Tommy Lee?"

Ray nodded. "That makes the most sense."

"And you're thinking that other person is Frank Clark? Seeking vengeance for Sara's infidelity?"

"It's a common motive."

Morgan shook his head. "I'm here to tell you, that ain't the Frank Clark I know. He worshipped Sara."

"Which could mean that her affair only cut that much more deeply," I said.

Morgan seemed to shrink. Get smaller. As if all the air had leaked from his body.

"Let me ask you," I said. "Do you think Clark knew about her affair?"

Morgan seemed to consider that for a few seconds. "Not that I ever saw. He never said anything about it, for sure."

"Could be an ego thing," Pancake said. "Not too many guys would shout out that their partner was cheating. Particularly someone like Clark." He opened his hands, palms up. "If I'm reading him correctly."

"Who was Sara Clark seeing?" Morgan asked.

Ray nodded to Nicole.

"We don't know," she said. "I talked with their neighbor Sally Foster. She wouldn't say who it was."

"But she knew Sara was involved with someone?" Morgan asked.

"She did. And she knows who it was. Saw him sneaking in and out. At least once. I suspect more than that. She and Sara talked about it and Sara admitted to the affair, but she wouldn't say who it was."

"You're sure Sally knows?"

"I am. But, like I said, she wouldn't tell me who."

"She give a reason why not?"

Nicole shook her head. "Not in so many words, but I got the impression she wanted to protect Frank's, and Sara's, reputations."

"Sally's good people," Morgan said. "Maybe I'll have a chat with her."

"Can I suggest something else?" Nicole said.

"Sure."

"Let me talk to her. Woman to woman. I got the impression that she wanted to tell me but just couldn't quite get there. I think she will. If she and I can sit down again."

Morgan nodded. "When?"

Nicole nodded toward me. "Actually, we stopped by earlier. Sally wasn't there. The lady across the street said she'd gone to a matinee play up in Panama City. With some friends. That they were going to grab some dinner. Sally apparently told her she'd be back around eight. I thought I'd call and see if we can chat after that."

Morgan nodded, then dropped his gaze to the tabletop. "This is a goddamn mess."

"It is," Ray said. "What's your next move?"

He sighed and looked up. "Not sure. I think I'll give Terry Munson a call. Get his take on this."

"Aren't he and Clark close?" I asked. "He might tip him off."

"If Frank's the one that answered that phone, I'd say he's already tipped off."

He had a point.

"But, one thing for sure," Morgan said. "Terry'll do the right thing. Even if it's Frank."

CHAPTER FORTY-EIGHT

MORGAN TUGGED OPEN the front door, stepped back, and let Terry Munson in. "Thanks for coming over."

"No problem, Chief. What's this about? You were a little mysterious on the phone."

He led Munson into the kitchen where they sat. The phone lay on the table near a pair of green, dancing alligator salt and pepper shakers. Morgan lifted it up.

"What's that?" Munson asked.

"A problem. A big problem."

Munson shifted in his chair. "You want to explain?"

"Everything said here tonight is between me and you. Got it?"

"Sure."

"Where's Frank?" Morgan asked.

"Home, I suspect. I got the duty tonight."

Morgan nodded. He tossed the phone on the table. "I have to say again, everything that's said here, stays here. Not a word. Clear?"

"Of course. Tell me what's going on."

Morgan did. He reeled out everything Ray and his crew had told him, ending with, "Did you know Sara was seeing someone?"

"No. And I don't believe it."

"Looks like she was. Do you think Frank suspected anything like that?"

"If he did, he would've told me."

"You sure?"

"Of course, I'm sure. We don't have secrets. Not now, not ever." Munson leaned forward, forearms on the table edge. "Fact is, I simply don't believe it. None of it. I've been to their house a thousand times. Known both of them for years. Better than anyone." He tapped an index finger on the table to emphasize his point as he said, "And I don't buy any of this. Sara having an affair? Not possible."

Morgan shrugged.

"Who said she was?"

"Sally Foster. She apparently saw the guy coming and going. And Sara confirmed the affair when Nicole, that girl with the movie group, asked her."

"Who was it?"

"She wouldn't say. A least not yet. Nicole's the one that got Sally to say even that much. She's going to have another talk with her. See if Sally'll say who."

"When?"

"Don't know. Maybe tonight."

Munson shook his head. "This is insane. You're sitting right here, right now, telling me that not only was Sara having an affair but that Frank and Tommy Lee cooked up some double murder scheme? Tommy Lee for money and Frank because his wife was seeing someone? Is that what you're saying?"

"I'm saying that's a strong possibility."

"Jesus."

"I'm just not sure what to do next," Morgan said. "I mean I could get a warrant and search Frank's place. See if the other phone is there. But I'm not sure that's the way to do this." He looked at Munson. "You know as well as I do that there are always several ways to look at evidence. That things aren't always as apparent as they seem."

"That's a fact."

"I'm open to suggestions."

Munson picked up the phone, turned it over in his hand, and laid it back down. "Let me talk to Frank. Feel him out."

"Don't tell him what we have. It could cause him to do something rash."

Munson sighed. "Wouldn't you? I mean, if all this came down on your head, wouldn't you do something about it?"

"Probably. That's why you need to be cool and calm when you talk with him. Don't spook him or give anything away. Kind of tease it out."

"I know how to do an interrogation."

"I know. I'm just—hell—I don't know what I am."

Munson stood. "I'm not looking forward to it. Fact is, I might sleep on it. Figure out the right approach. Chat with him tomorrow."

"Might be the best plan."

CHAPTER FORTY-NINE

"PLEASE, COME IN," Sally Foster said. She held the door for Nicole to enter.

"Thanks for seeing me."

"I just made some tea. Would you care for some?" Before Nicole could answer, she added, "It's herbal. No caffeine."

"That would be nice," Nicole said.

"Please, make yourself at home." Sally waved a hand toward the living room. "I'll be back in a sec." She headed toward the kitchen.

Nicole texted Jake. Two words: I'M HERE. She moved to the window. The one that faced Frank Clark's house. It was dark except for a single window toward the front of the home. Light fell through the curtains, highlighted by a slight flickering. Probably the TV.

From where she stood, she could see the entire house and the backyard to the property line, demarcated by a broken row of hydrangeas. Easy for Sally to see Sara's lover coming and going.

She returned to the living room and sat on the sofa.

It had taken her nearly half an hour to convince Jake she needed to talk with Sally alone. That she believed that was the only way Sally would open up. Tell all she knew. Jake countered that he didn't want her alone that close to Frank Clark. Frank Clark the murderer.

She called him a ninny. But he didn't give up, saying that it didn't really matter who Sara was sleeping with.

"Really?" she had said. "What if it was Tommy Lee?"

"Come on. Frank Clark getting into bed—no pun intended— with his wife's lover?"

"Why not? Frank was pissed. Tommy Lee was tired of her. Who knows what goes on inside these types of conspiracies?"

"That seems to be a stretch."

"Isn't all this a stretch?"

She had point. A murder swap conspiracy? Not something you read about every day.

She continued. "What if Sara was going to expose the whole thing? Tired of all the lies and secrecy. Both men would then have to live with that humiliation."

"What about her? She'd have to live with it, too."

"True. But people do reach the end of their rope."

Jake had simply shaken his head, obviously exasperated. But one thing she knew was she could grind him down. Men were sprinters; women marathoners. No contest.

She pushed on. "What if Frank knew about the affair? What if he was okay with it?" Jake started to say something but she raised a hand. "What if Sara felt trapped in the situation? Wanted out. Threatened to expose the whole thing? She'd come off as an abused woman and Tommy Lee and Clark as her abusers. For Tommy Lee that would be uncomfortable, at the very least, but for Clark it could be devastating. Maybe a career ender."

Jake sighed, shaking his head.

"Self-image," she said. "People will do a lot of crazy shit to maintain their self-image."

"Even if that's true, how would Sally Foster know all that?"

"She and Sara were close. Women talk."

"But to her, you're a stranger. Why do you think she'll tell you what she might or might not know?"

"A feeling." She shrugged. "The only way to find out is to have a sit-down with her. Alone."

"I don't like it."

She touched his arm, kissed his cheek, and said, "You'll get over it."

Finally, he relented but only if she would text him when she got there and when she left.

"Here you go," Sally said as she entered the living room, a tray in her hands. She placed it on the coffee table and sat in the chair opposite Nicole. The tray held a floral, porcelain teapot, two cups with saucers, a squeeze bottle of honey, a bowl of sugar cubes, and another of lemon wedges. A small plate held shortbread cookies.

"You didn't have to do all this," Nicole said.

"It's nothing." She smiled. "Besides, I don't get to sit and have tea often enough."

After they filled their cups, Sally rattled on about the weather and other small talk. She was nervous and wore it all over her face, her busy hands, her speech rapid and flighty. Nicole let her run on, until finally Sally said, "You said you had more questions for me?"

Nicole placed her cup in its saucer. She decided to get right into it. "Did Frank Clark know his wife was seeing someone?"

Sally shifted uncomfortably in her seat.

"It's important," Nicole added.

"I don't see how."

"You will. I promise I'll tell you everything. Once I know what everything is."

Sally sighed. "I don't think he did. And neither did Sara."

"She told you that?"

She nodded. "Yes. In fact, she was sure he didn't know." She started to say something but stopped.

"What?"

"Nothing."

"Sally, everything is important. Or might be."

"For your documentary? I don't see how."

Nicole leaned forward. "Sally, things have moved far beyond our project."

Now, concern blossomed on Sally's face. "What does that mean?"

"I'll get to that. First tell me what you wanted to say."

Sally hesitated, twisting her napkin into a knot. Her knuckles appeared white. She let out a long sigh. "Sara was going to confess to Frank. Tell him about the affair. She was just so eaten up inside." She used the napkin to dab one eye. "She was in so much pain."

"Guilt can do that."

"Sara was such a good person. A wonderful person. She made a mistake and she wanted to atone for it."

"Did she ever tell him?"

"No, I'm certain of that."

Nicole nodded. "Who was it? Who was she seeing?"

Sally shook her head. "I can't."

"Sally, this is important. Very important."

Her gaze turned toward the window that faced the Clark home. Another shake of her head. "I can't." She dabbed her eyes again, then directed her gaze to her lap where she worked the napkin again.

Time to roll the dice.

"Sally, look at me," Nicole said. She did. "What I'm about to tell you doesn't leave this room. Okay?"

"What?"

"Okay?"

Sally nodded.

"This project. This documentary is real. It's going to happen. But that's not how it started. It began as a cover story."

She now had Sally's full attention.

"I don't understand," she said.

"Just listen. This started because Billy Wayne Baker, or at least his benefactor, hired us to prove he didn't do two of the seven killings he confessed to." Sally's eyes widened, but Nicole pressed on. "I can't give you all the details, but we found evidence that there was a murder conspiracy here. Two women were killed in a complex murder swap. Sara Clark and Noleen Kovac."

"What does that mean? What are you saying?"

"I'm saying that all the evidence points to Frank Clark and Tommy Lee Kovac doing murders for each other. Each would have an alibi. Each without a connection to the other." Nicole sighed. "But we found the connection."

"You? How?"

"It's what we do. At least what Ray does. He's pretty good."

"I don't believe it."

"Does it help if I tell you that Chief Morgan believes it? He has all the evidence."

Sally seemed to melt into her chair. Her shoulders dropped, her face fell, and whitened.

Nicole stood, circled the coffee tables, and knelt before her. Repeating what she had done at her last visit. She took both of Sally's hands in hers. They were again cold, damp.

"I need to know who Sara was seeing," Nicole said.

Sally shook her head and barely breathed out, "I can't."

"Why? Are you afraid?"

Sally looked up, hesitated, then gave a quick nod.

"Tell me."

Sally's face screwed down into an expression of pain, her internal struggle evident. She seemed to be trying to will the knowledge she held out of her head. Finally, she sighed. "Terry Munson."

"Terry Munson? Frank Clark's partner?"

She nodded. Now tears welled in her eyes. "I've kept this buried for years. I told no one. Not a living soul."

Nicole squeezed her hands. "How long were they seeing each other?"

"I don't know."

"Sara didn't tell you?"

She shook her head.

"You're sure it was Munson?"

"Yes. I saw him. A couple of times." She sniffed. "And Sally confirmed it. I told her I had seen him so she fessed up."

"Was that why she was going to tell Frank?"

She nodded. "They're partners. Frank and Terry. She felt like she had betrayed them both. Betrayed everyone, really. Mostly herself. That's the way she was."

"Give me a sec." Nicole stood and pulled her phone from her pocket.

"What are you doing?"

"I have to let Jake know this."

"You said you wouldn't tell anyone."

"Jake will keep your secret. We all will. As long as we can."

"What does that mean?"

"Sally, this is a double murder investigation. Don't you think you're going to have to tell Chief Morgan what you know?"

Sally nodded. "I suppose." She buried her face in her hands, shoulders shaking with her sobs.

CHAPTER FIFTY

I WAS ANTSY. Even though I knew Nicole was okay, having tea and chatting with Sally Foster, I had that nagging feeling in the back of my mind. How did I know about the tea? Easy. Pancake and I drove by. He got tired of me pacing the floor in Ray's room, and Ray more than once said I was driving him crazy and distracting him from his computer work. So, Pancake dragged me downstairs to his truck.

We actually parked a block away and walked by Sally's house. There sat Nicole's car in the drive, and Sally and Nicole, in the living room, having what appeared to be a pleasant talk, teacups in hand. Very relaxed.

Okay, so I overreacted.

Since Frank Clark lived next door, I couldn't resist checking on him. Pancake suggested that sneaking up and peering in his window might not be smart. This coming from the guy who broke into Tommy Lee Kovac's house. A few hours before someone took off half of Tommy Lee's head. That someone likely Frank Clark. I told Pancake he had no credibility on the subject. He grunted, saying Tommy Lee wasn't a cop, and wasn't likely armed. He had a point. Yet, he relented and waited by his truck while

I crept up to the house, getting just close enough to the front window to peek through a half-open curtain. There was Clark. Asleep, in a lounge chair, the flicker of the TV dancing across his face.

Okay, okay. Strike two.

But I had to know.

After returning to the hotel, Pancake decided he was hungry and I could use a drink so we motored down The Boardwalk toward Woody's. Ray declined to join us. When I asked Pancake if maybe we should try somewhere else for a change, he simply said, "Why?" I dropped the subject.

I had a bourbon, Pancake a beer. I was in no mood for food, but he had a plate of nachos. And a pulled pork sandwich. And French fries. Right after the table was cleared, Angus Whitehead walked in. He saw us and headed our way.

"How you doing, Angus?" I asked.

"Good. Good." His head bobbed. "Thanks for the lunch and the drinks earlier today. Mighty generous of you."

I had received a call from the waitress at McGee's when Angus' tab topped a hundred bucks. Besides breakfast he had had eight bourbons. I assured her that all was okay and to let his tab run. She called before closing it out at just over a hundred and twenty bucks. Angus had gotten a good buzz going.

"I had to drop by the jail and grab me a nap afterward," Angus continued. "Now it's time for round two."

"What can I get you?"

"No, thanks though. I'm meeting a friend here." He looked around. "Don't see him yet but he'll be along directly."

He nodded and shuffled toward the bar. He only made it a couple of steps before turning back and dropping in a chair.

"Change your mind?" I asked.

"No. But I did me some thinking. About what we were talking about."

"Which thing?" I asked. "We talked about a lot."

"That night. When I was in the bushes and heard Munson on the phone."

"What about it?"

"Don't know why it popped into my head, but it did. Sometime while I was napping in jail." He laughed. "That kind of thing happens all the time. Stuff just comes to me. Sometimes I can be thinking or talking about something else and then my mind sort of does a hop, skip, and jump and I'm off on something else."

"Everyone does that," I said.

"Well, it happens to me all the time. Ever since I began hitting the bottle for sure. Don't remember doing it all that much before. Mama says otherwise. She says I've always been one to squirrel around in my head." He shrugged. "But even she agrees it's a mite worse lately."

"And what did you come up with?" I asked.

He tossed me a quizzical look. "About what?"

"You said you remembered something about Terry Munson's phone conversation."

He laughed and shook his head. "See? That's what I'm talking about. I plum forgot what I wanted to tell you."

"You forgot?" Pancake asked.

"No, no, I remember. I just forgot that that's what I wanted to tell you."

"Okay. What is it?" I asked.

"He sure had a bee in his bonnet. No doubt about that. Like the guy wouldn't listen to him—or wouldn't do what he wanted. Said something like it had to be that night. That he'd put it off long enough."

I glanced at Pancake. His wheels were turning, too.

"He say what?" I asked.

"Not that I heard," Angus said. "I don't remember it all that well. It's been a couple of years."

"Do the best you can," I said. "What were you able to pick up?"

"He told the person that it couldn't be put off forever. That that night, right then, was the perfect time. Something like quit whining and just do it."

"Any idea what *it* was?" Pancake asked.

Angus shook his head. "Don't think he ever said nothing specific. He did ask the guy if he had everything he needed."

Could we have been chasing the wrong rabbit the entire time? Focusing on the wrong guy? Was it Munson and not Clark? That made no sense.

"What kind of phone was it?" I asked.

Angus stared at me.

"Was it one of those smartphones or an old folding type?"

He thought about that for a full half a minute. "I don't know. I was more listening than watching."

"Think," I said. "Try to visualize that night."

He fixed his gaze on the floor, then shook his head. "I can't say." He looked at me. "I was hunkered down in the shrubs. Couldn't see all that well." His eyes narrowed, his brow furrowed. His eyebrows went up. "It was a flip phone."

"Are you sure? Maybe you're just remembering it that way?"

"Nope." He shook his head. "I might lose my train of thought sometimes but I remember things when my mind gets around to them. Recall them like they was yesterday." He smiled. "Or the day before." He laughed. "But I remember real good."

"How do you now remember it was a flip phone?" I asked. "I thought you couldn't see it."

"Couldn't. But I heard it. He snapped it closed. Those fancy new smart ones don't do that."

"You're absolutely sure?" Pancake asked.

"No doubt about it."

"And the conversation you heard Munson having. You sure you remember it correctly?"

"Sure. Why wouldn't I?"

"Tell me again," I said.

"He said something about right then was the time. That it had to be done quickly. Whatever it was. Said something about he'd done his part and now whoever he was talking to had to do theirs." He looked at me. "That make any sense to you?"

I nodded. "It just might."

Angus' head turned toward the bar. "There's my buddy. See you guys later." He stood and walked away.

I looked at Pancake. He looked at me.

"We been running in the wrong circle," Pancake said.

"Sure looks that way."

My phone chimed. A text. Nicole must be leaving. I checked it. It read: SARA CLARK WAS HAVING AN AFFAIR WITH TERRY MUNSON.

I texted back: ARE YOU LEAVING?

While I waited for her to reply, I showed Nicole's text to Pancake.

His eyes narrowed, shoulders squared, jaw locked. "And now we have a motive."

"To hide his affair?"

"Exactly." Pancake stood. "Let's go."

I tossed money on the table and we were out the door.

Still no reply from Nicole. I sent another text: WHERE ARE YOU?

Pancake called Ray.

I called Nicole. No answer. It jumped to voice mail. I left a short message. CALL ME. NOW.

Ray was standing by Pancake's truck when we got back to the hotel. We climbed in and Pancake sped from the lot.

"We were right about it being a cop," I said. "We just had the wrong cop."

CHAPTER FIFTY-ONE

NICOLE STOOD BESIDE Sally, a comforting hand on the sobbing woman's shoulder. "It'll be okay."

"Probably not."

Nicole spun toward the doorway that led to the kitchen. Terry Munson stood there, a chrome-plated revolver in his hand.

Sally's head jerked up and she gasped. Nicole squeezed her shoulder, hopefully relaying that it was best not to say anything right now.

"The phone," Munson said. "Toss it here."

Nicole still held her cell. She looked down at it.

"Now." The gun elevated, now pointed in their direction.

She underhanded it to him. He snatched it from the air, just as it chimed an incoming text. Munson looked at the screen. His eyes narrowed.

"So, now your boyfriend knows."

"He does. So does Ray and Pancake and by now I suspect Chief Morgan."

Munson's jaw tightened. His head swiveled. Nicole could feel his panic. The only question was would he fold—or fight? Was he willing to die and take them with him?

"Stop this now," Nicole said. "Give it up before it's too late."

"It's already too late."

"It can get worse," she said.

His jaw flexed, then a tight smile appeared. "It already is for you."

Sally whimpered. Nicole tightened her grip on the woman's shoulder.

"But—" Nicole began.

The phone chimed again. Another text from Jake no doubt. Munson looked at it.

"He's getting nervous," Munson said.

"He does that. But he's not the one you need to worry about."

"Oh, really?"

Nicole shook her head. "I'd worry more about Ray."

"Right. He's a fucking P.I."

"Oh, he's so much more than that."

Now the phone rang. Munson punched the off button, sending it to voice mail.

Keep him talking, she thought. And distracted. Buy time.

"Look," Nicole said. "You have no way out of here. It's over."

Munson smirked. "Not as long as I have two hostages I can trade for a head start."

"Won't happen."

"We'll see."

"Ray will kill you. And he won't hesitate to do it."

Munson looked around the room again. He waved the gun toward them.

"On the floor. Both of you." Neither Nicole nor Sally moved. "Now. Facedown. Arms and legs spread."

Sally lurched, suppressing a sob.

"It'll be okay," Nicole said.

She helped Sally to the floor and then lay prone on the thick carpet, arms spread wide.

"What now?" Nicole asked. "You going to shoot us?"

"If I have to."

"Okay. So you use us as your bargaining chip. Where are you going to go?"

"I'll figure that out later."

"Sounds like a plan doomed to fail."

"Shut up."

"Why?" Nicole said. "If we're going to die, I might as well say my piece."

Munson walked to where she lay. Stood over her. "There's dying and then there's dying. It can be quick and easy or slow and painful."

"You've got to stop watching the Turner Classic Movie Channel."

"What?" Munson asked.

"You sound like James Cagney. Just not delivered as well."

"Are you trying to piss me off?"

"It's what I do. Ask Jake."

CHAPTER FIFTY-TWO

PANCAKE FLIPPED OFF his truck's headlights a block away and parked three doors down from Sally Foster's place, opposite side of the street. He, Ray, and I stepped out, easing the doors closed. The street was quiet. Light fell through the pair of front windows that flanked Sally's front door. At this angle and distance, I couldn't see inside but did sense shadows moving around.

"I don't like it that her car's in the drive, but she isn't answering her phone," I said.

"Don't see another car," Pancake said.

Ray said, "If you were going to do something stupid, or desperate, would you just pull up out front?"

Pancake grunted. Meant Ray had a point. Ray always did.

We crossed the street and made our way across several yards, including Frank Clark's. I saw him inside. Just as I had seen earlier, he was kicked back in his lounge chair, TV glow still flickering. We settled behind Nicole's car. Through the multi-paned front window, I now saw Munson. Standing in the living room. Gun in his right hand. Head down.

Where were Nicole and Sally? My gut tightened. Ray must have sensed it.

"They're in there somewhere," he said. "I'd bet on the floor."

"How do you know?" I asked.

"Body language, head position. Besides, if he'd done something he'd be gone. He's holding them. Probably wants a deal."

"But what if he's willing to die?" I asked.

"That'd complicate things."

"We might be able to fulfill his wish," Pancake said.

"Which?" I asked. "Escaping or dying?"

"Either." Pancake shrugged. "Maybe one and then the other." He raised slightly and peered over the shrub. "Don't anybody move," he said. Then he was gone.

Staying low, he left the cover of the Mercedes and scurried up the driveway. His grace and agility always amazed me. How could someone so big get so small when need be? He slowed his movements and moved to his left, quickly reaching the front corner of the house. He crept forward until he was below what I knew was the dining room window. He peeked inside, then ducked. He gave a thumbs-up sign.

"They're in there and they're okay," Ray said.

"What are we going to do?"

"Say hello."

"What?"

Ray smiled. "Either we start a dialog, or we storm the Bastille."

My cell buzzed. Nicole? No, Tammy. I swear, she had the absolute worst timing of anyone I'd ever known. Like when we were setting up an ambush of Tony Guidry and his crew. Bang. There's Tammy calling about some stupid shit. And here we were. Basically, the same situation and she calls. It was uncanny. Annoying, but uncanny. I pressed it over to voice mail.

Pancake returned to our side. "On the floor. They look okay." He looked at Ray. "But Munson looks panicked."

"Then let's introduce ourselves." Ray nodded toward the house, and then to Pancake said, "You take the back. I'll take the front."

"What's the plan?" I asked.

"Not ring the doorbell, for sure."

I nodded toward Clarks' house. "What about Clark?"

Ray looked that way, then gave a slow nod. "He might be able to help."

"He's in there. Asleep in front of his TV," I said.

"Go wake him up. Pancake and I are on the move."

And they were off. Pancake scurried back up the drive and disappeared around the rear corner. Ray dropped low and sprinted around Nicole's car toward the front of the house. He settled in the shrubbery just to the right of the front stoop.

I reached Clark's front porch just as my cell phone buzzed again. Tammy. I turned it off this time, knowing she'd keep it up. Relentless being her style.

It took a half a minute after I rapped on Clark's dark green front door for it to swing open. His eyes were sleep swollen, but that didn't hide the surprise on his face. I didn't give him much time to sort things out.

"Listen to me. Terry Munson and Tommy Lee conspired to murder your wife and Tommy Lee's sister. Munson probably killed Tommy Lee."

"What are you talking about?" Clark asked.

"No time to explain. Right now, Munson is next door. He's taken Nicole and Sally Foster hostage."

Clark stepped outside and looked that way. "What?"

"Just what I said. Ray and Pancake are getting ready to confront him. Maybe go in. You might be able to reason with him."

"This makes no sense."

"It will. But, right now, we need to act."

Clark hesitated a short beat, his eyes seemed to clear, and he nodded. He stepped inside briefly before returning with his service weapon in his hand. "Let's go."

We joined Ray near the front door.

"You sure about all this?" Clark asked.

"Take a look. What do you think?"

Clark rose slightly and crab-walked to his left. Apparently, he now had a clear view into Sally Foster's living room. He repeated the low walk back to us. "Jesus. Has he lost his mind?"

"I think he did that a couple of years ago," I said.

"Why? I don't understand."

"He was having an affair with Sara."

Clark's jaw literally dropped, his mouth agape. "No. No way."

"He did," I said. "Sally confirmed it."

Clark literally deflated. "I had no idea."

"We can go over all this later," Ray said. "Right now we have to clean up this mess."

"What's the plan?" Clark asked.

Sally had a neat, well-maintained planting area to either side of the front stoop. A few shrubs and wads of flowers of various types. Each area was demarcated by a brick perimeter, the bricks tilted against each other, like leaning soldiers, creating a sawtooth pattern. Ray loosened a brick and picked it up.

"This."

"He's got a gun, you know?"

"Which means chaos is our friend."

Then things happened quickly. Chaos did indeed rule.

Ray coiled and hurled the brick through one of the panes of the front window. The sharp shattering of the glass seemed amplified by the still night air. Ray didn't hesitate. He sprang forward, lowering his shoulder, blasting through the front door. The frame splintered. Clark and I followed. Munson looked up, shock and confusion on his face. He raised his gun in our direction. Ray and Clark elevated their weapons. Everyone froze.

Pancake had apparently found the back door unlocked since I heard nothing breaking. He was good at breaking things. He came through the dining area and into the living room, standing just behind us. Munson waved the gun back and forth, unsure what to do, obviously unable to determine which threat was the most immediate. He finally decided on Ray and settled his aim on him.

Sally scurried behind the sofa and balled up.

Munson, to his credit, brushed off his initial shock and reacted. He reached down and grabbed Nicole by the hair, lifted her, pulled her against him, and backed against the wall. Behind him, a picture came unanchored and dropped to the floor, its glass cover shattering. His weapon never wavered from Ray.

Time stopped. The sudden silence almost made my ears pop. As if the air had been sucked from the room. The four of us faced Munson across the coffee table that fronted the sofa. Sally whimpered softly.

"Don't move," Munson said.

"Shoot him," Nicole said. "Shoot him in the head."

Munson yanked her head back, pressed the muzzle against her neck. "Shut up."

"Shoot him, Ray," Nicole repeated. "Shoot this son-of-a-bitch."

She had balls. I had to give her that.

"Be cool," Ray said. Then to Munson: "Put the weapon down and we can sort this out."

Munson shook his head and smiled. "I don't see much sorting going on here. But I can tell you what will happen. Me and her are going to walk out that door and climb in her car. Once I'm away, I'll let her go."

Pancake took a step forward. "Ain't going to happen."

Munson turned the muzzle his way. "Don't move."

Pancake crossed his arms over his chest and smiled.

"Terry," Clark said. "Don't do this. Don't make things worse."

"Frank, things can't get any worse, I'm afraid." He swallowed hard. "I'm so sorry. I never meant any of this to happen. Never wanted to hurt you. Betray you. Neither did Sara. It just happened."

"Is it true? Did you and Tommy Lee kill her and Noleen?"

Munson's eyes squeezed shut, then popped open. He blinked, as if fighting back tears. "Worst decision ever. Sara was going to tell you. She hated the secrecy. Hated it. I couldn't let her do that. It would have crushed you. Destroyed our friendship. Torn up everything. I tried to explain that, held her off for a few months, but in the end, she needed to unburden herself."

"So you killed her? Did you really think that was a better solution?"

Munson shook his head. "Not me. Tommy Lee did."

"And you killed Noleen?" I said.

"That was our deal. Tommy Lee wanted money. I wanted . . . I'm not sure what I wanted." He shook his head. "I wanted everything to be like it was. Wanted my mistake to disappear."

"Shoot him," Nicole said.

"Nicole, be cool," Ray said. "Nobody's going to shoot anyone."

"You know you can't run," Clark said.

"I can try."

"And, I can't let you." Clark extended his weapon, broadened his stance. "You know I'm pretty good with this."

Munson angled his own weapon toward Clark.

I realized I wasn't breathing. It seemed that no one was. My chest hurt. My mouth felt like the Sahara and my heart fluttered like a couple of squirrels trapped in a burlap bag. I searched for some weapon. As if Clark's gun—hell, Ray's gun—wasn't enough. My gaze fell to the snow globe on the coffee table before me.

A snow globe? Really? Everybody had guns pointing here and there and I'm looking at a freaking snow globe?

Then I looked at Nicole. Her jaw flexed. Her eyes narrowed. Her shoulders tensed. What the hell?

No, no, no, my brain screamed, but before my mouth could join the chorus, it happened. With Munson's gun no longer pressed against her neck, Nicole sprang. She jerked her head back, smashing it into Munson's nose. His head literally bounced against the wall. She dropped low, spun, and punched him in the throat. Hard. Munson staggered. One hand went to his face. The other waved his gun wildly before him.

I didn't think; I jumped into motion. I scooped up the snow globe and let it fly. I could almost hear the ump yell, "Strike three." It struck Munson's forehead with a sharp thud/crack. The gun fell, his eyes glazed. He wobbled to his left, his legs gave way, and he folded to the floor.

CHAPTER FIFTY-THREE

RAY SNATCHED UP Munson's weapon, while Clark knelt beside him. Munson's nose yawed to one side, blood streamed down his face, chin, and onto his shirt. I saw the beginning of a goose egg on his forehead. Good. His gaze seemed to be searching for some anchor.

I hugged Nicole. "You okay?"

"Fine." She slipped from my grasp and looked down at Munson. "Can I kick him?"

I grabbed her arm and pulled her away. "I think he's more or less done."

"I'm not."

I hugged her to me again. This time more tightly. "Take a breath."

"Let go of me."

"No. You did good. Real good. Leave it at that."

She resisted, but I held on.

Finally, she said, "Okay, okay. I give."

I kissed her forehead. "You sure?"

Now, she laughed. "Yes."

I let her go. Sally struggled to her feet, and Nicole moved to help her.

Sally looked at Munson's bloody face. "Oh, my God."

"It's not as bad as it looks," Nicole said. "Unfortunately."

Sally began to cry. Nicole held her, looked at me. I gave her a smile.

Munson had now reentered reality and sat up, his back against the wall.

"Want me to call the medics?" Clark asked.

Munson shook his head.

"We'll take you over to the hospital and get this checked out."

"I'll be fine."

"Not negotiable," Clark said. "Your nose is busted and you were out for a while."

Munson offered no further resistance.

"I'll go with you," Ray said. "Pancake can follow us."

"We'll stay here with Sally," I said.

Ray gave me a quick nod.

Pancake found a towel in the bathroom down the hall and brought it to Munson. He looked at Sally. "This okay?"

She nodded. "Sure."

Munson took the towel and pressed it to his face. He grimaced. "Hurts like a bitch."

Nicole smiled at me. I gave her a thumbs-up.

I suggested that Sally might want to go with us. That we'd get her a room over at the hotel. She refused, saying she wanted to be alone. What about her fractured front door? It wouldn't lock.

"I'll be fine," she said.

"You sure?"

She nodded to Clark. "Frank's right next door."

"Once I get Terry settled, either in the hospital or the jail, I'll stop by and check on you," Clark said.

"Thanks," Sally said.

Clark helped Munson to his feet. He and Ray guided him to Clark's car and settled him in the back seat. No cuffs so he could hold the towel against his face. But with Ray sitting next to him there was no chance he could escape.

They left, Pancake's truck lumbering along behind them.

We secured Sally's front door as best we could. Not bad. The lock still worked. Sort of. It at least held the door closed.

We then climbed in Nicole's car.

"Want to swing by the hospital and see how things go?" I asked.

"Yeah. Let's do."

I pulled out my phone and turned it on. Six missed calls, four texts, all from Tammy, of course. My phone rang. "Guess who?"

"What is it?" I asked.

"Where have you been?" Tammy asked.

"Busy."

"With what?"

"Let's see. Three guys with guns. Nicole held hostage. The usual."

"Can't you make up a better story than that? If you don't want to talk to me, just say so."

"I don't want to talk to you."

"Ass."

"I am."

"But, I need you." She sounded like she might cry. I knew better. Tammy whined, she complained, she screeched, but crying wasn't part of her vocabulary.

"For what?"

"Walter. He saw his urologist. He doesn't have cancer. Just an enlarged prostate."

"Good for him."

"But what about me?"

"It's not your prostate," I said.

"But we can't even go to dinner. He has to run off to the boy's room every five minutes. It's so annoying."

So Tammy.

"Probably more so for Walter," I said.

"He's not the one that has to sit there. Alone. People stare."

"Maybe it's time to trade Walter for a younger model."

"Like I did with you?"

"Walter's older than me. A lot older."

"It's the principle. He's nicer."

"Well. Except for his prostate."

"See? That's why I dumped you. You have no compassion."

"For Walter's condition? Sure I do. Enlarged prostate and all. He is, after all, stuck with you. I really feel for the guy."

She hung up. Mission accomplished.

CHAPTER FIFTY-FOUR

THE NEXT MORNING, I called Gloria Whitt, the reporter for the
Pine Key Breeze. She had been helpful and I thought she'd appreciate a look inside the case before we left town. Nicole and I sat in her
office and told her the entire tale. Even though she recorded it, she
took four pages of notes. She was delighted to have the scoop but
saddened by the entire story. Said she knew Tommy Lee and Terry
Munson well. Had even been out with Munson a few times. Seemed
to me everyone had at some time or the other. The guy did get
around. "Back in the day" as she put it. Said she never saw anything
but a fun-loving, if womanizing, guy. And Tommy Lee? Hard
worker. Good guy. No way she would ever have predicted him being
involved in something like this. She concluded with, "I guess you
can never really know other people."

As she walked us to the door, she asked if she could email me the
story to go over before she published it. Of course.

We then returned to the hotel and finished packing before
hooking up with Ray and Pancake for a visit with Chief Morgan.
As we followed them to the station, we talked about last night.
Again. We had stayed up until nearly two going over everything.

"You really wanted Ray to shoot him? With you standing right
there?" I asked.

"Of course."

"What if he hit you by mistake?"

"You ever seen Ray make a mistake?"

She had me there.

"Anyway," I said, "I'm glad you paid attention in our Krav Maga classes."

She laughed. "And I'm glad you're such a stud baseball player. That snow globe fastball was a thing of beauty."

Yes, it was.

Chief Charlie Morgan was in his office with Frank Clark. He had arranged folding chairs for us. We sat.

"To say that this is a hell of a mess doesn't quite cover it," Morgan said.

"Not what this town needs," Nicole said.

"That's true." Morgan pinched his nose. "Last night, we had a long talk with Terry. Over at the hospital." He looked at Nicole. "You did a number on his nose."

She shrugged.

"And he's got a big old goose egg on his forehead," Morgan said. He nodded toward me. "Good to see you haven't lost your stuff."

Now I shrugged.

"I'm just glad no one got shot," Morgan said.

"It was touch and go for a minute there," Ray said. "If I'd left it up to Nicole, someone would've." He smiled at her.

"I was a little hyped up," she said.

You think?

"The docs admitted him," Morgan said. "They straightened his nose. Somewhat. Did a CT scan. Said he had a concussion but nothing more serious. Kept him overnight for observation."

"He's still there?" I asked.

"Yep. Cuffed to the bed. One of my guys is sitting with him."

I nodded.

Morgan continued. "Terry confessed to the entire deal. He and Tommy Lee cooked up the murder swap. Tommy Lee bought the phones. Terry grabbed the DNA from the evidence locker. Said he simply took a swab of the stain Billy Wayne left behind at Loretta Swift's. Kept it in a vial of saline in his freezer." Morgan opened his palms. "Got to admit, it was pretty clever." He leaned back in his chair. "Then it was simply a matter of time. Waiting for the right evenings for the murders."

"And he did kill Tommy Lee?" I asked.

"He did. Said when he got the phone call from the other phone he knew something was wrong. He went to see what Tommy Lee's story was. Was he the one that made the call? Did he flip on him? If the phone was missing, did he know who had it?" Morgan sighed. "Ultimately, he decided that Tommy Lee was a liability."

"Secrets can only be kept by one person," Pancake said.

I looked at Frank Clark. "We're sorry."

He nodded. "I still miss her. Always will."

"For more than that. For the lies we had to tell each of you."

"You mean about the documentary?" Morgan asked.

"No," Nicole said. "That's real. In fact, we'll have a crew in here to do the interviews in a couple of weeks. We're working on that schedule right now." She smiled. "Each of you can expect a call in the next day or so."

"It'll be good to see you again," Morgan said.

"It won't be me," Nicole said. "Just a producer and camera and sound people. We'll then edit in my parts and put it all together."

"I'm glad to hear that," Clark said. "That it's going to happen. I think Sara would have liked it."

"I need to clear up something else," I said. Clark gave me a quizzical look. "This started because Billy Wayne Baker said he didn't do two of the killings he confessed to. He had to confess to all of them to get off death row. Then he found a pen pal. Guy with a love for true crime and lots of money. Billy Wayne confided in him and the guy believed him. Paid for our investigation."

"Who is it?" Morgan asked.

I shook my head. "Can't say. His anonymity was part of the deal." I looked at the floor and then back to Clark. "Once we looked into all of Billy Wayne's murders, the only place that even remotely made sense was here. Three killings when there was only one everywhere else. A cop's wife one of the victims."

"A cop who could stage the crime and plant the evidence?" Clark asked.

I nodded. "We came in here expecting it was you." I sighed. "And we're sorry for that."

Clark rubbed his chin. "Truth be told, I'd have come to the same conclusion." He raised an eyebrow. "If I'd believed Billy Wayne in the first place."

"If you talked to him, you just might," I said. "He's very convincing."

"Which was part of his MO," Morgan said.

"Yes. He's very good at making you feel relaxed around him."

"And, Jake's gullible," Nicole said. "At least as far as Billy Wayne and I are concerned."

She's funny. I swear to God she is.

"But Billy Wayne was telling the truth," I said. That even sounded defensive to me.

"So do I." She smiled. "Mostly."

"Women," I said with a headshake.

Morgan laughed. "I'd say you got a good one."

That I do. Most definitely.

CHAPTER FIFTY-FIVE

BEFORE WE LEFT the police station, Morgan told us he didn't suspect he'd need us to come back and testify or anything like that. That since Munson had confessed, there wouldn't be a trial. We said we would if anything changed and that we'd each write up a statement and get it to him within the week.

He and Clark walked us outside.

"You have a wonderful town here," I said. "A pleasant place to live."

"It is," Clark said. "Despite what you've seen of it, it's pretty boring around here. And that's how we like it."

We all shook hands. Then, Nicole gave each of them a hug.

We had one more stop to make. Woody's. To say goodbye to Betty Lou and so Pancake could see Laurie Mae, tell her he'd be back in a few months. Once the documentary was completed. It was emotional. Betty Lou actually cried. Laurie Mae, too.

Nicole took my hand as we followed Ray and Pancake back to the hotel.

"I love this town," she said.

"The mortality rate's high," I said.

"That aside, it's pretty cool."

"It is."

We lugged our bags downstairs and loaded up for the drive back to Gulf Shores. I told Ray and Pancake that we needed to detour by Union Correctional for a chat with Billy Wayne, so we'd be an hour or more behind them.

Pancake grunted. "With Nicole driving, the detour means we'll all get there about the same time."

By the time we crossed the bridge and headed toward the highway, I had Billy Wayne's attorney, Winston McCracken, on the line.

"Billy Wayne was telling the truth," I said.

"Really?"

I told him the story.

His take: "Now I've heard it all."

"What's your next step?" I asked.

"Get the wheels of justice turning. Get a couple of Billy Wayne's confessions overturned."

"Will that be a problem?"

"Shouldn't be. Since Munson confessed, we won't have to wait on a trial."

"Good. I'm headed to Raiford to chat with him now. Okay if I tell him we've chatted and what you're planning?"

"Absolutely. I'm sure he'll be pleased. It won't change his address, but it'll for sure satisfy his fair play rule."

An hour later, I sat waiting for Billy Wayne to appear behind the glass. Seems I was now on a first-name basis with a couple of the Union Correctional guards. Not sure that was a good thing, but it made the transition from outside to inside smoother.

Billy Wayne sat and picked up the handset.

"What brings the great baseball player by?" he asked.

"I wanted to be the first to tell you that you were right."

"I knew that. What's the story?"

I told him.

"So it was the cop. Just like I said."

"Yeah, but not the one you thought."

"I never said who I thought it was," he said.

"Come on, Billy Wayne. You thought it was Clark, too. No way you knew it was Munson."

He laughed. "Just messing with you, man. Yeah, after I read all the investigative stuff that McCracken gave me, I believed it was Clark. He was the husband, after all."

"You'll also be happy to know that I talked with Mr. McCracken. He's getting the ball rolling on overturning two of your confessions."

"Good."

"He said he didn't see any obstacles, so hopefully all that will be resolved soon."

"My friend, the one who's paying you guys."

"Jason Levy."

"So, you know?"

"We wouldn't be very good if we didn't."

Billy Wayne smiled. "I guess that's true. Well, seems he has a guy lined up to write my story. Ain't that a hoot?"

I had no response for that. Neither did I feel the need to tell him of the documentary. In which, of course, Billy Wayne just might not come off so well.

In the end, I wished Billy Wayne well and walked out of Union Correctional. Hopefully for the last time.

CHAPTER FIFTY-SIX

We didn't return to Pine Key for several months. Early December. Nothing had changed. Except for the weather and the buzz. It was cold, even some predictions that it might snow. In the Sunshine State? Go figure. The buzz, however, was electric. Everyone in town was talking about the documentary.

Saturday night. The high school gym since the local movie theater was too small for the premier of *Aftermath: Pine Key*, the first installment of the eight-part documentary Uncle Charles was shepherding. The screening on TV wouldn't be for another month, after the holiday season, but we felt a showing for the residents of Pine Key would be a good deal. From the reaction of the town folks, it was.

Posters lit up every building. They even had over-the-street banners. And Gloria Whitt had splashed it on the front page of the *Pine Key Breeze.*

Nicole was serving as host and doing the voice-overs for the entire series. We had spent a week in LA recording the first four episodes. The others would require a return visit next month.

A low stage had been constructed at one end of the gym. The bleachers were filled, as were the army of folding chairs on the floor. I suspected the local fire marshal had waved the rules.

The murmuring that filled the space was filled with excitement, laced with a palpable layer of sadness, even dread. After all, this was their story. It might be a little slice of Hollywood, but it was also a revisiting of the town's worst nightmare. The anticipation of seeing friends and family reveal their innermost pain on a large screen, naked, exposed for all to see, had to be an unnerving feeling. One of those things that you wanted to see but dreaded doing so.

I stood stage right with Nicole. The lights dimmed, the murmurs waned. A single overhead spotlight fell on the center of the stage.

"Showtime," Nicole said.

"Break a leg."

She walked onstage, into the cone of light. The applause was real, but nervous. She looked magnificent. Tight black jeans and a coral RGP shirt. Her hair glowed like a halo. She held a wireless microphone. She waved to the crowd and waited for the noise to fade.

"Thank you all for coming out tonight for this very special event. I'm Nicole Jamison and I'm the host of this series. This entire project is special to us at Regency Global Productions, or RGP as we call it. It is an eight-part documentary series that focuses on the victims of serial predators like the one that visited your community. It's not the story of Billy Wayne Baker. It's not the story of any of the killers the series will profile. It's the story of the victims and their friends and family. It's your story."

Another smattering of cautious applause.

"The episode you will see tonight will be the premier episode of the series."

The applause this time was louder and longer.

"You will see many of your friends interviewed in the film. You will unfortunately relive a very sad and stressful time for your community. The purpose is in no way to add to your pain, or feed on your tragedy, but rather to celebrate the strength and courage of this town and especially those so closely affected by Billy Wayne Baker. We want to thank you all. You opened your doors and your hearts to us and we are eternally grateful. This is a wonderful town and we love it. And all of you."

Now, applause and shouts erupted.

"Before we begin the film, I have an announcement to make. To show our appreciation for you and to say thank you for welcoming us into your lives, RGP has a couple of special gifts for Pine Key." She shielded her eyes from the light. "Will Police Chief Charles Morgan join me onstage?"

A murmur rose from the crowd. Morgan climbed onstage and moved to where Nicole stood.

"Chief Morgan," Nicole said. "Regency Global has purchased a pair of new, state-of-the-art cars for your department."

A picture of the two vehicles parked in front of the Pine Key police station appeared on the screen. People stood, chairs scraping the floor. The applause was enthusiastic.

"We want to present you with the keys to your new vehicles, which, as you can see, are now parked at the station."

He took the keys, shaking his head. Nicole held the mic toward him.

"This is a surprise. We had no idea. I mean, you had mentioned a car a few months ago, but I never imagined it would happen. Let alone two." He shook his head. "We are very grateful."

When the applause died and Morgan left the stage, Nicole took center stage. She gazed over the crowd. Smiled.

"Now I want to present to you, *Aftermath: Pine Key*."